GATORS
AND
GARTERS

A Miss Fortune Mystery

NEW YORK TIMES BESTSELLING AUTHOR
JANA DELEON

MISS FORTUNE SERIES INFORMATION

If you've never read a Miss Fortune mystery, you can start with LOUISIANA LONGSHOT, the first book in the series. If you prefer to start with this book, here are a few things you need to know.

Fortune Redding – a CIA assassin with a price on her head from one of the world's most deadly arms dealers. Because her boss suspects that a leak at the CIA blew her cover, he sends her to hide out in Sinful, Louisiana, posing as his niece, a librarian and ex–beauty queen named Sandy-Sue Morrow. The situation was resolved in Change of Fortune and Fortune is now a full-time resident of Sinful and has opened her own detective agency.

Ida Belle and Gertie – served in the military in Vietnam as spies, but no one in the town is aware of that fact except Fortune and Deputy LeBlanc.

Sinful Ladies Society – local group founded by Ida Belle, Gertie, and deceased member Marge. In order to gain membership, women must never have married or if widowed, their husband must have been deceased for at least ten years.

Sinful Ladies Cough Syrup – sold as an herbal medicine in Sinful, which is dry, but it's actually moonshine manufactured by the Sinful Ladies Society.

CHAPTER ONE

THE SALESWOMAN in the bridal shop stood holding the tray of wine she'd been trying to push on us and glancing back and forth between Ida Belle and Gertie. She looked scared. Whether it was for herself, Gertie, or the dress Gertie was clutching, I couldn't say. I had taken a chair in the corner as soon as we walked in, committed to my vow of staying all the way out of whatever happened.

"Just try it on," Gertie pleaded. "A couple of seconds is all I ask. If you hate it, you don't have to wear it."

"I don't have to try it on to know that I hate it," Ida Belle said. "I can tell that just by looking. Probably I didn't even have to see it."

"Come on," Gertie said. "It won't kill you."

"Might kill *you*," Ida Belle said. "Last time I checked, I could draw faster than you, and if you keep pushing that dress on me, we might see an exhibition."

I had to laugh, which earned me a dirty look from Gertie and a fearful one from the saleswoman. It wasn't the first time I'd laughed today and not even close to the first time I'd gotten a dirty look from Gertie, and I predicted that trend would continue until we got past Ida Belle's wedding and Gertie's insistence that she do normal bride things.

Like wear a dress.

"I haven't worn a dress since my father gave me my first gun," Ida Belle said.

"Did you pull it on your mother?" I asked.

Ida Belle waved a hand in dismissal. "There was an Easter sermon at church. She had this frilly pink lacy thing that would have itched and made me look ridiculous. She asked for it."

The saleswoman made a noise that sounded something like 'eep' and fled the consultation room. Unfortunately, she took the tray of wine with her.

"You were six years old," Gertie said. "And pulling a gun on your mother over an Easter dress is the reason the South gets a bad name."

"*The* reason?" I asked.

"Well, one of them," Gertie said. "It's still the best place in the world but I will admit to a few quirks."

"A *few*?" I asked.

The saleswoman chose that moment to ease back in, this time with a tray of sweets. She was going for either alcohol poisoning or diabetic coma.

"You decided to move here," Gertie said to me. "The quirks must not have been bad enough to scare you away."

"She was an assassin, for Christ's sake," Ida Belle said. "You can't scare assassins."

The saleswoman's eyes widened and the color drained from her face. I jumped up to grab the tray of food before she dropped it but when she saw me hurrying toward her, she threw the tray and ran. It was either catch the tray and hope some goodies remained on it or block for the dress. The goodies ended up claiming the floor mostly, but a few remained on the tray.

"Hey, what's the ruling on pastries on a wedding dress train?" I asked. "Five seconds, ten?"

"Five," they both answered at once.

I grabbed a raspberry croissant and hopped back in my chair.

"Just under the wire," I said and took a big bite.

Gertie shook her head and turned back to Ida Belle. "Well, you can't scare me, either. Will you at least consider a white pantsuit?"

"You want me to wear white to a crawfish boil?" Ida Belle asked. "Look what happened to that dress from just one pastry. If Fortune hadn't blocked the rest of them, it would look like a B horror movie prop. And I'm not paying for that, by the way. That saleswoman needs to work on her fortitude. This is Louisiana, not the Hamptons."

"You're the one who insisted on crawfish," Gertie said. "I tried to suggest grilled fish with rice and salad."

"On what planet is that representative of what I eat?" Ida Belle asked. "Shouldn't the bride actually like what's being served at her wedding?"

"I think the bride should and the bridesmaids as well," I said. "I appreciate the crawfish. And the lack of dresses."

Gertie gave me a look of dismay. "I should have known you'd take her side. The two of you together might have one drop of estrogen between you."

"Maybe half a drop," Ida Belle said. "Estrogen decreases as you age. Besides, grilled fish would be a mess. This wedding is happening in Fortune's backyard. A couple of tents, some folding chairs and we're good. You can't have a formal sit-down dinner in the middle of the summer in a backyard."

"Finally!" Gertie threw her hands in the air. "You understand the problem."

"There's no problem for me," Ida Belle said. "I don't want to get dressed in a way I never have before, then sit down to a fancy dinner that wouldn't be my first choice in some building that would charge too much and insist on throwing flowers everywhere."

"But this is your wedding," Gertie said. "It only happens once and quite frankly, as long as you waited to say yes, I'm surprised one of you isn't already in the grave."

"Look," Ida Belle said, "I appreciate that you want to make it special, but Walter wants to marry me, and God knows, he's had plenty of time to get a fix on who I am. If I put on some fancy gown and have a fancy dinner in a fancy building, then he's not marrying me at all. That's me pretending to be someone else."

"Oh, good point," I said, storing that one in case I ever took the scary plunge into permanency with Carter.

"Fine," Gertie said. "Then what do you plan on wearing to be married to the man who has waited patiently for a million years for you to wise up?"

"Don't worry," Ida Belle said. "Wedding wardrobe is our next stop."

Gertie eyed her suspiciously. "Where exactly are we going?"

"Army-Navy store," Ida Belle said.

The dismayed look on Gertie's face was so hilarious I snapped a picture of her.

"You're *not* wearing camo to your wedding!" Gertie insisted.

"It will be new camo," Ida Belle said.

I laughed. "Gertie, you haven't looked this upset since Ida Belle told you Francis couldn't sing in the church choir."

"An idea almost as ridiculous as me wearing a wedding dress," Ida Belle said.

"The choir needs another tenor," Gertie said. "And Francis loves singing."

"He also loves talking," I said. "He'll hijack the sermon and since he spent half his life with nuns and the other half with criminals, I hesitate to think what kind of trouble that would cause. Maybe you could check with Celia. Francis *is* Catholic, after all."

Gertie gave me a dirty look. "I would never allow Francis in the Catholic church, especially as long as Celia's running the show over there. Any congregation that has Celia in charge of their events doesn't deserve to have Francis's talent to entertain them."

"She called animal control on you again, didn't she?" Ida Belle asked.

Gertie threw her hands in the air, chucking the dress behind the couch. "All I was doing was walking down Main Street with Francis on my shoulder. It wasn't like I was going into the café with him or anything. I just wanted to grab some fruit for him at the General Store, and he likes to pick his own."

"Yeah, I can't see why she would have a problem with that at all," Ida Belle said.

"I know, right?" Gertie said, clearly missing the sarcasm. "It's like she wakes up every day trying to figure out how to make the entire world as miserable as she is."

"That seems a fairly accurate statement," I agreed.

I heard someone clearing their throat behind me and turned around to see an older woman with the word 'Manager' on her name tag. She was wearing a forced smile until she caught sight of the ruined dress, then it changed to a pained look.

"I understand there was a problem with the dress," she said.

"The dress was fine until your saleslady threw a tray of dessert at it," I said.

"Yes, well," the woman said, looking increasingly more uncomfortable. "She was under the impression that you were going to harm her."

I shook my head. "I was just trying to save the desserts before she passed out. Unfortunately, I didn't make it."

"So you're not..." The woman's voice trailed off.

"An assassin?" I asked. "Not anymore. Nowadays, I try to apprehend people without killing them. Doesn't always work out, but you know how it goes—you have the best intentions when you head off to work and sometimes things just don't go the way you planned."

She paled a bit. "You're joking, of course."

"Heck no, she's not joking," Gertie said. "Fortune was one of the CIA's best operatives."

The woman relaxed a tiny bit. "CIA. I see."

Gertie smiled. "So it's all aboveboard. Government-sanctioned killing, and you know our government always gets everything right."

The pained look returned.

"Well, is there anything I can help you with?" she asked, looking at me but not directly in the eyes. "Are you the bride-to-be?"

"Good God, no," I said and pointed to Ida Belle. "That's your victim."

"And you need a wedding dress?" she asked.

"No way I'm wearing one of those things," Ida Belle said. "Besides, do you know how much ammo I could buy for that price?"

"Then what can I help you with?" the woman asked, her exasperation starting to show.

"A garter," Ida Belle said. "Preferably one in blue. That way I cover two of those superstitious wedding things."

"You dragged me all the way out here for a garter?" Gertie said. "Why don't you just order one online like you do everything else?"

"It's going to be on my thigh," Ida Belle said. "I don't want anything that close to my privates to come from an online store. God only knows how many people would fondle it before it got to me."

"You buy your underwear online," Gertie said. "And they're kissing your privates."

"My underwear come in a package," Ida Belle said. "Less handling by strangers. Besides, I wash them in bleach and hot water before I wear them and that wouldn't be good for the garter. Please tell me you're not wearing drawers right out of the package."

Gertie suddenly grew interested in the stained wedding dress.

Before anyone could launch into the questionable state of Gertie's drawers or the potential risks to her privates, I motioned to the manager. "We'll take a blue garter, please. Here's twenty bucks. Keep the change. And I'm sorry about the mess."

The manager took my twenty bucks and met us at the door as we prepared to leave. She opened the bag wide enough for Ida Belle to look inside. "They're individually wrapped," she said. "So your, uh...everything should be fine. Just fine."

"Perfect," Ida Belle said. "Two things down. I've got my garter and I can officially cross going out to shop off my annual list of things to do."

"You have an annual list?" I asked as we hopped in her SUV.

She nodded. "I know I can be stubborn, so there's a few things that some people suggest are normal or polite things to do. I refuse to work them into my daily life, so I have a list. As long as I do things on that list once per year, I consider that broadening my horizons."

"But you shop all the time," I said, confused. "We just stocked up on ammo yesterday, and the day before we both bought meat at the butcher."

"Food and ammo are essential items," Ida Belle said. "My list requires that I shop for something nonessential and at a place I wouldn't normally frequent."

"You're cheating," Gertie said. "The garter is essential."

"No. The garter is for Walter," Ida Belle said. "I'm already marrying him. Do you think he would have the bad judgment to say he won't go through with it unless I'm wearing a garter?"

"You shouldn't challenge wedding superstition," Gertie said. "Bad things could happen."

"I've been friends with you since Jesus was in diapers," Ida Belle said. "I'm pretty sure I'm prepared for whatever life throws at me."

"You're impossible," Gertie said.

"You're going to break a finger trying to shove a square peg in a round hole," I said to Gertie. "If the bride and groom are good with it, then everyone else should be."

"The groom would skydive naked if that's what Ida Belle said it would take to tie the knot," Gertie said. "So what Walter will settle for is not the same as what he might like, given that he's unlikely to have more than one wedding, especially after being married to Ida Belle."

"I thought he had a cardiac workup last week to prepare," I said.

"Here's an idea," Ida Belle broke in. "Stop thinking about it as a wedding and consider it a party with a bit of ceremony at the start. I mean, honestly, we're going for the short version here. The entire I-do-do-you-exchange-rings thing won't last ten minutes. It's the rest of the afternoon that's going to be more important, and that is going to be stellar."

Gertie crossed her arms and slumped in her seat. "I don't see what's so stellar about boiled crawfish and kegs of beer. We're invited to one of those parties just about every week."

"Because those parties don't have a cake and other goodies that Ally baked," Ida Belle said. "And the sides aren't catered by Miss Molly."

Gertie perked up. "You hired Miss Molly?"

Ida Belle grinned and nodded. "I thought that might make you happy."

"Who's Miss Molly?" I asked.

"Only the best caterer in southeast Louisiana," Gertie said. "Her potato salad is legendary. There's been three shoot-outs over it just in the last two years alone."

"I'm not shooting anyone over potato salad," I said. "Maybe over cake."

Ida Belle nodded. "Anyway, Miss Molly is one of Sinful's more colorful residents."

"How come I've never heard of her?" I asked. "I thought I'd cornered the market on anyone who could provide great food. Why have you been holding out?"

"She just got out of jail a couple weeks ago," Ida Belle said.

I raised one eyebrow. "Jail?"

"Oh yeah," Gertie said. "There was this situation with twice-baked potatoes at a wake."

She stopped talking, as if that was all she needed to say. "Seriously? You're going to hold out on me after that statement?" I asked.

"Oh, sorry," Gertie said. "Sometimes it feels like you've been here forever, so I forget that you don't know about Miss Molly or her dark side."

"A caterer with a dark side," I said. "Only in Sinful. What did she do? Poison someone with the potatoes?"

"God no!" Ida Belle said. "Miss Molly would never compromise her food. If she had that big a problem with you, she'd just break your neck like she did her husband's. That's how she learned to cook—in prison."

Gertie nodded. "Miss Molly always loved food but when she got to prison, she found out everything was cheap and tasteless. She begged for kitchen duty until they gave in, and she managed to work wonders with very little. Even the guards started eating there."

"The warden was so impressed, he gave her run of the kitchen and an improved budget," Ida Belle said. "So inmates got some of the best food they'd ever had in their lives. When she got paroled, she worked for a caterer in New Orleans for a while to learn the business end of things. Then she turned all that skill and knowledge into a business and Miss Molly's Catering was born."

"What did she do before catering?" I asked.

"Cage fighting," Gertie said. "She was Molly the Mauler. Had an excellent record."

"A cage fighter from Sinful?" Even for the town that invented crazy, that one sounded strange.

"She isn't an original local," Ida Belle said. "She's from New Orleans, best anyone knows. That's where she was living when she was a fighter, anyway. Had a great-uncle or a fifth cousin or something that used to live here so she knew of the area from when she was a kid. Thought a change of pace would be good when she got out and didn't think she had the looks to compete with the caterers in NOLA."

I stared. "Best anyone knows? How is it possible that the woman has lived here for more than a day and the local gossip contingent hasn't hounded her for every detail of her life since she emerged from the birth canal?"

"Easy," Ida Belle said. "They're scared of her, and she has a reputation for being rather a hothead."

"Which is exactly what got her into trouble over the twice-baked potatoes," Gertie said.

"Did someone sneak seconds without permission?" I asked.

"Worse," Gertie said. "They salted them without tasting."

"Molly dived over that table like she was in the Olympics and tackled the offender like she was back in the cage," Ida Belle said. "The over-salter was unconscious before she ever hit the floor."

"Given Molly's prior conviction," Gertie said, "we were afraid she'd go away for longer than a year, but the judge took pity on her."

"Over salt?" I asked. Clearly I didn't have as good a handle on this whole Louisiana thing as I'd thought.

Ida Belle grinned. "The salt offender was Celia."

"Oh no," I said, and started laughing. "But wait, this was at a wake, you said. What about the family of the deceased? Weren't they mad?"

Gertie shook her head. "They didn't think the potatoes needed salt either."

"Well, Miss Molly sounds like the perfect person to cater your shindig, then," I said. "At least she won't be traumatized by random gunshots, fights over the cake, or a certain alligator who shows up when he smells food."

"Oh no!" Gertie said. "What am I going to do about Godzilla? Gator tail is one of Miss Molly's most requested appetizers."

"She's not going to shoot him and fire up the grill with

Carter standing right there," Ida Belle said, but she didn't look completely convinced.

"Don't worry," I told Gertie. "She won't get a shot off before I do."

Gertie looked relieved. "It's really nice to have friends who can handle all these domestic issues."

I shook my head. Only in Sinful were a begging alligator and a murdering cage fighter considered domestic issues.

"So why did she kill her husband?" I asked. "Did he put ketchup on his steak?"

"No. He changed the television channel," Gertie said.

"And she killed him for that?" I asked.

"It was the last five minutes of the final episode of *Justified* and they didn't have a DVR," Gertie said.

"Well, that explains everything," I said.

"That's what I thought," Gertie said.

"Word was her husband was a bad dude," Ida Belle said. "The whole TV thing probably isn't even true. Rumor has it he tuned Molly up on the regular. That's probably how she learned to fight so well."

"Why didn't she just leave him?" I asked.

Ida Belle shrugged. "One of life's mysteries. And since no one is willing to ask her, we'll probably never know. We're headed to her place after the Army-Navy store. You can give it a go if you'd like."

"No!" Gertie said. "Not before the wedding. Fortune's trying not to kill people and if Miss Molly gets her on the ground, then she'll be sporting black eyes for your wedding."

"Yeah, I'm good with not knowing," I said. "It was just a basic curiosity, but not the kind I want to die over. Besides, if I get her too wound up, she could be sent back to jail and I'm really looking forward to the food now. Are we doing taste-testing, I hope?"

"Nope," Ida Belle said. "Just dropping off money. Molly doesn't do taste tests. You tell her about the event, what other food you'll have, and what your budget is, and she picks the menu."

"Well, it's not very customer-friendly, but I suppose it's better than being tackled," I said.

"Trust me, you can't lose," Gertie said. "Everything that woman sends out of the kitchen is magic."

Ida Belle pulled into the Army-Navy store parking lot and smiled. "You guys ready to find my wedding duds?"

Gertie sighed. "Might as well. Hey, they have camo in white and black."

"Crawfish boil," Ida Belle reminded her. "This is the one thing I'm going traditional on."

"Of course it is," Gertie grumbled as she climbed out of the truck.

CHAPTER TWO

We headed inside the store and Ida Belle called out to Big Chappy, the owner. He looked up from the counter and gave us a wave and a smile. I didn't know much about him, but I did know his real name wasn't Chappy and he wasn't big. But he'd served as a chief of chaplains in the Army, so I figured the nickname had stuck from his service days. And the smile. Leave it to an Army chaplain to be both deadly and optimistic.

He finished up checking out a customer and headed our way just as Gertie spotted a rack of camo miniskirts. She dashed over and yanked one off the racks.

"Oh my God!" she said. "Look at this skirt. It's too cute."

Ida Belle frowned. "You're disappointing me, Chappy. Don't tell me you're selling that trendy crap in here now."

Chappy shrugged. "The kids like 'em, and the parents are happy to spend a fortune for that strip of stretchy nonsense just to shut them up. Heck, I've had more new customers in here since I started stocking those skirts than I have in the past ten years. And once the kids get the parents in here, there's usually something else I can convince them they need.

Flashlights, knives, coolers...it's been a real boon to the business."

"Well, I can't knock capitalism," Ida Belle said and looked at Gertie. "Don't even think about buying that. It's a disgrace to people who wore the real thing."

"Why?" Gertie asked. "You can run in it. It's not long enough to trap your knees."

"It's not long enough to trap your important parts," Ida Belle said. "You run in that, your heinie will be showing in about five steps."

"Depends on your heinie," Chappy said. "It's that stretchy stuff. If you've got enough for it to tuck under, you'd probably be okay."

I stared. "Exactly what kind of religious leader were you?"

"The kind that wasn't blind," Chappy said.

"You keep looking at young girls' tuck-unders and that could change," I said.

He grinned. "What can I help you ladies with today? Got some great .45 rounds in yesterday. And a couple new semis."

"Actually, we're here for Ida Belle's wedding outfit and the bride has chosen camo," I said.

"Great choice," Chappy said. "I've got pants with zipper pockets and snaps. Do you have a preference?"

"Snaps," Ida Belle said. "It's easier to draw your gun."

I shook my head. "You know, it's a little disconcerting the amount of discussion that has gone into the need for self-defense at your wedding. Are you sure you don't want to just fly to Vegas and do this thing?"

"I'm not leaving Louisiana," Ida Belle said. "Look what happened when we went to Florida. Chaos. Can you imagine what could happen in Vegas?"

"Without Gertie?" I asked. "It would probably be as boring as one of Pastor Don's sermons."

Ida Belle shook her head. "Walter's not big on shows or gambling and I'm not big on people. That doesn't leave us much else to do in a place like Vegas."

Gertie stared at her in dismay. "You're getting married! There's only one thing you *should* be doing."

Chappy looked a bit uncomfortable.

"Walter's as old as me," Ida Belle said. "Without medical assistance and a respirator, that one thing isn't going to occupy days."

"So you're not going to have a honeymoon?" I asked. "I thought you said you'd be gone for a couple days after the wedding."

"We're going deep-sea fishing," Ida Belle said. "Got a spiffy charter booked as soon as we set a date."

"You're going to spend your honeymoon on bunk beds with a boat captain and other fishermen?" Gertie asked. "I just can't even with this anymore. I've officially given up hope."

"You could always get married yourself and have it your way," Ida Belle suggested.

"Just as soon as I find a man who can handle a woman like me, I'll see about it," Gertie said.

Ida Belle looked at me. "Looks like you're safe from having to wear a bridesmaid dress."

Gertie gave her the finger and stomped toward the dressing room, waving the miniskirt above her head. "I'm wearing this to your wedding, even if I have to grease up to get it on. I might even run."

"Maybe you should just pick out one of those frilly, ruffled monstrosities for her to wear," I said. "At least you could avoid the potential for a bare-buns scene."

"It's half of Sinful's residents, outside in July, with five hundred pounds of crawfish and five kegs of beer," Ida Belle said. "We'll see someone's buns before the night is over. That's a given."

I grimaced.

"At least Celia's not invited," Ida Belle said.

Chappy nodded. "Thank the Lord and pass the beer. Camo for the adults in the room is over on the rack near the AR-15s."

"See," Ida Belle said. "I can buy clothes and accessories all in the same spot."

I grinned. I really loved this woman.

————

MISS MOLLY LIVED off the highway, down a long dirt road with only a few houses on it. I was pretty sure we'd driven to Canada and was relieved when Ida Belle finally turned into a makeshift driveway. We'd already had to stop for Gertie to pee in a bush, and the subsequent round with her and an overly friendly snake had taken up more of my time and energy than I'd wanted to expend. Ida Belle cheering on the snake hadn't helped matters. Neither had the fact that the bottom of Gertie's pants had been caught on her tennis shoe.

The house was a rather unusual one. It looked like a giant barn or airplane hangar, depending on what mode of transportation you preferred. Added to the oddity of the architecture was the choice of paint color. The entire structure was painted bright purple.

"What's with the house?" I asked. "This is the house, right?"

"The barn and a surrounding thousand acres or so used to be owned by a cattle rancher," Ida Belle said. "He sold off the land in pieces years ago and retired to a small section with the barn and the house. There was a big colonial-mansion-style home over in that clearing to the right but it got taken out by a tornado. The only thing left standing was a refrigerator, which, lucky for the owner, was where he went to hide when he saw the tower of doom coming straight for him. Didn't take a single board off the barn, though. After that nightmare, he sold the rest of the land with the barn, and Molly scooped it up for a song."

"It's a shame the tornado didn't strip the paint," I said.

"The paint is all Molly," Ida Belle said. "The original owner had it done up in traditional red with white trim. Looked way better in my opinion."

"See," Gertie said. "There is something to be said for a traditional take."

"It looked better to *me*," Ida Belle said. "But Molly prefers it like this and she's the one who has to look at it every day."

"Good thing it's not in our neighborhood," I said. "People would have to wear sunglasses just to live nearby."

"She wouldn't be allowed to paint that color in Sinful proper," Gertie said.

"Don't tell me there's an approved list of colors," I said.

"Not exactly," Gertie said. "Back years ago, a former mayor's wife ran off with a musician with a traveling band—the Purple Experience. He managed to sneak a law in that prohibits purple houses in the town limits."

"How did he manage to sneak a law in?" I asked.

"He got the council drunk first," Gertie said.

"That explains a lot about Sinful laws," I said.

Gertie nodded. "If we removed all the laws from the books that came about as part of a drunken stupor, it would be a free-for-all."

"Of purple houses?" I asked.

"And probably a lot more public nudity," Gertie said.

Ida Belle knocked on what I presumed served as the front

door. I heard yelling inside, then a huge crash, like someone had taken down a wall. Then more yelling.

"Maybe we should come back when someone isn't being murdered," I said.

"Might be a while," Gertie said. "I heard she spent a ton of money having her own fighting cage built in the house. I'll bet she's having a round with someone."

"Hopefully, it's not someone she likes," I said.

"I think that's probably a really short list," Ida Belle said and rang the doorbell.

Disturbed's "Stupify" blared from speakers inside and outside the house, and we all covered our ears. When it finally stopped, I looked over at Ida Belle.

"Is this woman staying for the whole shebang?" I asked, praying that she was just flinging plastic containers out of her vehicle as she drove by. I was really looking forward to an event where I probably wouldn't have to pull my gun, but Molly was a curve I hadn't seen coming.

"I doubt it," Ida Belle said. "She hates weddings. Not overly fond of people, really. She's mostly in love with a healthy profit."

"Thank God for capitalism," I said.

The door was flung open and I doubled down on my words. Molly was a sight to behold—if you were into sights that combined MMA and horror movies.

Early thirties. Six foot even. Two hundred and sixty pounds. Enough muscle to worry anyone who got stuck in an enclosed space and couldn't run. Bright purple hair in giant spikes all over her head. The one detriment I could see was the strip of spandex shoved up her personals but at the moment, the only casualty was the bike shorts she wore beneath. Well, and maybe her personals.

"Ida Belle," Molly said and smiled. "Sorry about all the noise. Me and the boyfriend were just roughhousing a bit."

Since no more sound came from inside the barn, I wondered if the boyfriend was still conscious, but I was more disturbed by Molly's smile. At least, I think it was a smile, but somehow it seemed more sinister than the scowl she'd worn when she first opened the door. Then she grabbed Ida Belle in what appeared to be a bear hug but could have been a wrestling maneuver. My hand hovered at my waist. I didn't hesitate often, but this one had me stumped. Finally, I glanced over at Gertie, but since all she'd done was take a step back and wasn't scrambling to dig something out of her purse, I figured the worst threat was being next up for a hug.

Molly finally released Ida Belle, who now looked sort of like a rumpled bedsheet, and gave Gertie a nod. Then she turned her attention to me and I felt my hand itch. Was it gun time now?

She looked me up and down, then shook her head. "I've heard about you. I have to say, the looks don't fit the stories, but then I guess that gives you an advantage, doesn't it? I mean, people see me coming and figure I can do some damage, but they see you and think pretty little thing. I bet you have more confirmed kills than I've got knockouts."

"Maybe, but the day's still young," I said.

She laughed—one of those huge laughs where your head goes all the way back. "I like her," she said to Ida Belle.

Thank God. Although I really hoped liking me didn't mean I was in for a hug.

"I brought you the money for the catering," Ida Belle said and pulled an envelope of cash from her pocket.

"Sure, sure," Molly said. "Come on in. I've got your contract—better late than never. Just need to get a signature. I'll scan it later and shoot you a copy. Plus, I just finished a batch of crab cream cheese dip and need someone to test it for me."

Molly flung open the door and we stepped inside just as a man headed toward a stairwell to our left.

Six foot two. Three fifty if he was a pound. Fortyish. Long gray-and-black hair in a ridiculous ponytail. Far too many tattoos to count. Some of them even spelled correctly. Very recent broken nose. Like five minutes ago recent. Threat level zero now that Molly had worked him over.

"Get some ice on that before it's bigger than your face," Molly said. "And stop falling for my backhand."

He shot her a look that would have scared normal people but she didn't even blink an eye as she waved us down a hallway. I fell in step behind Ida Belle and Gertie, certain that even if the dip tasted like the cat's butt and dirty socks, I was going to declare it the best thing I'd ever eaten. The hallway opened up into a kitchen that was something to behold. It looked as though it belonged in a five-star restaurant, not in a barn in the middle of the swamp. I didn't know anything about kitchen domestics, but even I could tell there had been a serious outlay of cash on her equipment, not to mention the miles of marble countertops.

"Wow!" Gertie said. "Your kitchen is a dream. I couldn't do something like this justice, but I'd pay to spend a day in here baking."

Molly frowned. "I'd loan you my boyfriend before I'd let you use my kitchen."

I worried for a second that Gertie might take her up on that loan. She had been on a bit of a manhunt lately, but apparently Molly's boyfriend wasn't on Gertie's menu. She said thank you so politely that I had to cough to cover my laugh. I supposed even Gertie had a line in the sand when it came to men.

"Here you go," Molly said and pulled a container of dip from one of the two huge refrigerators. Then she dumped some crackers in a bowl. "The presentation isn't up to my normal fare but I just need a quick opinion. Normally, I wouldn't ask as I don't care much for what other people think, but this one is a little spicy—candied jalapeños."

Which she'd bothered to tell us after I'd dumped a cracker with a load of the dip into my mouth. I braced myself for hell-fire and doom but this wasn't bad. It tingled a bit but that only added to the taste. And the taste was awesome.

"This might be one of the best things I've ever eaten," I said. "Can you sell this to me by the gallon or the pound—whatever a really, really big container is?"

Molly laughed, and I could tell she was pleased as Gertie and Ida Belle doubled down on my thoughts.

"I'm surprised you didn't ask for the recipe," Molly said. "That's usually what most people do."

"I'm not domestic," I said. "But I'll gladly pay people who are."

"You wouldn't sell a recipe anyway," Gertie said. "Would you?"

"Ha!" Molly said. "I wouldn't give this recipe to Jesus even if he guaranteed me forgiveness and a seat next to the big man."

"I can offer you an old recliner and money if you give me an ice chest of this," I said.

She shook her head. "If you ate that much, it would make you sick and it's best fresh. But I could probably sell you a good-sized container of it if you like it that much."

"I will mortgage my house if I have to just to pay for it," I said.

"Good," Molly said. "'Cause it's a pain in the butt to make so it's not going to be cheap like some ranch dressing dumped in a bowl. But since you girls like it so much, I'll add it to Ida Belle's wedding list."

"I'll get you more cash," Ida Belle said.

Molly waved a hand in dismissal. "Consider it my wedding gift. You and Gertie were the first people to give me a chance with my business, and your recommendations helped me launch. Without your backing, I would have never gotten off the ground."

"You could have force-fed people this dip," I said.

Molly laughed. "Fierce *and* creative."

"Thank you," Ida Belle said, and I could tell she was really happy about the addition. "I cannot wait to see the rest of the items on the menu. I am sure everyone is going to be thrilled."

"Heck, what's not to be thrilled about?" Molly asked. "Crawfish, beer, my sides, Ally's baking. It will be like everyone died and went to food heaven."

"Isn't that the truth," I said, then looked at Ida Belle. "You should have gotten married months ago. Look at what we've been missing out on."

"If Ida Belle would have said yes to Walter when he first asked, I would have still been in the pen," Molly said.

"If she'd said yes when Walter first asked, you wouldn't even have been born yet," Gertie said.

We all laughed and Molly checked her watch. "Okay, girls, I have to cut this short. I've got a match scheduled with two ex-cons in fifteen minutes. Unless, of course, you want to give the cage a whirl."

We all politely declined, and Molly grinned and shoved the bowl of dip at us as we left the kitchen.

"We might need a cage match to decide who gets to keep that dip," Gertie said as we got in the SUV.

"I have an unopened box of Wheat Thins," I said. "And a new bottle of wine that the clerk at the liquor store up the highway said tasted like raspberries."

"Oh, that sounds great," Gertie said. "Unless, of course, Ida Belle has any more nontraditional wedding errands to run."

"My list for today is complete," Ida Belle said. "I was thinking about fishing this evening, but sitting inside with the AC, wine, and that dip beats out fishing by a long shot."

"Sitting quietly in a corner with AC and no dip should beat out fishing," I said. "I swear this summer is hotter than last year."

"Nah," Gertie said. "You'd just come here from the sandpit, so you were more acclimated to really hot. It didn't seem as bad. Now that you're a regular, you'll eventually give up and fish and sweat. It's the Southern way."

"Why would I go out in a boat and sweat when I never actually fish?" I asked.

"I keep hoping that one day it will look like so much fun that you'll want to do it regularly," Gertie said.

"You people aren't regular," I said. "You're insane. You fish when it's ninety-five degrees and when it's thirty degrees. You fish in hurricanes. You'd probably fish in tornadoes as long as you thought your boat could outrun it."

Gertie nodded.

"Same goes for hunting," Ida Belle said to Gertie. "Remember that year we went hunting when we hit that record low of twenty degrees? I had on two pair of pants, three shirts, and five pair of socks. Thought I'd never get my waders on."

"Would have bagged that duck if I hadn't fallen in the bayou," Gertie said. "Man, that was cold."

"You almost died of hypothermia," Ida Belle said. "Cold is a bit of an understatement. And I told you not to walk that close to the ledge. That overhang was just waiting to break off. All her yelling scared the ducks away for a week."

"Quit your grousing," Gertie said. "You still got your limit. All I got was pneumonia."

"So I take it you learned your lesson?" I asked.

"Heck yeah," Gertie said. "I wear a dry suit under my clothes now."

Ida Belle shook her head as I laughed. Gertie logic.

CHAPTER THREE

IT WAS GETTING on toward late afternoon and Ida Belle, Gertie, and I were semi-comatose in my living room after consuming the entire box of Wheat Thins and the dip. I think we drank two bottles of wine but I honestly couldn't remember. I was in a cream cheese and cracker haze. We'd turned on the television but no one was watching. I was certain that was the case as it was showing a golf tournament. Most likely, Merlin had walked on the remote and no one had the energy to fix the situation.

Gertie groaned. "I'm going to have to have water and air only until your wedding, or I'm not going to fit into my dress."

"You aren't going to fit into that dress unless you die and decay for a year or two," Ida Belle said. "Why didn't you just order it in your size?"

"I thought I'd be thinner by the time the wedding came around," Gertie said.

"You ordered it two weeks ago," Ida Belle said. "Were you planning on getting a horrible stomach flu?"

Gertie waved a hand in dismissal. "I can take a water pill

and lose ten pounds in a day. I didn't think another ten was out of the question."

"You can take a water pill and spend all day in the bathroom," Ida Belle said. "Remember what happened last time you went that route?"

"I don't know what you're talking about," Gertie mumbled.

I opened one eye. "This I have to hear."

"Gertie had a hot date with the new widower in town," Ida Belle said. "His wife's body wasn't even cold before the casserole queens lined up to get a shot at him, but that's small-town living for you."

"He had all of his teeth and hair," Gertie said. "What did you expect?"

"Pension plan?" I asked.

"No one's perfect," Gertie said.

Ida Belle grinned. "So *someone* thinks she's going to take a water pill and squeeze into a skirt she bought back when JFK was still alive."

"It lifted my butt," Gertie said.

"It squeezed your butt so tight it scared gravity," Ida Belle said. "Anyway, Gertie took the water pill, thinking she had a few days before the wife kicked it, but she went early. So she grabs her casserole and heads over there the next day, then promptly runs past the eligible widower and straight into his bathroom...and didn't leave until the next day."

I grinned. "I hope you had enough toilet paper."

Gertie grimaced. "There was only half a roll and the bathroom wasn't even clean. Who has a death in the household and doesn't think to clean their guest bathroom?"

Ida Belle chuckled. "It was a narrow miss—not catching the guy with all his teeth and a dirty bathroom."

"It was clean when I left," Gertie said. "I asked for Comet

28

and a scrub brush. I could reach the sink and the tub from where I was sitting."

I laughed. "Oh my God! I wonder what he was thinking when you asked for cleaning supplies."

"Probably thinking about what his house would sell for," Ida Belle said. "He listed it the day after he got Gertie out of there."

"I'm sure he got more for it since I cleaned his bathroom," Gertie groused. "Anyway, that was a fluke."

"Oh Lord," I said. "Another fluke. What does that make, like ten million flukes in your lifetime?"

"Keep laughing," Gertie said. "But one day, Carter will have less hair and teeth and you'll be lucky if he ever leaves the seat down."

"Less hair and teeth I can deal with," I said. "But he knows I'll shoot him if I fall in the toilet in the middle of the night."

"Threat of death is a good motivator," Ida Belle said. "I'll have to remember that for when Walter thinks he's going to impose man stuff in my space."

"So is Walter moving into your house?" I asked.

Ida Belle had never been one to talk at length about her personal life, but she'd been even quieter than usual when it came to her and Walter's future, especially their living arrangements.

"We haven't really decided," she said. "But I'm making a note of things. I like to be prepared."

"You're getting married next Saturday," Gertie said. "How can you not know where you'll be living after that?"

"I know where *I'll* be living," Ida Belle said. "It's Walter who's unsure."

"Is he unsure because he doesn't want to leave his house or because he's not sure if he'll be shot for moving a toothbrush into yours?" Gertie asked.

"Don't be silly," I said. "There's plenty of room for Walter's bathroom essentials and his clothes. Not like Ida Belle is girling it up in either of those areas. The question is whether he gets any garage or freezer space."

Ida Belle nodded. "So you see my dilemma."

"I'm sure you'll figure it out," I said. "Maybe you should add on to the garage. Or just keep extra frozen goods at the General Store. He's got tons of freezer space."

Ida Belle threw her hands in the air. "Which is exactly what I keep telling him. But then he's all like 'this law' and 'that inspection' and you just can't reason with the man."

"I think you should build a guesthouse in the backyard," Gertie said. "At least then he'd have a place to go when he's tired of everything being your way."

"He already has a place to go," Ida Belle said. "His house."

Gertie shook her head in dismay, then looked at me. "Please tell me you aren't going to make Carter live in his own home when you two tie the knot."

I held my hands up. "Whoa! I'm not even to the point where marriage is a passing thought. No way am I having a conversation about it."

"Is Carter aware that he's not a passing thought?" Gertie asked.

"I think about Carter all the time," I said. "I just don't think about marrying Carter."

Gertie gave me a mischievous grin. "Is he naked when you think about him?"

"Oh good God!" Ida Belle threw her hands in the air.

My cell phone rang and I checked it.

"Speaking of naked thoughts," I said.

"I knew it!" Gertie said.

I laughed and answered, but I could tell right away that something was wrong.

"What happened?" I asked.

"Is Ida Belle with you?" he asked.

"Yeah, she's right here," I said. "Why? Was there an explosion somewhere? Because I swear, we spent the last couple hours eating ourselves into oblivion and then crashing in my living room."

"Were you by any chance at Miss Molly's house earlier today?" he asked.

"Sure, hence the eating ourselves into oblivion," I said. "Ida Belle dropped off the catering money."

"Did you see Molly?" he asked.

"Well, we didn't break into her house and steal her food," I said. "What's going on? Did something happen to her?"

"I don't know," he said. "I'm trying to figure that out."

"What do you mean?" I asked. "She's either okay or she's not."

"She's missing," he said. "So I can't tell you whether or not she's okay."

"We just saw her shortly after noon," I said. "How long could she possibly be missing?"

"I don't know," he said. "I got a call about an hour ago from a woman saying Molly called her but the call was cutting in and out and was hard to hear over engine noise. All she could make out was 'he's going to kill me.' Then she heard Molly yell and the phone went dead. I came out here right away to check. Her boat's gone from the dock and there's no sign of Molly."

"What about her boyfriend?" I asked. "He was there when we were."

"That idiot claims he didn't know she'd left."

"Do you buy it?"

"I don't know if I do or not. It's too weird right now. Anyway, there was a contract on her desk with Ida Belle's name on it dated today, so I figured I'd call and ask."

"Was the money there?"

"I, uh, listen, I need to stop talking about this. If this turns into a missing persons case..."

"I know. I know. Civilians can't be involved in law enforcement business. But will you at least call as soon as you know something about Molly? Friend business trumps law enforcement."

"I will. Gotta go."

He disconnected and I relayed the conversation to Ida Belle and Gertie, who'd already figured out from my tone and just half the conversation that something was seriously wrong.

"Oh no," Gertie said. "I hope something hasn't happened to her."

"I think we have to assume something has," Ida Belle said. "Otherwise, why would she have made that phone call?"

"Maybe not," I said. "The call was cutting in and out and this friend was trying to listen over engine noise. For all we know, Molly could have called her to talk about an upcoming cage match and then a statement like 'he's going to kill me' takes on a whole different meaning."

"What about the yelling?" Gertie asked.

"Someone passed too close or too fast in a boat," I said. "Birds swooped down. Someone waved from across the lake. People yell in boats all the time."

"I see your point," Ida Belle said. "I'm just not sure Molly would ever admit that someone was going to get the best of her."

"And why call in the middle of driving your boat?" Gertie asked. "Why not wait until she stopped when it was easier to talk? You have to be pretty worked up to try both at the same time."

I shook my head. I didn't want to believe that something

bad had happened to Molly, but I couldn't disagree with Ida Belle and Gertie either. The truth was, it sounded odd.

"We should go look for her," Gertie said.

"Wouldn't that be interfering with police business?" Ida Belle asked.

"I don't think so," I said. "Last time I checked, taking a ride in a boat wasn't a crime. Around here, people's boats probably have more hours logged on them than cars."

"Very true," Gertie said and jumped up from the couch. "And a lot of people have been known to take a boat ride during hot weather to get some outside air but not sweat to death. If you guys wouldn't mind hosing me down before we leave, that would be great."

It actually didn't sound bad, now that she'd mentioned it.

"Good idea," I said as we headed outside. "If we get caught, we tell Carter we're playing wet T-shirt contest."

"As long as I get to win," Gertie said.

"You're not winning if Carter's voting," Ida Belle said.

Gertie shook her head. "The game is always rigged."

"Only if you're playing," Ida Belle said. "Let's get going. I'd like to think Molly can take care of herself and she just went boating for peace of mind or fishing for a new dish she thought up. But anybody can be got if the desire is strong enough."

"And accidents can happen on boats," Gertie said.

"Sort of an understatement coming from you," Ida Belle said. "I'm surprised boats don't flee when they see you coming."

"Or insurance companies," I said as I grabbed the hose.

Five minutes later, we were soaking wet and flying down the bayou. The water, which had felt like bathwater when it was hosed on, combined with Ida Belle's driving speed, was now offering up a bit of cool. If I hadn't been worried about Molly, I might have enjoyed myself.

Ida Belle had indicated that Molly's property had a bayou out back where her dock was. That bayou fed into a larger channel that split off in a million directions, a few of which dumped into the lake. So we were going to scan the lake first, then start down that larger channel and hope that Carter wasn't coming straight toward us. He couldn't arrest us for boating, but no way he was going to buy our wet T-shirt story. He'd know exactly what we were doing.

We hit the lake in record time and Ida Belle slowed as she headed for the center. Gertie handed me binoculars from the storage bench and I scanned the area, looking for Molly. I spotted a couple of commercial fishing boats and a ski boat full of teens, then several bass boats, but they all held men.

"Anything?" Ida Belle asked when I lowered the binoculars.

"No," I said. "All the bass boats are guys."

"You sure one of them isn't Molly?" Gertie asked. "I mean, they're wearing caps and from a distance..."

"Heck, from up close she could look like a guy," I said. "But they all have beards. I don't care how much testosterone she has, she still can't grow a beard in one afternoon."

Ida Belle nodded. "Then we'll head up the channel."

I barely got the binoculars tucked in by my side before she took off across the lake at two billion miles per hour. It might have been terrifying if it hadn't been so exhilarating. Gertie was hooting from her seat in the bottom of the boat when Ida Belle made a sharp right and the boat skimmed the top of the water sideways as we turned into the channel.

She slowed down in the narrower body of water. Not because she couldn't go faster and definitely not because she didn't want to, but because I needed to be able to hold the binoculars to my eyes and scan the marsh for any sign of Molly. Gertie pulled out another set and hopped up on the bench seat now that we were slow cruising and helped me look. We did ten minutes of scanning up the channel but never spotted her.

Ida Belle cut the accelerator. "There's her dock and her bigger boat isn't there."

"Does the bayou continue past her dock in the other direction?" I asked.

"It does," Ida Belle said. "But it dead-ends at a freshwater dam. It's decent fishing there, although more so at night, but if that's where she was, you would have already heard from Carter. Deputy Breaux was on boat patrol today and he would have been sent there first to check."

"Do many people come this way?" I asked.

"Not really," Ida Belle said. "There's better fishing a dozen other places."

"So it's unlikely someone would have seen Molly unless she went into the lake," I said.

Ida Belle nodded. "Maybe we should head back to the lake and ask around."

"I think so," I said.

"Grab your butts," Ida Belle said.

Gertie flopped down in the bottom of the boat on her custom cushion, and I moved to the very back of my seat and gripped the arm bars with both hands, clutching the binoculars in between my thighs and hoping I had the strength to hold once she got going. She took off at full speed and it was worse than a day at the gym. Weaving around the corners, barely skirting overhangs and cypress roots. Even fish fled in the other direction, skipping across the top of the water as they made their escape.

When we reached the lake, she took a hard right and Gertie involuntarily vacated her cushion. At least she was already in the bottom of the boat. The first couple times we'd gone out in my airboat, Gertie had attempted to sit on the bench but the potential for disaster was so high, I'd had her a memory foam cushion specially made so she could be secure in the bottom of the boat. Well, mostly secure.

She pushed herself upright and gave Ida Belle the finger without looking back. I held in a grin and then suddenly, Ida Belle cut speed completely and I leaned forward, clutching the handrails so that I didn't pitch out of my seat. She pointed ahead of us and I saw a couple of older local guys in a bass boat. They were some distance away but it was beyond rude to approach people quickly when they were fishing. Even if someone was missing.

She inched closer to the fishermen and lifted her hand to wave. They recognized us and lifted a hand back. We pulled up within loud talking distance and they both stared at us, expectantly and just a tad bit impatiently.

"You guys seen Miss Molly today?" Ida Belle asked.

They both shook their heads.

"But if she's fishing, I don't think I'd go tracking her down for food and stuff," one man said. "That woman is scary."

"It's not that," Ida Belle said. "Her boat is missing and there seems to be some concern that she's in danger. So we were trying to find her and reassure ourselves that she's all right."

"Can't imagine who could take that woman out," the second man said. "Unless maybe it was you with a long-range rifle, or that pretty blonde there that you run with."

"If you see her, will you tell her we were looking for her?" Ida Belle asked.

Their eyes widened and they both shook their heads.

"No ma'am, we won't do that," the first man said. "But I'm happy to call and let you know if we spot her."

"Cowards," Gertie grumbled.

I couldn't say that I blamed them. If Miss Molly was really out fishing, either for dinner or relaxation, then accosting her probably wouldn't end well. She struck me as the type of person who liked to choose when she interacted with people. And heading out on your boat alone said only one thing to me.

Ida Belle started up the boat and continued on. About halfway around the lake, we spotted another boat. As we inched up, the man with the pole in the water looked up from what appeared to be a nap. He spotted us and waved.

"Hey, Nickel," Ida Belle said. "Good to see you out in the fresh air."

Nickel and his brother, Whiskey, owned the Swamp Bar, but it was usually Whiskey who kept things running. Nickel, who'd gotten his nickname from a five-year stint in prison, was a repeat jail visitor. Mostly his offenses were minor now but with his record, judges didn't tend to give him any slack.

He grinned as we approached. "I don't know how fresh it is, but it's still good to be out in it."

"Maybe you can cut your brother a break and stick around for a while," Ida Belle said.

"Oh heck, Whiskey's got that bar running on autopilot," he said. "If anything, I get in the way. Best thing I can contribute is fresh seafood, which is why I'm out here today."

He reached over and opened an ice chest to show us a couple of large redfish.

"Nice," Gertie said.

He nodded. "Couple more and we'll have enough for a big stew tomorrow night. Whiskey's redfish stew always brings in the crowd."

"How's your daddy doing?" Ida Belle asked. The brothers'

father had terminal cancer and doctors had said he didn't have much longer back last year. Apparently, their father wasn't in agreement and was still hanging in.

"He's in bad shape," Nickel said. "But you know the old coot is too stubborn to go. Can't walk much anymore without help, and we can't keep any weight on him no matter what we feed him. But ain't none of that stopped him from dressing us boys down, so I'd say he's doing all right."

"He always was a tough guy," Ida Belle said. "Let me know if we can do anything."

"I appreciate it," he said. "So what are you ladies doing out today? I don't see any fishing gear."

"We're looking for Miss Molly," Ida Belle said. "You seen her?"

"Nope," he said. "Hadn't seen any womenfolk out today at all, not that I'd ever refer to Molly as womenfolk. Least not to her face." He gave Ida Belle a curious look. "Why you looking for her?"

"Her boat's gone from the dock and no one can raise her by phone," Ida Belle said. "Apparently, she called a friend who couldn't make out much of the phone call, but she heard enough to think something was wrong. She called Carter and he went to check but so far, hasn't no one seen hide nor hair of her since this afternoon."

"She's got that aaaaasss...boyfriend."

I smiled. I knew what he'd been about to say. "The boyfriend doesn't know where she is, either," I said. "I take it he's not on your fishing buddy list."

"No way," he said. "That dude is bad news. Comes into the bar and gets stinking drunk, hitting on wives and girlfriends. Like anyone's going to take him up on that crap. First off, he's obnoxious and not all that pretty to look at. More importantly, everyone knows he's with

Molly. Ain't nobody fool enough to jump in front of that train."

"Does Molly know he does that?" Ida Belle asked.

Nickel shrugged. "No idea. Guess someone might have told her, but it would have to be someone with big ones. I wouldn't want to deliver that kind of message to Molly. Would you?"

"No," I said. "It might affect life expectancy as sometimes the messenger gets taken down with the guilty party."

"Exactly," he said. "Anyway, if I see her, I'll give you a call but it's been quiet out here today. Too hot for most people. They'll come out in an hour or so when the sun starts setting. I wouldn't worry much about Molly, though. She can take care of herself. If people can't find her, it's probably 'cause she don't want to be found."

"Probably so," Ida Belle agreed. "Thanks, Nickel. And stay out of trouble."

"I'm going to try," he said.

"I wonder if Molly knew her boyfriend was trying to pick up other women at the Swamp Bar," I said as Ida Belle pulled slowly away.

"Hard to say," Gertie said. "Normally, you can't keep something that blatant a secret in a place like Sinful, but Nickel's right—people might be afraid to tell her. Still, I suppose someone could have made an anonymous phone call or sent her an email from a fake account. Her email is on her website."

"Or sent pictures or video for that matter," Ida Belle said. "The days of 'he said, she said' about public displays of bad behavior are over. Seems most everything you do outside your house is recorded by something."

I frowned. "Her boyfriend looked awfully mad today."

"You mean after he got his butt whupped?" Gertie asked. "Maybe someone did tell her."

"You think he did something to her?" I asked.

They looked at each other, then shrugged.

"I don't know anything about him," Ida Belle said. "Never even knew she had a boyfriend until today. Molly isn't one for small talk and definitely not for personal talk."

"I couldn't even tell you his name," Gertie said. "He's not from around here. That's about all I know."

"Maybe she imported him from New Orleans," I said. "Where to now? There's no one else on the lake. I guess everyone's headed home."

"I don't want to give up," Gertie said. "If Carter had found Molly, he would have sent a text at least."

"I don't want to give up, either," I said. "I just have no idea where to start. There's a million places a person in a boat could go around here. You two are going to have to make your best guess and we'll start there."

"That's a tough one with Molly being such a private person," Ida Belle said. "If this was a regular search-and-rescue, we'd have a dozen or more volunteers and could split up territory, but with only us..."

She scanned the lake for a bit, then shook her head. "Since we know Molly didn't like the stop-and-chat, maybe we start on some of the lesser-used bayous."

"That makes sense," I said. "Maybe the ones closest to the channel that runs by her house first, then we can spread out from there."

Ida Belle nodded and Gertie and I prepared for launch. A couple minutes later, she turned into a smaller channel and slowed so that Gertie and I could use the binoculars to search.

"I picked this one because there's not so many trees in between bayous," Ida Belle said. "From this one, you should be able to see two or more to the right."

"Will we be able to see her boat with the grass?" I asked.

"Her console is high enough that I'm hoping you can, but I can't be sure," Ida Belle said.

She continued down the bayou as Gertie and I scanned the area for any sign of a boat. We'd probably traveled a mile or better when I spotted sunlight reflecting off something one bayou over.

"There!" I said and pointed.

CHAPTER FOUR

IDA BELLE LET off the accelerator and Gertie swung her binoculars the direction I'd indicated.

"I don't see anything," Gertie said.

"I saw sun reflecting off something," I said. "Maybe a boat console?"

Ida Belle nodded. "Let me turn around and head back out."

"Wait a minute," Gertie said. "It will take longer for you to drive back up this bayou and then down the other than it will for me to walk across this narrow patch of land and see for myself."

"I don't think that's a good idea," I said. "What if there are gators in the marsh?"

"That goes without saying," Gertie said. "But they usually take off when they hear people coming."

"'Usually' is not always," I said.

"Oh, for Christ's sake," Gertie said as she stood and set her binoculars on the bench. "I've been traipsing through these bayous since I could walk. A gator hasn't gotten me yet and one isn't going to."

"I'm more afraid you'll come back with another one in your pants," Ida Belle said.

Gertie waved a hand in dismissal and stood on the bench. We were only a foot from the bank, and she could easily step off onto it but where Gertie was involved, things rarely went to plan. She was just stepping off when Ida Belle yelled to wait.

But it was too late.

The patch of dirt that looked like land was, in fact, a mat of marsh grass and mud, floating on top of the water. Gertie took one step on it and down she went.

"At least she had the sense to take the binoculars off first," Ida Belle said as we leaned over the side of the boat. A second later, Gertie's head broke the surface—the mat of dead marsh grass sitting on it like a hat—and she coughed water everywhere.

"Do you have to hack that up on all of us?" Ida Belle asked.

Gertie grabbed the side of the boat and we hauled her back into it. She slumped in the bottom, still coughing, and Ida Belle banged on her back a couple times until she was breathing normally.

"Do I have your permission to drive around now?" Ida Belle asked. "Maybe we can blow some of those weeds off your head. You look like a rerun of *Hee Haw*."

I was waiting for the inevitable finger but all of a sudden, Gertie's eyes widened and she bolted up like she'd been ejected from her seat, flinging the patch of weeds off her head. She grabbed her T-shirt and started pulling it, yelling at the top of her lungs. Ida Belle appeared as lost as I was, but the one thing I knew was that she wanted that shirt off and T-shirts just didn't tear in real life like they did for sexy guys in movies. I grabbed the bottom of her shirt and yanked it up over her head, and that's when I got a firsthand look at the problem.

There was a water moccasin in her bra.

The long venomous snake had gone in between her boobs and was looped around the front of the undergarment, its head forward and hissing at me. It struck out once and I jumped back. Gertie had her hands over her mouth, probably to keep from yelling and drawing its attention her way.

"Unhook her bra!" I yelled at Ida Belle, who was standing behind her.

"It's a front clasp," Ida Belle said, sounding a little panicked.

"Cut it!" I said as the snake lunged at me again.

I heard a knife click open and a second later, the bra flipped forward over Gertie's shoulders. The snake dropped to the bottom of the boat with the bra, and Gertie shifted her hands from her mouth to her chest and jumped up into my chair. The snake fled the bra and slithered into the T-shirt, so I grabbed the whole bundle and tossed it overboard. When I looked up at Gertie, standing in my chair and holding her chest with her hands, I realized we might have a logistical problem.

"I don't suppose you keep spare shirts on your boat," Gertie said.

"In hindsight, I probably should," I said. "What is it with you and snakes this week?"

"Give her your shirt," Ida Belle said. "You wear a sports bra. That's more coverage than a bikini top."

"I'm not wearing a bra at all today," I said. "It's too hot for multiple layers, and my T-shirt is the thicker kind."

"Wait until you have gravity issues," Gertie said. "You won't be going without one then."

"What about your shirt?" I asked Ida Belle.

"My bra is lace," Ida Belle said.

Gertie stared. "That seems awfully girlie of you."

Ida Belle shrugged. "Combine too hot with the gravity

problem and you get a really thin bra. Seemed more of a practicality, really."

I picked up the bra from the bottom of the boat. "We can salvage this. Tie it back together."

Gertie turned her back to us and slipped the bra into place while Ida Belle worked on tying the back into a knot. Gertie grunted as she stretched the fabric to its limit, finally managing to get a small knot. Gertie turned around and we couldn't help laughing. It was so tight it had her chest not far from her chin.

"Maybe pull it down all over," I said.

Ida Belle adjusted and Gertie looked down and sighed. "I look like a white trash dirty movie."

I pulled a life jacket from the storage bench and handed it to her. "Wear this. It covers the important things."

Ida Belle nodded. "And now that they're strapped in, that whole gravity thing won't have parts peeking out the side of that jacket."

Gertie glared. "You two are enjoying this entirely too much."

She pulled on the jacket and flopped back down in her seat, waving a hand at us to get going. Ida Belle looked over at me and grinned before she started up the boat and took off. It didn't take too long to backtrack on the bayou and then traverse the other, and as we approached the bend where I'd seen the boat, Ida Belle slowed. We rounded the corner and she nodded.

"That's Molly's boat," she said.

Since the name on the back read *The Mauler* I figured that was the case but there was no sign of Molly anywhere. I scanned the bank behind the boat but didn't see any evidence of human passage.

"It's not anchored," Gertie said. "This is bad."

I nodded, the impact of her words not lost on me. If something had happened—an injury, a mechanical problem—and someone had given Molly a ride, they would have towed her boat. And if that wasn't possible, she would have secured it. Ida Belle had told me the make and model before we set out, and I'd been in Louisiana long enough to know a boat like that ran upward of sixty grand. No one was going to leave sixty grand floating loose.

"What's that on the side?" Gertie asked. "Is that blood?"

Gertie had barely finished the sentence before I jumped onto Molly's boat and hurried to the back edge where the dark stain was. I dipped one finger in it and nodded.

"It's blood," I said.

"Jesus!" Gertie said. "We need to dive in. She could be down there somewhere."

"No," I said and held up a hand to stop her from leaping into the bayou. "We don't know for sure the blood belongs to Molly, and even if it is hers, it's been here a while."

I spotted a mark in the inside hull and squatted to get a closer look. "There's a hole here. Looks recent."

"Bullet hole?" Ida Belle asked.

I frowned. "Could be. Is there an exit on the opposite side?"

"Not that I can see," Ida Belle said.

I took out my phone and took a snapshot of the hole. It looked like a bullet hole but had left a slightly imbalanced tear in the metal that caused more of a rip on one side. But then, it might also be a puncture from a gaff hook or even a sharp anchor tip. I didn't want to get ahead of myself, but it didn't look good.

Ida Belle and Gertie both frowned at me as I stood. I didn't have to spell it out to them. They knew the score. If Molly had been shot and fallen overboard, then she'd been down there too long to think she'd be catering Ida Belle's or anyone else's wedding.

"The hole could be from something else," Gertie said. "Maybe she fell and hit her head and went over the side. She might have walked up the bank and could be lying in the grass, injured."

"If she'd fallen in the water, she'd have pulled herself right back into her boat," Ida Belle said. "I've seen her lift a full keg of beer like it was a pillow. I don't think pulling in her own body weight would faze her."

"No," I said, "but she could be confused or have an injured arm or shoulder. We should check the bank but first, I need to call Carter."

"Crap," Gertie said. "He'll probably be mad."

"I think he'll be worried first and mad later," I said and dialed.

I heard a boat engine cut out as Carter answered his phone. I told him what we'd found and then handed the phone to Ida Belle to give directions. When she was done, she passed it back to me.

"I'll be there in about ten minutes," he said. "Don't move until I get there and don't go onto that boat again. Don't leave your boat. And definitely do not go into the water. That area is full of gators."

He disconnected and I relayed the message. Gertie sat on the bench and sighed.

"I knew I should have brought a casserole," she said.

"They're not all casserole eaters like Godzilla," Ida Belle said.

"If Godzilla can be trained, the others probably can too," Gertie argued.

"Now she's the alligator whisperer," Ida Belle said. "Do I

need to remind you that Godzilla ate a guy at Fortune's house?"

"He was a bad guy," Gertie said. "He didn't count."

"I think Wildlife and Fisheries might have a different opinion on that one if they ever got wind of it," I said.

"Well, at least we can see if she's collapsed somewhere on the bank," Gertie said.

"Because that one went so well for you the last time," Ida Belle said.

"I'll do it," I said.

Gertie could be right. It was possible that Molly had cracked her head on the boat, fallen over the side, and then crawled up the bank and passed out. Unfortunately, that would indicate a head injury and that was never a good thing to wait on. I grabbed a pole we used to push the boat around and poked the bank to make sure it was real ground and not floating grass disguised as land. When I was satisfied that I had a good landing pad, I sprang from the boat and onto the bank.

"Go back toward the lake," Ida Belle said. "The tide's been going out for hours. It would have taken her that direction."

I nodded and headed down the edge of the bank, scanning the ground for Molly and the edge of the bank for any sign that a person had traveled up it. I had to stop several times to scan an area around flattened grass, but never saw any sign of Molly, blood, or anything else that would indicate a person-sized object passed this way. I was probably thirty yards away from the boat when I found a large depressed area of grass at the edge of the bank that led into taller grass to my right. I stepped onto the grassy trail and pushed forward into the thicker brush.

I heard the rumble before I saw it, but unfortunately, I'd already taken that last critical step.

The gator was at least twelve feet long and was in the center of a small clearing. His head was lifted, his mouth open, and he stared right at me. I considered pulling my pistol, but I knew there was no way I could get off a shot that would kill the gator. Not from this angle and not with a nine-millimeter. I took one slow step backward, then another. The gator tossed his head from side to side and I took another step, praying that he was posturing and as soon as I vacated his sunning spot, he'd let my trespass go.

No such luck.

Before I could take another step, he launched forward at a speed that people wouldn't think possible from something so large and long. Except for people who'd been in a footrace with an alligator, of course. I whirled around and set off at a dead run.

"Gator!" I yelled as I went.

I saw Gertie toss a rifle up to Ida Belle, who stood on her seat and took aim.

"I don't know him," Gertie said. "Shoot the sucker!"

CHAPTER FIVE

I COULD HEAR the gator closing in on me as I approached the boat. Just another ten yards and please God, don't let me trip over anything. If I went into the water, it was all over but the funeral. I was about ten feet from the bank when Gertie yelled, "Jump!"

I took two more steps, then launched into the air, using every inch of muscle in my legs to propel me up and out. I heard the gunshot and more yelling from Gertie but it was as though everything was in slow motion. I couldn't have been in the air more than a couple seconds, but I swear, I had time to look and consider every blade of grass and every drop of water beneath me. The side of the boat was closing in but not quickly enough.

I wasn't going to make it!

I hit the water right in front of the boat, my hands clutching the side as I fell. I pulled myself up and flung my body over the side so quickly, my moves would have made a cat jealous. I hit the bottom of the boat and rolled to a stop before sitting up. Gertie and Ida Belle stared down at me and Gertie laughed before patting the top of my head.

"You came up so fast the top of your head's not even wet," she said.

"Where's the gator?" I asked.

"He went in right behind you," Ida Belle said. "Sorry. I didn't have line of sight."

"At least you slowed him down long enough for me to jump," I said. "I'm pretty sure I felt his breath on my leg."

"I'm pretty sure you did too," Ida Belle said.

"He was a big one," Gertie said. "I wish you could have bagged him. We could have fired up the grill big-time."

"I'm just happy we're not firing up the coroner's office," I said. "I didn't see any sign of Molly as far as I made it. Do you think she could have drifted farther than that before reaching shore?"

"Anything is possible," Ida Belle said. "But if she was conscious, she would have tried to get onshore as soon as possible so she could try to get back to her boat and in the worst case, it makes it easier for people to find you when they come looking."

"Well, that's not a good place to take an unwelcome nap," I said. "There were a lot of smaller trails out of the water and onto the bank and they all looked fairly recent. This place must be popular with the gators."

Ida Belle gave me a grim nod, then pointed. "There's Carter."

I sighed. "And me dripping wet and Gertie still damp."

"Wet T-shirt contest, remember?" Gertie said.

"You're not even wearing a shirt," I said. "I'm never going to hear the end of this."

"Sure you will," Ida Belle said. "You'll do something worse and this will all be forgotten."

"Always the optimist," I grumbled.

"More of a realist," she said.

Carter approached in his boat and gave us all the once-over. I'm sure he'd only needed a couple seconds to take in the condition of Gertie and my clothes and the fact that Ida Belle was holding a rifle to know we'd ignored his directive.

"I thought I told you to stay put," he said.

"Gertie fell in before we got here," I said. "There was a situation with a snake, and clothes had to be sacrificed."

"I fully expect an overboard incident with Gertie in the boat, and I'm not touching the whole clothes-snake thing," he said. "I was referring specifically to *you.*"

"We were afraid Molly had fallen overboard, cracked her head, and might have crawled up a bank," I said. "The sooner you get to a head injury the better."

"I take it you didn't find anything?" he asked.

"A sunbathing alligator," I said. "He was not happy to be interrupted."

Carter sighed. "These banks are dangerous. This whole area is dangerous."

"I heard it was good fishing here," I said.

"Of course it's good fishing here," Carter said. "Which is why the alligators love it."

"Oh yeah," I said. "Didn't quite put that one into perspective."

He looked up at Ida Belle. "Did you tag him?"

"No line of sight," she said.

"Well, at least that's one set of paperwork I don't have to worry about," he said. "Did anyone step onto Molly's boat besides Fortune?"

"Just me," I said. "But as soon as I spotted the blood on the side, I called you."

"Really?" he asked. "The very second you spotted it?"

"Well, I might have checked the blood to see how old I

thought it was," I said. "It's not overly fresh but with this heat…"

Carter stepped from his boat to Molly's and went to inspect the blood. He squatted down and looked closely at the side, then touched a bit with his finger.

"It's bad, isn't it?" Gertie asked.

"It's not good," Carter said.

He pulled out his phone and made a call requesting a forensic unit, two boats to make drags on the bayou, and as many people as could volunteer to do a search. He slipped his phone back into his jeans pocket, then scanned the bottom of the boat. I had no idea what he was looking for, but he must not have found it because his frown got bigger and he opened the bench chest to look inside.

A couple seconds later, he pulled out an anchor and I saw his jaw flex.

"Is there blood on it?" I asked.

"Can't say," he said. "And even if there was, we wouldn't know that it's Molly's. For that matter, we don't know that the blood on the side of the boat is Molly's. It could be from fish."

"Then where is Molly?" Gertie asked.

He didn't answer. He couldn't.

———

IT WAS 8:00 the next morning before I crawled out of bed. Even Merlin's complaining about his late breakfast hadn't fazed me. After ten minutes of opera yowling and one run across my forehead, he'd probably decided I was dead. I suppose I was lucky he didn't start eating me. I had read up on house cats. You didn't want to die alone with one. Not if you weren't going to be missed for a while.

I trudged into the kitchen and put on a pot of coffee, then

flopped into a chair. Carter had finally called off the search at
3:00 a.m. and was planning to regroup this morning. But we all
knew the score. It was no longer a search-and-rescue mission.
It was a recovery and in one of the worst environments
possible.

The two boats had dredged the channels in the area
surrounding where we found Molly's boat and at the opening
of the lake for hours without success. But it wasn't an easy job.
So many things were submerged in the water that they had to
constantly stop and untangle nets before starting again. It
seemed a tedious and never-ending process.

After Gertie was properly dressed and could take in a full
breath again, we were assigned bank lookout but under no
circumstances were any of the volunteers to leave their boats.
It was pitch-dark with no moon and the area was full of
hungry gators. We used spotlights and poled our way slowly
along the bank. If we spotted an area that looked as if a person
could have passed that way, then we were to alert Carter and
he would access the ground with Deputy Breaux. Ida Belle and
Gertie showed me the gator claw marks to look for, and all of
the breaches of the bank from the water that we found
contained them. That would probably have been good information to have had earlier that evening before I ran the thirty-
yard dash while chased by a man-eater.

By the time we got back to my house, we were all
exhausted and sad. I had just met Molly but I had liked her.
And I hated that right now, everything was a big unknown.
Had someone been chasing her? Had he caught up with her
and hit her over the head with the anchor before dumping her
into the bayou? Or had she been talking in generalizations to
her friend and then had a tragic accident? While I didn't envy
Carter the job he had in front of him, my curiosity wanted
those answers as badly as he did.

I grabbed two coffee mugs and poured them both almost to the rim. No creamer, milk, or sugar for me. Today was straight-up caffeine day if I planned to move beyond the kitchen. I had just sat down when I heard my front door open and Carter called out.

"In the kitchen," I said and he appeared several seconds later.

"Did you know I was coming?" he asked, pointing to the two cups.

I shook my head. "Despite all the conspiracy theories, the CIA didn't teach psychic perception. I poured two for myself, figuring it was going to take at least that to get me back out of this chair."

"Good idea," he said and grabbed two cups for himself.

He filled them up, then sat across from me. "I hate this," he said.

"Me too. I hated it in the sandbox and I hate it here. People need a body. They need a coffin or an urn. Something."

Carter nodded and gave me a sympathetic look. "You thinking about your father?"

"Not really. Well, maybe he's crossed my mind. The first time, I buried teeth. It's hard for a teenager to wrap their mind around a death when all you have to go on is a couple of molars."

"But you did it."

"And then he came back. And look how fabulous that was."

"The two of you saved this country and others from a serious breach of national security and God knows how many people from being assassinated—important people."

"I know. But it still sucked. I'd put all that behind me. And now it's all right there again."

"Do you think Morrow is still looking into his second death?"

I shrugged. The official narrative was that my father was spotted on the deck of a boat just seconds before it exploded. Of course, his body wasn't recovered because due to the blast, there wasn't much left over the size of a quarter. And retrieving any body parts from an ocean explosion was mostly a fool's mission. But a couple weeks after his 'death,' I'd received a gift that I was certain had come from him. I'd told Carter, Ida Belle, and Gertie about it because someday, he might be the catalyst for trouble again. But I hadn't told Morrow. I didn't agree with the way my father had handled things but I couldn't fault his accomplishments. I was sure he figured 'dying' was the best possible outcome for both of our futures. And he was probably right.

"If Morrow's looking into anything, he's not telling me about it," I said. "But I'm sure at some point Jesus Redding will rise once more and we'll get to play ball all over again."

"Hopefully, next time he can leave you out of it."

"As long as I'm his daughter and he's breathing, I'll always be in it."

Carter frowned. I knew he wasn't happy about the situation. Neither was I. As long as my father was alive, there was always that chance that something would surface again and drag me back into my former life. It didn't mean I was going to spend my time looking over my shoulder. Neither was Carter. We were both trained professionals. If anything was off, we'd know it long before it was visible. I had to believe that intuition would alert me if things ever shifted. Otherwise, every day would begin with a cloud over my head, and that's not the way I chose to live.

"What's the plan for today?" I asked. "Are we going on land since it's daylight?"

"No. I know no one wants to hear this but I'm going to do

a couple more drags of the lake at the opening of that bayou and some surface scouting, but then I'm calling it."

"Is that going to fly?"

"Yeah. No one likes it but everyone knows the score. Molly isn't the first person that's come up missing in those bayous and she won't be the last. She's not even the first this year. I'd say we haven't found a body over half the time in circumstances like these. It's hard but it's reality."

"What about the anchor? They're testing it, right?"

"You know I can't comment about that," he said.

I sighed. "Your job and your ethics really get in the way of all the good gossip. But have it your way. When you start an investigation, we'll all know it was murder."

"I'm really hoping it wasn't. This town has had enough bad things happen lately. It would be nice to have something be just a tragic accident."

"We have plenty of those—but mostly Gertie causes them and usually no one dies."

He gave me a small smile as he stood. "Anyway, I just dropped by to check in. I've got to get down to the sheriff's department and coordinate those sweeps. Then I've got a mountain of paperwork to start on. I assume if I ask you to stay off the water, you'll completely ignore me, so instead, I'll just ask that you call me immediately if you feel that anything is off. Anything at all. Your intuition is better than most people's eyesight."

I nodded and he leaned over to kiss me, then left. I waited until I heard the front door close, then poured the rest of the coffee in my mugs and started another pot. Then I grabbed my phone and sent a text to Ida Belle and Gertie.

Meeting at my place whenever you're up and moving. Just started another pot of coffee. Use your key. I don't want to get out of the chair again.

About fifteen minutes later, the front door opened and I heard them arguing as they walked toward the kitchen.

"I'm just saying that a bouquet would be nice," Gertie said. "No one's telling you to carry a bush around. You're so drama these days."

"I already told you that these hands carry exactly two things when I'm wearing camo—guns and dead things. I'm guessing neither would be appropriate for a wedding."

Gertie threw her hands in the air and flopped into a chair as Ida Belle poured them some coffee. They both looked as bad off as I felt.

"Looks like we could all use another round of sleep," I said.

"I had cucumbers on my eyes for thirty minutes," Gertie said. "I finally gave up and pulled out the Preparation H."

Ida Belle gave her a look of dismay. "Those kinds of problems have nothing to do with a lack of sleep. And we don't want to hear about them."

"I put it on my eyes," Gertie said. "It reduces inflammation. Doesn't matter if it's your eyes or the thing you don't want to talk about. Those beauty pageant girls have been doing it for years. I've told you about this."

"I probably zoned out when you got to the Preparation H part," Ida Belle said.

Gertie shook her head and looked over at me. "I have some in my purse if you'd like a swipe before Carter sees you looking like a *Walking Dead* extra."

"Carter has already seen me," I said. "I sent that text right after he left and since he didn't look any better than we do, I'm calling it an equal rights thing and moving on. Plus, I don't care, which pretty much solves everything."

Gertie looked at Ida Belle and sighed. "She's you. A younger, better, prettier you."

Ida Belle grinned.

"So what did Carter have to say?" Ida Belle asked. "Are we on search duty again? What time are they starting?"

"They're not," I said and relayed what Carter had told me. They both frowned but neither seemed surprised by the news.

"I figured we'd go out and do our own thing, though," I said. "I mean, if you think that's the best plan."

"What do you think?" Ida Belle asked. "Does this feel like something more than an accident?"

I shrugged. "I don't have enough information to know. But I don't like it. Molly seemed more than capable of handling herself but if you combine her disappearance with that phone call, then it doesn't sound good. I'd love to know if that blood on the anchor was Molly's. Because if it was, and it was recent, then no way she slipped and hit her head on it, then fell overboard but somehow managed to put it back in the storage bench before she drowned."

"Seems like a really stupid thing to do if you were the killer," Gertie said. "Why not just throw it overboard?"

"Because most criminals are dumb as rocks," Ida Belle said. "And thank God for that."

"It might be nothing," I said. "For all we know it could be from fish or an older injury."

"If Carter keeps investigating, then we'll know, right?" Gertie asked.

"I thought the same thing earlier," I said, "but now that I've had a couple cups of coffee, I'm not sure. I don't know anything about insurance and estates and all that legal mess, but I'd think anyone standing to gain would have to have some sort of evidence that Molly was deceased. I mean, the CIA has its own set of criteria for operatives, but I figure it's got to be worse for civilian cases, which means he'll need as much information as he can get for a report, right?"

Ida Belle nodded. "It's one of the biggest problems around

here when it comes to drownings. They don't find the body a lot, and families are stuck trying to prove that if someone didn't reappear from a boat trip, then they likely aren't around anymore."

"How long do they have to wait?" I asked.

"In general, five years," Ida Belle said. "But if you have circumstances that indicate death is the most likely event, then you can get it pushed through sooner. In this case, she went out on her boat, she's missing, and if the blood on the side is hers, then that's an indication of some kind of accident. Then if she doesn't reappear and there's no changes to her cell phone, bank accounts, and credit cards, heirs can make a case for having her declared legally dead before that five-year mark."

"Which is good," Gertie said. "Can you imagine being a widow with kids to support and having to wait five years for an insurance payout because your husband is a commercial shrimper or fisherman and went missing in a storm? We saw that play out several times with Sinful residents. It was always a hassle to get it pushed through earlier, but at least no one lost their house."

"So what do you guys think?" I asked. "You know Molly way better than me, although it doesn't sound like anyone around Sinful knew her well. Do you think she could have been careless enough to get herself killed?"

"It seems rather a long shot in good weather," Ida Belle said. "These bayou towns are full of old people. Despite how it sometimes appears, it's harder to accidentally kill yourself than one might think, even in a place with as many dangers as Sinful."

"Unless you're drunk," Gertie said. "All bets are off with the stupid things drunks get up to."

I shook my head. "I'm really sorry about Molly. And your catering, Ida Belle."

She nodded. "I think people would have enjoyed her food even more than me and Walter finally tying the knot. Oh well, I'll figure something out."

"You've got less than two weeks," Gertie said.

"Need be, we'll bake a ton of beans and make potato salad," Ida Belle said. "It won't be nearly as good as Molly's but there will be plenty of beer. People won't complain."

My cell phone rang and I saw Ally's number in the display.

"Speaking of great food," I said and answered.

"Fortune! Come quick. There's a crazy guy at my house. I called the police but no one's available except Sheriff Lee and he's hopeless."

"Stay inside with the doors locked," I said and jumped up from the table. "We'll be right there."

CHAPTER SIX

IDA BELLE and Gertie had no idea what was going on, but the great thing about awesome friends is they just rolled with it. They were right behind me as I ran out the door and jumped into my Jeep. I tore out of the driveway backward and told them what Ally had said as I broke every traffic law as I raced through the neighborhood.

"What in the world is going on now?" Gertie asked.

We made it to Ally's house in record time and sure enough, there was a man standing on her porch, yelling and shaking his fists at her front door. I recognized him immediately as Molly's boyfriend.

Sheriff Lee was on the front lawn, messing with a bag on his horse's tail.

"Darn bag keeps him blocked up," Sheriff Lee said as the Jeep slammed to a stop. "Stupid laws."

I had no idea what that meant and given the position of the bag, I was certain I didn't want to know. Besides, the bruiser at Ally's door was definitely my biggest concern. I jumped out of the Jeep and ran for the porch, pulling out my gun as I went.

"You're going to want to back away from that door," I said.

He turned around and sneered. "You're big and bad with your gun, aren't you?"

"And you're big and bad threatening a woman one-third your size," I shot back. "If you want to step off that porch and test me, I'm happy to put my gun down and finish what Molly started."

He gave me a nasty grin and called me an even nastier word, then lumbered down the porch straight at me, gaining speed as he moved. Which made everything so much easier. He was going to help knock himself out.

When he got within kicking distance, I spun around and nailed him on the side of the head with a spinning hook kick. His eyes grew as big as an owl's just before snapping shut, then he crashed headfirst into the ground and didn't move.

"Did you kill him?" Gertie asked.

I shook my head. "I just knocked him out."

"That's a shame," Gertie said. "I really don't like him."

"Neither do I," I said. "But I don't want Carter stuck with the paperwork."

Ally flung open her door and ran out onto the lawn, throwing her arms around me.

"Oh my God!" she said. "Thank you so much. I was terrified. I've never seen that guy before in my life and he shows up at my door yelling a bunch of nonsense at me."

"Got it!" Sheriff Lee yelled and we looked over to see him holding the bag triumphantly over his head. His horse promptly jogged over to Molly's boyfriend and expressed his relief at being freed of the bag—right on his head.

We all laughed and Sheriff Lee started clapping as he approached his horse.

"That's a good boy," he said. "Don't we feel better now?"

"One of us doesn't," Ida Belle said.

I heard an engine racing up the street and looked over to see Carter's truck pulling up to the curb. He jumped out of his truck and hurried over, took one look at the guy on the ground with a steaming pile of horse poo sitting on his head like a hat, and smiled.

"I see you decided not to wait for backup," he said, looking at me.

"I had backup," I said. "Sheriff Lee's horse finished him off."

His lips quivered. "Really? And here I was afraid you'd handled the whole thing yourself and I was going to have to reassess my choice of a girlfriend."

"I'm still cocked," I said. "Keep talking."

"My horse is still cocked too," Sheriff Lee said. "No way that was all of his breakfast."

Carter shot him a look of dismay, then looked back at us. "Someone want to tell me what's going on?"

I shrugged. "Got me. Ally called in a panic about some crazy man threatening her. When we got here, we spotted Poopyhead banging on Ally's door. I suggested he pick on someone more suitable, a fight ensued, Sheriff Lee got the bag off the horse's rear, and here we are."

Ida Belle gave me an approving nod. "That was both descriptive and brief."

"It wasn't much of a fight, though," Gertie said. "Just one kick and lights-out."

Carter looked at Ally. "Do you know this guy?"

"Lord no!" Ally said. "And I don't want to."

"Did he bother to allude to the source of his anger while he was yelling?" Carter asked.

Ally frowned. "He just kept calling me a thieving b-word and said no way Molly was cutting him out of everything, not after all the support he'd given her. Is he talking about Miss Molly?"

"That's her boyfriend," I said. "Did you know Molly well?"

"No one knows Molly well that I'm aware of," Ally said. "*Knew* her well. Knows her well?" She gave Carter a hopeful look.

"I'm afraid past tense might be more accurate," he said.

"Oh no," Ally said. "That's too bad. I didn't know her but her food was legendary. The few times we interacted she was very nice and extremely complimentary about my baking. I'd kinda hoped if I ever got my bakery opened that we could partner up a bit—you know, recommend each other for gigs, maybe cater together with her providing the main meals and me the desserts."

"Looks like we're going to have to wait until that kick wears off before we find out what this is about," Gertie said.

"*We* are not going to wait on anything," Carter said. "I am going to handcuff this idiot, hose him down, then call for some help to get him into the bed of my truck. No way he's riding up front."

"The hose part might wake him up and then he can get in himself," Gertie said.

Carter secured the handcuffs on Poopyhead, then nodded. "Let's give it a shot."

Ally indicated a hose tucked on the side of her porch and Carter turned on the water and stretched it out. He stood back far enough to avoid splatter and pulled the trigger on the hose nozzle. The water hit the poop, scattering it across the lawn.

"Good fertilizer right there," Sheriff Lee said. "If you'd like, I can save you up some more and you can do the whole lawn."

"I'll pass," Ally said.

Sheriff Lee shrugged. "Suit yourself, but you're going to have dark spots everywhere that crap takes up residence."

"She'll live," Ida Belle said. "Why don't you get that horse back to the barn before he makes the whole neighborhood look like a green leopard?"

"Might as well," Sheriff Lee said. "It's almost our nap time anyway. And one of us hasn't had our constitutional yet this morning. Might need to drink some prune juice."

"That's an overshare!" Gertie yelled as Sheriff Lee climbed on his horse and headed off.

Carter had managed to get all the poop off of Idiot Boy's head, and he was starting to move a little. Then he came to and realized his arms were in a bind and started flopping around like a giant, poop-smelling fish that badly needed a shave and better tattoos.

"What the heck?" he yelled and managed to flip over so he could glare up at us.

Carter flashed his badge. "Hello, Dexter. Remember me?"

The man's face flashed with anger. "I told you it's Nutter Butter."

"Because that's better than Dexter?" I asked.

"That's my stage name and it's what I prefer," Dexter said.

"What the heck kind of fighting name is Nutter Butter?" Gertie asked.

"Last name's Nutters," he said. "And I like the cookies. You got a problem with that?"

"Your name is Dexter Nutters?" I asked.

Ida Belle shook her head. "No wonder you're a fighter."

"And angry," Gertie said. "Don't forget angry."

"Mr. Nutters," Carter said, "you and I are going to have a talk down at the sheriff's department."

"I ain't going nowhere," Dexter said.

"We can do this the easy way or the hard way," Carter said.

"Either you climb in the bed of that pickup truck and ride nicely down to the sheriff's department, or I'll call the sheriff back over and he can drag you behind that horse with digestive problems. Your choice."

"Whatever." Dexter scowled.

"I take that to mean I should help you up and we'll head down to the station," Carter said. "Here we go."

Despite the fact that Dexter outweighed Carter by well over a hundred pounds, Carter grabbed him under one arm and hauled him to his feet. Dexter looked at the three of us and glared. "If you think I'm going down on this one, you're wrong. I'm going to get my due. Molly and I had an agreement and she ain't weaseling out."

"I'm pretty sure dying isn't the same as weaseling," Ida Belle said.

"Whatever," he said again. Apparently his manners *and* his vocabulary needed work.

He lumbered off with Carter and we all stared as they left.

"What the heck is he talking about?" Gertie asked.

"That seems to be the pertinent question," Ida Belle said.

"It sounds like Molly promised him something and now he thinks he won't get it because she died," I said. "But what in the world does Ally have to do with it?"

"I don't have a clue," Ally said. "And honestly, I don't want to know. I never had any agreement with Molly about anything. I barely knew the woman and I know all I need to about her choice in men."

"I don't suppose Carter will bother filling us in," Gertie said and sighed.

"Not us, but he has to say something to Ally," I said. "He can't keep Dexter locked up forever, and Ally needs to know what he thinks is going on so she can set him straight and keep him from coming back."

"You think he'd be stupid enough to do that?" Gertie asked.

"I think some people are stupid enough to do anything," I said.

Ally crossed her arms across her chest and glanced around. I could tell the entire thing had spooked her.

"Come on," I said and motioned to her house. "Let's go in and have something to drink. We'll wait with you until Carter offers up an explanation."

"Really?" Ally perked up.

"Of course," Ida Belle said.

I felt a tiny bit guilty as we strolled inside. Yes, I'd suggested we wait with Ally to help quell her fear, but I had to admit that I was dying to know why Dexter had made that scene.

"This is perfect, actually," Ally said as we walked into the kitchen. "I was just working on icing for your wedding cake. I have several made. I'd love for you to test them. I also have some new cookies that I was thinking about adding to the list but I'm not sure if it will fly—mint chocolate chip. I thought the mint might be refreshing since it will be so hot out, but I'll have to keep them chilled to keep the chocolate chips from melting."

"Flies with me," Gertie said. "I love the ice cream. If the cookies are half as good, I want them. Of course, if Ida Belle would have an indoor wedding and reception, like a normal person, 'refreshing' wouldn't be necessary."

"Don't start again," Ida Belle said. "Even if I decided to lose my mind and say I'd do this all your way, you couldn't come up with an indoor location in time for the wedding."

"You've waited a hundred and fifty years to do it at all," Gertie said. "What's another couple months?"

"The difference between a summer wedding and interfering with hunting season," Ida Belle said.

Ally and I laughed as Gertie flopped into a chair, waving her hands in defeat. Ally grabbed a tray of cookies off her counter and placed them on the table, then poured us all some sweet tea. I didn't even bother to wait for the tea or for Ally to take her seat before snagging one of the cookies and stuffing half of it in my mouth.

"Oh my God," I said, dripping crumbs onto the table. "This is so good!"

Gertie wiped up the crumbs and handed me a napkin. "I swear, we can't take you anywhere."

"Me?" I asked, giving her an incredulous look.

Ally laughed again, looking pleased at the compliment.

"It is really fabulous," Ida Belle said. "Mint is so hard to get right. Too little and there's no point. Too much and it overpowers everything and you might as well have eaten a breath mint."

Gertie nodded. "It really is perfectly balanced. You have so much talent, Ally. When are you going to ditch the café and open your bakery? I really need a batch of those cookies before I die."

"Well, unless you plan on dying today, I have enough dough made for another batch," Ally said. "I can put them on now if you'd like."

"I'd definitely like," Gertie said. "And my question about the bakery?"

Ally shrugged and rose from the table. "I don't know. I mean, I have money saved and could probably swing a small shop now, but I worry about things. There's no way I could keep waitressing and run the bakery, so I'd be cutting my income off immediately and I do pretty well at Francine's. She's got good food and tons of regulars and most of them tip well."

"How long can you get by without working?" Gertie asked. "And feel free to tell me it's none of my business."

"It's none of your business," Ida Belle said.

"I wasn't talking to you," Gertie said.

"I know," Ida Belle said. "But since Ally's too polite to say it, I figured I'd help out."

"It's okay," Ally said. "My expenses are pretty low so I could probably swing a year or better with no income at all. But that's if things don't change with Mother. Right now, her expenses are mostly covered but if anything changes, I'd have to find a way to pay. I wouldn't want her moved and I'm not capable of taking care of her myself."

"How is she doing?" Ida Belle asked.

"It's hard to say," Ally said. "Her doctors didn't figure she'd be around this long, so they can't really give me an idea of a timeline. She's so stubborn she's probably sticking around just to prove the doctor wrong. She's never liked him although I don't think she remembers that now. She doesn't remember much. They said it's the meds."

"If stubbornness is the secret to longevity," Ida Belle said, "Gertie is going to live forever."

"You might give me a run for my money," Gertie said. "I'm pretty sure 'stubborn' is your middle name.

"My middle name is Belle," Ida Belle said. "You only call me by it ten times a day."

"I'll get out that icing," Ally said.

I gave her an approving nod. Distraction was always the best course of action when Ida Belle and Gertie were in one of their disagreements. I usually distracted them with gunfire and explosions and bad guys, but Ally's way would probably work. And it would be a lot less exercise.

She sat four containers of white icing on the table and a stack of disposable spoons.

"No double dipping," she said.

"They all look the same," Gertie said.

"A wedding cake needs white icing," Ally said. "But they don't taste the same. I don't want to tell you the flavors because I want an unbiased opinion."

We started dipping into the icing and I swear each one got better and better—another mint flavor, traditional white, buttery creamy, and one that I swear tasted like cotton candy. Gertie, Ally, and I waited until Ida Belle did a second round, then when she selected the cotton candy flavor, we all cheered.

"I'm so glad you picked that one," I said. "I was afraid I was going to have to push Carter into marriage just to get it."

"I don't think you'd have to push all that hard," Ally said. "You two are practically tied at the hip unless you're working."

"Well, since one of us is almost always on the job, I guess that works out well," I said. "How in the world did you make icing taste like cotton candy?"

Ally smiled. "Magic."

"I believe it," I said and grabbed a new spoon to load up a huge scoop. "I wish the wedding was tomorrow."

"Not me," Ida Belle said. "We still have to figure out the sides."

Ally gave her a sad nod. "I'm happy to help but I won't have enough time for anything that needs to be done that day or the day before. The cake and other desserts will take every spare minute."

"You're already doing enough," Ida Belle said. "I'll pull together the Sinful Ladies and have a chat with Francine. I'm sure among all of us, we can fill in the gaps."

Ally bit her lower lip. "I guess there's no chance..."

"I wouldn't say there's no chance," Ida Belle said. "But you know the odds."

"Yeah," Ally said. "It's just so wrong. A strong, capable woman like Molly going out like that. I mean, not that there's a pleasant way, but it doesn't seem right."

"It doesn't," I agreed.

I'd been thinking about nothing else the entire night when we combed the marsh and then when I'd showered for an hour to try to get saltwater residue off me and the smell of dead fish and bayou mud out of my nose. Then I'd pondered it some more while I tried, marginally successfully, to fall asleep. But no matter how many angles I looked at it from, it still smelled as rotten as the dead fish I'd inhaled.

There was a knock at the front door and Ally jumped up. "Oh my God, you don't think he's come back, do you?"

"Don't worry," I said as I stood. "Dexter wouldn't knock that politely. My guess is Carter got something out of him and is coming to try to fill in the blanks. I'll let him in."

Sure enough, Carter was standing at the front door when I opened it. He didn't look surprised to see me, but he didn't look overly pleased either.

"Ally was nervous, so we stuck around until you knew something," I said as we walked.

"And we got to try excellent icing," Gertie said as we entered the kitchen. "You should try it. Might make you want to get married just to get it."

Carter's expression was a blend of a tiny bit of fear and a bit more dismay, and I struggled not to laugh. I had no doubt about his commitment to me or mine to him. But neither of us was ready for legally bound and definitely not ready to cohabitate. The best icing in the world couldn't rush that one.

Ally jumped up and started pouring Carter a glass of tea. I could tell she was nervous.

"Did you find out what he wanted?" she asked as she handed him the glass.

He nodded. "Sit down, please. I would ask to speak to you alone, but there's no point as I'm sure you'll tell them anyway."

Ally sat but she was perched on the end of her chair, not relaxed at all.

"Molly had a safe in her bedroom," he said. "I was hoping to get someone in today to open it but apparently, Dexter decided to beat me to the punch with a blowtorch. There was an empty bank envelope inside that had Ida Belle's name on it in Molly's handwriting. I assume that was your catering money."

Ida Belle nodded. "I just handed her the envelope straight from the bank."

"How much was in it?" Carter asked.

"Fifteen hundred, all in hundred-dollar bills," Ida Belle said.

"Well, that matches the amount I just pulled out of Dexter's glove box," Carter said. "There was also another document inside."

Carter reached into his pocket and pulled out a folded piece of paper and handed it to Ally. She took the paper and started to read, her eyes widening as she went.

"This can't be right," she said. "I didn't know her. This can't be right."

"What does it say?" I asked.

"It says that Molly was leaving her business to Ally," Carter said. "I asked a lawyer about the legality of the document, but it's Molly's handwriting and notarized. My lawyer said it might be a fight if a family member wanted to contest it, but someone like Dexter, who had no legal relationship to Molly, wouldn't stand a chance."

"I still don't understand why he's so mad," I said.

"He claims he helped Molly with the business," Carter said.

"And that she promised to make him her partner as soon as she could have documents drawn up. Furthermore, if anything happened to her, he claimed the whole shooting match would go to him and that he did sign something to that effect."

"But nothing like that was in the safe," I said.

"Of course not," Carter said. "Most likely because it never existed. Dexter's reaching."

Ally frowned. "This document was signed just a month ago. If Molly was really making promises to Dexter..."

"And I pointed that out," Carter said. "But Dexter is sticking to his story. He's worked up some nonsense about how you stole the business out from under him. You're sure you never had a discussion with Molly about anything like this?"

"Lord no!" Ally said. "We only ever talked about food, and even that was brief. Molly isn't—wasn't—much of a talker. And to be honest, she scared me a little, so I never tried too hard to work her into conversation."

Carter nodded. "I figured as much but I had to ask."

"Dexter isn't going to believe that Ally didn't know," I said. "How long can you hold him?"

"He'll go before the judge tomorrow probably," Carter said. "There's not a lot on the docket, so we can't count on a delay there. And he'll get bail. He's got some priors, but a cage fighter getting into fights is hardly a smoking gun. As long as he can come up with the cash, he'll be out in a couple days."

"Do you think he'll cause more trouble for Ally?" I asked.

"I've advised him that's a bad route to take," Carter said. "And I pointed out that since I have the legal document, it's now known to law enforcement and would be made known to Ally. I've also explained to him that since there was no requirement on Ally's part as far as numbers of days living beyond the deceased, if something were to happen to her, then *her* next of kin would inherit the business."

"Do you think he has the mental capacity to understand that?" Ida Belle asked.

"Unlikely," Carter said. "Especially since it doesn't suit him to believe it. But I also explained that if he threatened Ally again, he was likely to get shot by one of her friends and they didn't miss."

Ally gave him a small smile. "The best thing is, that part is true. But Carter, what in the world is going on? I didn't ask for Molly's business. I can't even find the time to get my own bakery up and running. How in the world would I take hers on? And unless she left me recipes and the skill to do them just like her, I wouldn't stand a chance at keeping clientele."

I frowned. "What, exactly, does inheriting the business entail?"

"I don't know," Carter said. "Estate attorneys would have someone separate business assets from personal assets."

"And no indication of assignment of her personal assets?" I asked.

"Not that Dexter had on him," Carter said. "And I didn't find anything else in the safe."

"You have to check her phone records," I said. "If Molly had an attorney, then she would have called them—"

Carter held up his hand. "I know what I need to do. The question is, do you three know what you need to do?"

"Stay out of it?" Gertie asked.

"You say that like it's a question," Carter said.

"I'm optimistic," Gertie said.

"Well, don't be," Carter said. "This is an open investigation and I need the three of you to stay out of it. Ida Belle, I'll need you to sign some documents about your catering payment, but once all this clears up, you should get it back. Sorry it can't be sooner."

Ida Belle waved a hand in dismissal. "I'm not concerned

about the money. I'm more concerned about what really happened to Molly."

"Let me handle that," Carter said and rose. He gave us all a stern look. "I mean that."

He headed out of the kitchen and a couple seconds later, I heard the front door close.

"You're not going to stay out of it, are you?" Ally asked.

"Of course not," Gertie said.

"Technically," I said, "we don't have a valid reason to be in it. So if we're going to poke around then we have to do it on the sly."

"On the sly is my specialty," Gertie said.

"You haven't known sly since the wheel was invented," Ida Belle said.

"I can be sly," Gertie said. "You'll see."

"It would be the first time," Ida Belle said.

CHAPTER SEVEN

ALLY FINALLY CALMED down and we headed back to my house. As soon as we sat down at the kitchen table, Gertie started in.

"So what are we going to do about this?" she asked. "We have to do something. That awful man can't get away with killing Molly."

"Let's not get ahead of ourselves," I said. "We don't know that Molly was killed and if she was, we don't know for certain Dexter did it."

Gertie stared.

"Okay," I said. "I agree that it looks bad, but we don't have proof and without a body..."

Ida Belle shook her head. "The whole thing is a mess. Do either of you believe that Dexter is qualified to run Molly's catering business? I mean, it's not like she took orders and someone else did all the work. Molly did everything. I just can't see Nutter Butter in the kitchen whipping up fabulous dishes. Feel free to call me sexist."

"I don't think it's sexist as much as it is a personality thing," I said. "I can't see Molly teaching someone her secrets and I can't see Dexter taking direction. But then, he gets in a ring with her knowing she's going to kick his butt, so who knows? Mostly, I've decided people are unpredictable and often strange."

"That's true," Ida Belle said. "And Walter is a great cook. Better than me. Just not at grilling, although he thinks he is."

"So if Molly didn't promise Dexter the business, why make it up?" Gertie asked.

"I have a feeling that it comes down to what assets are considered business assets," I said. "I mean, all that kitchen equipment was super pricey. If it was all claimed by the business, then he could sell it off for a nice little profit. And I noticed a van parked out front. I assume she uses it to haul her food around. If those things aren't financed, then that's all cash in his pocket. Not to mention actual cash in bank accounts."

"I hadn't considered the equipment or the van," Gertie said. "I bet you're right. But boy, what a long-shot claim. And unless he has video proving Molly said it, I don't see where Dexter has a leg to stand on with that one."

"He doesn't," I said. "But you realize that if Dexter has no real motive, he's unlikely to be our killer."

"Maybe it was personal," Gertie said. "Lover's quarrel. Carter did say he had a record for fighting. That implies a temper."

"Everything about him implies a temper," Ida Belle said. "And if Molly had been beaten to death then my entire catering money would be on Dexter. But following her in her boat and making her disappear? Tempers dissipate. Following her out into the bayou implies specific purpose, not temporary rage."

"Maybe he didn't follow her," Gertie said. "Maybe he poisoned her and it didn't kick in until after she left. She fell overboard and that was it. Or maybe she made that call and her cell ran out of battery so she went back home where he killed her, then took her body out into the bayou and dumped it, figuring it would be filed as an accidental death."

"That was a really long sentence," I said.

"If he dumped her body and left her boat, then how did he get back home?" Ida Belle asked.

"Towed her small boat behind the big one," Gertie said. "She kept her small flat-bottom even after she bought the bigger one. It was tied at the dock when we went by yesterday. Or he could have gotten on the bank and walked most of the way. He would have only had to swim across one channel."

"And avoid alligators along the way," I said.

"But people manage to do that every day," Gertie said. "They don't usually attack unless they have a nest or feel threatened."

"Or you interrupt their napping," I said.

"Or they're hungry," Ida Belle said. "And that area is full of hungry gators. Our friend Dexter strikes me as a coward. I can't see him risking a swim."

I put my hands up in the air. "At this point, anything is possible but nothing seems plausible. And without knowing how she was killed or where, we're shooting so many moving targets it's like a carnival game."

"So where do we start?" Gertie asked.

I thought about it for a minute. On the one hand, we couldn't even be certain a crime had occurred. If it hadn't, then all this speculation was for nothing. If it had, we had no reason to go butting in. But I couldn't help but believe that something was wrong. Beneath all the frenzy, I sensed calculation. I knew Gertie wasn't going to let it go and suspected Ida Belle wouldn't either. And even though I'd known Molly for less time than I spent on a good shower, I had liked her and wanted to know what happened to her. If someone had killed her, then I wanted them to go down for it.

"I suppose the first thing we do is dig deeper into Dexter and more importantly, Molly," I said. "We need to know if there's family lurking around, waiting on an inheritance. And given that the collective gossips in Sinful haven't managed to get anything out of her, I have a feeling running down facts on Molly isn't going to be a simple matter."

Ida Belle nodded. "We don't even know for certain that Molly is her real name."

"What did that document Ally read say?" Gertie asked.

"Miss Molly of Miss Molly's Catering," I said. "I looked over her shoulder."

"Well, that's no help," Gertie said. "And is it even legal?"

"If it's in Molly's handwriting and she's known for that name, I would guess it is," Ida Belle said. "And for all we know, she has a will stashed in a safe-deposit box somewhere that says the same thing."

"Or had an attorney working on one and drew up that document in case something happened," Gertie said.

I nodded. "Which begs the question—did something happen?"

"Or did she think something might happen?" Ida Belle asked.

"Let's start with Molly," I said and grabbed my laptop.

It didn't take long to find out that there was very limited information on Molly. The catering business had a website, but everything referenced 'Miss Molly.' I couldn't find a business listing for her name that provided ownership information but for all we knew, the legal name of the business was completely different from the d/b/a. Public records were public but not always easy to find and with only a first name, it was going to be difficult to track anything from the business angle. So I started with her professional fighting name, but none of the articles I found on Molly the Mauler referenced a real name either. After thirty minutes of frustration, I slouched in my chair.

"It's going to be difficult to get information on a woman when we don't know her legal name," I said.

"Try the property," Ida Belle said. "There has to be a name on the deed."

"Good idea," I said and accessed the tax roll. I found the property, no problem, but when I spotted the name, I groaned. "Miss Molly's Catering."

"Smart," Ida Belle said. "More tax benefits that way."

"Does that mean it's paid for?"

"No," Ida Belle said. "The loan could be in the company name and Molly could have cosigned for it."

"So whoever got the catering business might make off with a nice piece of property," I said.

"Not necessarily," Ida Belle said. "The argument could be made that since Molly lived in the house and had a fighting cage, that it was also her personal residence and not solely used for the catering business. Assuming she had a CPA set up her books, my guess is she was paying the catering company rent."

"So part of the house would go to next of kin along with her boats and money in bank accounts," I said.

"This blows," Gertie said. "No way a bank would give us her real name."

"We might have to wait for the death announcement," I said. "They'd make her legal name known then."

"We can't wait for the funeral announcement," Gertie said. "If Dexter did it, he's long gone when he makes bail."

"Before you even suggest it, Carter is *not* going to tell us," I said. "Surely this woman had one close friend who knew her real name...besides that idiot Dexter, because Carter would tell us before that guy would."

"There is a way to get her real name," Gertie said. "You can't put a nickname on your driver's license."

"Unless you can pull her license out of your butt, I don't see how that helps us," Ida Belle said.

"She was boating, right?" Gertie said. "So she wouldn't have had her license with her. All we have to do is make a quick trip to her house and check out her license."

I shook my head. "We are not breaking into a potential crime scene. I'm pretty sure Carter would consider that above and beyond 'sticking our noses in.'"

"Why not?" Gertie asked. "No one thinks Molly was killed there so technically it would be trespassing, not entering a crime scene. Heck, we don't even have to wear gloves. Our fingerprints are all over the kitchen from yesterday."

"And everyone keeps their wallet in the kitchen?" Ida Belle asked.

"Okay, so we bring gloves just in case," Gertie said.

"What do we bring 'just in case' Carter shows up?" I asked. "Because I'm pretty sure anything short of that memory-erase wand thingy that they used in *Men in Black* isn't going to pass muster. What you're suggesting is not trespassing. It's breaking and entering."

"We've gotten around Carter plenty of times," Gertie said.

"We got around Carter when I was CIA and he was doing his best to maintain my cover, even when I was making it next to impossible. He's not going to extend that courtesy to me as a civilian. And having seen me naked will not stop him from arresting me if he has no other choice. Like if a forensic team rolls up on us while we're digging around in Molly's house."

"So I'll do it," Gertie said. "Then he can't put it on you."

"Sure he can."

Ida Belle and I both spoke at once.

Gertie sighed. "You were a lot more fun when you were still in the CIA and before you started having slumber parties with Carter. So if you won't take my advice, then what do you recommend?"

"I'm a private detective, not a magician," I said.

"Well," Gertie said, "we could always hang out here and go over my plans for Ida Belle's bachelorette party. There's the whole G-string selection process and things like whether or not you like body hair."

Ida Belle cringed. "I suppose it wouldn't hurt to take a boat ride over toward Molly's place. Could be there's a trash can that hasn't been emptied. I might have lost a trailer hitch off my SUV when we went last time and we could drop by there while looking for Molly to see if it's lying around."

"The only thing you've ever lost off that SUV is Gertie," I said. "The items you've put on that vehicle would be afraid to fall off."

Ida Belle shrugged. "Well, you think about it while I use the restroom."

She said 'restroom,' but I heard the front door open. I motioned to Gertie and we headed to the living room and looked out the window as Ida Belle removed her trailer hitch and tossed it in my flower bed.

"I'm charging you for those flowers if they die," I called out the door.

"Since I'm the one who put them in, I don't figure you have a leg to stand on there," Ida Belle said as she walked back inside. "So, trash?"

I blew out a breath. Walking onto Molly's property, even tying off at her dock, was trespassing. But that wasn't nearly as bad as breaking and entering. It would be better, of course, if it was trash day and we could haul the trash to the road and if we got caught, swear that we'd found it there, where it was fair game. But trash pickup wasn't for two more days, and we had a limited amount of jail time to get the goods on Dexter, assuming he had done anything besides make up a stupid lie and yell at Ally's front door.

"Fine," I said. "We'll take the boat out under the auspice of searching for Molly some more. And it only makes sense that we'd comb the bayous around Molly's house as that's where her boat was found and where she would have tried to get back to had she gotten disoriented and separated from her boat. But if there is any sign of law enforcement, we're not setting foot on that dock."

"Fair enough," Gertie said. "But do you think Carter will even send forensics to process the house? I mean, it's unlikely anything happened there and even if it did, Dexter had all night to get rid of the evidence."

"Now there's a question I wish I had an answer to," I said. "Why wasn't Dexter out searching last night with the rest of us?"

"Because he was too busy figuring out how to blowtorch a safe?" Gertie asked.

"I'm sure that's the real answer," Ida Belle said. "But you're right. Molly had another boat. Why wasn't he using it?"

Ida Belle pulled out her cell phone and called Myrtle, one of their good friends and also the night dispatcher at the sheriff's department. She woke her up from her normal sleeping time but Myrtle had the answer. It just wasn't a good one.

"Dexter would like us all to believe that he doesn't know how to drive a boat," Ida Belle said after she hung up.

"So he could have ridden with someone else," Gertie said.

"Apparently, he would also like us to believe he can't swim and is therefore scared of the water," Ida Belle said. "That part I might actually believe."

Gertie let out a string of complaints with a few choice words and I nodded.

"Isn't it like a Louisiana law or something that you learn how to swim and drive a boat before you can walk?" I asked.

"Pretty much," Ida Belle said. "But then we don't know where Dexter is from. I'm not saying I buy his reasons, but I suppose Carter couldn't force him onto a boat to help if he didn't want to go."

"I bet I could have," Gertie said.

"I wonder if Dexter lived with Molly?" I asked.

Ida Belle shrugged. "I didn't even know she had a boyfriend until we saw him at her house and she said as much. Molly didn't exactly run in the same circles as we do."

"I'd bet Molly didn't run in any circles except her fighting ones," Gertie said.

"Well, Nickel knew about Dexter," I said. "So some people in Sinful have more information on Molly than we do. I just don't know how reliable thirdhand information from the Swamp Bar clientele would be."

"But I bet it would be interesting," Gertie said, looking hopeful. "At least we should talk to Nickel again."

"We'll worry about that once we get past this trash heist," I said.

"Then let's get to digging," Gertie said and hurried toward the back door.

Ida Belle shook her head. "She is entirely too happy for someone who is about to head out in ninety-five-degree heat to dig through garbage. The garbage of a caterer, I might add. You do the math on that one."

I groaned. I hadn't yet considered that any paperwork in the trash would be covered with remnants of Molly's catering jobs.

"Maybe we'll get lucky and she has one of those things

where you turn dead stuff into fertilizer," I said.

"A compost pile?" Ida Belle asked. "Did Molly look like someone who gardens?"

"Herbs?" I asked.

"Keep wishing," Ida Belle said. "And grab some extra gloves and the raincoats from the garage. I have a feeling this one is going to be a mess."

"When is it not?"

———

IT WAS OFFICIALLY ONLY ninety-three degrees but felt like 10,002. Even with the air current flowing across my body from Ida Belle pushing the boat at least one mile per hour beyond its capacity, sweat was still dripping down my body in a matter of minutes. I felt like I'd gone ten rounds with Mike Tyson. On the upside, I'd probably sweated out all the calories I'd eaten at Ally's house.

It didn't take long to get to the channel that led to Molly's house. Because it was a lot narrower than the one behind my house, Ida Belle had to slow to merely warp speed, and I mourned the loss of the additional airflow. When we stopped completely, I was going to be tempted to jump in the bayou, gators and all. The only thing stopping me was that I already knew the bayou was going to feel like a warm bath, so without the airflow, being wet wouldn't help matters.

Ida Belle let me know when we were closing in on Molly's dock, and Gertie handed me my binoculars so I could scan for potential problems. There was a big clump of cypress trees directly behind the house, but I could still see some of the purple shining through. Fortunately, I had a reasonably clear view of the driveway and the only vehicle I saw was Molly's van.

"Looks clear," I said.

Gertie clapped her hands, entirely too happy about our upcoming task.

"Then let's get this over with," Ida Belle said.

I tied off the boat, wondering just what lengths Ida Belle would go to in order to avoid discussing her upcoming bachelorette party. Not that I blamed her. Gertie had insisted it had to happen, and in theory, I kind of agreed with her. After all the time Ida Belle had waited to say yes to Walter, a party was probably in order. But we were both worried about what shenanigans Gertie would come up with. Mind you, I wasn't worried enough to get involved in the planning, because that way led to fear and ultimately blame. At least this way, I'd only have to live through one night of whatever Gertie had cooked up instead of anticipating the potential horror for weeks on end until finally culminating in what was certain to be a disaster in one way or another.

We climbed out of the boat and headed toward the house, eyes trained on the road to watch for approaching law enforcement. But so far, everything seemed quiet. When we reached the house, we stopped at the edge, scanning the area for trash cans.

"Surely she doesn't set everything out in bags, right?" I asked.

"No way," Ida Belle said. "No one wants to clean up that mess and the wildlife around here wouldn't waste two seconds tearing into a stack of bags. Besides, it's not allowed. No one wants the trash blowing into the marshes and bayous. We have enough pollution without adding unnecessarily to it."

"Then where might she keep her cans until trash day?" I asked. "You think she keeps them in the garage?"

"Lord no!" Gertie said. "The heat inside is worse than outside. The smell alone would kill half the parish. But she's probably got them tucked against a solid structure, as far from the house as she can get them."

"And upwind from southern breezes," Ida Belle said.

We looked around and I pointed to the lean-to storage attached to the far side of the garage.

"Maybe on the other side of that?" I asked.

"Probably," Ida Belle said. "Looks like it has the best access from the back door as well."

We tromped to the other end of the house and around the back side of the lean-to and sure enough, that's where Molly kept her cans. At least, I assumed that here was where Molly expected them to be, but there were no cans in sight. Instead, shredded black plastic bags mixed with paper, plastic, and rotting food were strewn all over the ground and into the woods.

I involuntarily reached up to squeeze my nose and switched to mouth breathing.

Then something rattled inside the lean-to and I pulled out my gun just as a raccoon shot out and ran between my legs and into the woods. I jumped back from the lean-to, in case he was partying with friends, and Ida Belle and Gertie laughed.

"Sure, you can laugh," I said. "You never shot a hole in your roof over one of those things."

"That's not entirely true," Ida Belle said. "Not for all of us, anyway."

"How was I supposed to know it wasn't a ghost in my attic?" Gertie said. "And I was shooting rock salt because that's what those paranormal hunters do on television. It didn't leave a hole in my roof. Not exactly."

"Why on earth would you assume you had a ghost in your attic instead of one of the many critters around here that seem to crave air-conditioning and a fully stocked pantry?" I asked.

"I was being optimistic," Gertie said. "Having a ghost

would be a lot more interesting than a raccoon. Everyone gets raccoons in their attic at some point, but no one in Sinful has had a ghost."

"Maybe because they don't exist," Ida Belle said.

Gertie started to argue, so I held up a hand. "I think this discussion needs to wait until we're not in the middle of trespassing on what could be a crime scene. Where are the cans? Did raccoons do this?"

"No way," Ida Belle said. "They have been known to get a can flipped over and they can work off a lid, but they don't have any use for carrying them off. They just shop on the spot."

"So did someone beat us to the trash-digging games?" I asked.

"Most likely, it was a bear," Ida Belle said.

I cast a worried glance at the woods. We'd had a run-in with a bear during an investigation and it hadn't ended well for us, a man's house, or the bear. I wasn't anxious to visit with one again.

"So did they pull the lid off and get on top of the cans so they could roll away?" I asked, still trying to understand why the cans were nowhere in sight.

"This is Sinful, not a circus," Ida Belle said. "Well, maybe that sentence could be restated to more accurately reflect things. This isn't an official circus with tickets, and tents, and roasted peanuts."

Gertie nodded. "Smart bears have learned that people will come out and run them off, so they'll roll a can into the woods. The lid usually pops off as they're going, and this mess is the fallout after all the other critters come out and take advantage of the situation."

"But the bear is gone with his spoils, right?" I asked.

"Probably," Ida Belle said. "Maybe."

"Probably-maybe is not the answer I was looking for," I said.

Ida Belle shrugged. "Bears are unpredictable."

"At least we don't have to tear into all the bags," Gertie said. "And everything is kind of sorted. I mean, what's left. If we don't find anything in this mess, I suppose we can try tracking the cans into the woods."

"No!"

Ida Belle and I responded at once.

"I am not running from a bear today," I said. "Or any day, if I can help it. I did that once and it wasn't any fun. Besides, I just ran from an alligator, so I've gotten in all my fleeing-dangerous-man-eaters steps for the week."

"You know," Gertie said, "they should make a special Louisiana Fitbit edition that tracked that stuff. You should get double or triple steps when fleeing for your life."

"If that were the case, we'd have racked up enough steps for two lifetimes," I said.

"I sometimes feel like I've lived two, so that would work out fine," Ida Belle said. "Shall we try to wade through this mess?"

I pulled gloves out of my backpack and handed sets to Gertie and Ida Belle. "I wish I had thought to bring trash bags," I said. "We could have cleaned up as we went along. I hate to think of Molly's backyard turning into a battlefield for wildlife."

"The food will be gone soon enough," Ida Belle said. "The paper, unfortunately, will blow away with the first decent wind."

Thunder boomed so loud I almost jumped, and I looked up and saw storm clouds rolling over the top of the cypress trees. I stared at the sky in dismay.

"Or it will get beaten into the ground by a torrential rainstorm," I said. "I thought the forecast said no rain."

"Heat thunderstorms," Ida Belle said. "They come up fast and leave fast, but they can be a doozy."

"I remember," I said. "I just keep hoping Mother Nature will forget about them. We'd best get to work before anything useful is destroyed."

We took off in three different directions, picking up and scanning anything that looked like a piece of an envelope or statement. Small containers that still had shipping labels. Basically, anything that might have a name on them. I'd located a ton of shipping boxes and several envelopes but all of them were addressed to the catering business. I figured that would be the case but still, Molly had to have a personal bank account, legal documents for her business, tax filings, and the like. But it was probably our luck that none of those things had been mailed in the past week.

I reached the edge of the marsh, close to the bayou, when I heard something moving through the brush. It didn't sound big, so I assumed it was another raccoon. I left my pistol in place and crept into the line of cypress trees, hoping to snag an envelope I'd spotted clinging to the top of a bush. The bush had thorns, so I carefully reached up on my tiptoes and leaned forward just a tiny bit where my fingers barely clenched the corner.

I heard the noise again, this time from the bush I was perched above, but now it sounded like something bigger. I snagged the envelope and shoved it in my pocket, then took one slow step backward, pulling my pistol from my waist as I went. Before my foot touched the ground, the bush exploded with action and the source of the noise rushed out at me.

Rats! Huge rats!

CHAPTER EIGHT

I TURNED AROUND and ran like I was going for a gold medal in the summer Olympics. I hated rats. I'd seen them clinging to too many bodies when I was overseas and if I never saw one again, it would be too soon. I glanced back, hoping to see empty grass but instead, the entire horde was racing right behind me. What the heck was happening?

I fired over my shoulder as I ran, hoping to scare them back into the marsh, and Ida Belle and Gertie whirled around, their eyes huge as they surveyed the current and ridiculously awful situation that was transpiring.

And also hurtling right at them.

"Run, Fortune, run!" Gertie yelled, and I had a flashback to that Tom Hanks movie she'd had me watch. I had the advantage of two good legs but the disadvantage of more pursuers, and they apparently weren't scared of gunfire.

Ida Belle and Gertie must have approved of my reaction because they set off toward the house in front of me, but it didn't take me long to catch up. When we reached the driveway, I stuck my pistol back in my waistband and did a flying leap, pulling myself up onto the top of Molly's van. Then I dropped and reached down to help haul Ida Belle and Gertie up.

I felt my knees burning and realized the top of the van was probably about two thousand degrees due to the sunlight that had just disappeared behind the storm cloud. We all stood there and watched the flood of nutria as they caught up, then breathed a sigh of relief as they continued past the van and across the driveway into the marsh on the other side.

"What the heck was that about?" I asked.

Ida Belle shook her head. "I have no idea."

"It looked like a crazy scene from one of those *Jurassic Park* movies," Gertie said. "You know, where all the plant eaters suddenly race off because a meat eater has arrived."

I stared at Ida Belle and her eyes widened. We whipped around to look back at the trees we'd fled, just in time to see a huge mama bear with two cubs come racing out of them.

"It's T. rex," Gertie said.

"Flatten!" Ida Belle yelled and dropped down onto the hot metal.

I dropped beside her, cringing as the metal burned through the thin cotton I was wearing. I tucked my arms behind my back and kept my head lifted, noticing Ida Belle and Gertie were doing the same. We looked like a lineup for handcuffs on one of those reality cop shows. But the burns could be fixed with some aloe vera. Maybe a skin graft. A single bear claw across your body left it shredded beyond repair.

"Why don't these things ever happen in the winter when we're wearing jeans and jackets?" Gertie asked.

"These things aren't supposed to happen at all," I said. "I'm starting to believe in curses. On me, one of you, this town, the local wildlife...something is clearly wrong."

"It's just another day in the bayou," Ida Belle said, looking completely relaxed. I swear, if she were a smoker, she would have pulled out a cigarette and lit up.

"How is it there's a killer bear coming right toward us," I said, "and you're lying there like we're sunbathing, but you were scared to marry Walter?"

"I wasn't scared," Ida Belle said. "I just wasn't ready."

"Well, it wasn't because you hadn't found your perfect dress," Gertie said.

"Shhhhh," Ida Belle said. "She's getting close."

We all went silent and I heard the bear lumbering toward us. I prayed that she'd go past with her cubs, chasing the trail of tasty nutria. Did bears eat nutria? Now that I wasn't able to ask, I desperately wanted to know. But at least we'd solved the mystery of how the trash cans disappeared. Mama probably hauled them into the woods to give her babies a snack. And with Molly running a catering business at her house, I imagined her trash cans had a fair share of goodies.

The bear slowed and I silently cursed. Could she smell us? Probably, right? Heck, it was July in southern Louisiana. Humans could probably smell us over in Mississippi, and it didn't help that we were all wearing gloves that had been holding stinky paper. I looked at Ida Belle and now I could see the worry in her expression. We were sitting ducks. Pistols might take the bear down, but how quickly? And we couldn't outrun her, so making a dash for the boat was out. I could send a text but if she decided to attack, no one would get here in time to help. And where was that rain that kept threatening to come down? At least that would help with the smell thing, not to mention the burning skin thing.

Deciding it was better, at least, to let someone know where to start looking for bodies, I eased my phone from my pocket to send Carter a message that we had a life-and-death emergency at Molly's house, knowing full well that if we lived through this, I'd never, ever hear the end of it. That whole trailer hitch story of Ida Belle's wasn't even going to fly.

But just as I started my text, Mama Bear decided she knew the location of the enemy.

Her roar coursed through my body, making my hair stand on end. Then her entire weight hit the side of the van and she started pushing. I spread my arms out, trying to maintain my balance, and my cell phone slipped from my hands and fell to the ground. With every hit by the bear, the van swayed farther and farther to the side, then violently rocked back in place. It was probably the first and only time in my life I gave serious consideration to the monumental importance of a luggage rack on a minivan.

I heard a worried cry and glanced back to see Gertie losing her balance and tipping to the side, almost rolling over the rack bar. The van rocked back into place and she flopped back on top, but part of her body was over the rack bar. Another push like that one and things would be dire. I had to do something but had no idea what. I couldn't even keep my pistol in my hand with all the rocking, much less get off a perfect shot, and a perfect shot was exactly what was called for because anything less would just piss her off long enough to reach me and shred me like tissue paper.

Then I ran out of time to decide.

The bear hit the van so hard that I thought it was going to topple completely over. It held suspended in midair for what seemed like minutes. I stretched my pinkie finger over, because it was the only thing I could risk moving, trying to get every bit of weight I could shifted to bring the van back down. That whole pinkie thing must have worked because finally, the van left its stationary hold and crashed back down upright.

Unfortunately, Gertie did not make it with the van.

I heard the impact and jerked my head back to see she was

gone but had to give her enormous props for not making a sound when she went. Other than hitting the ground, that is, and that one couldn't be helped. If we all lived through this, I was going to have to tell her just how impressed I was. But I couldn't linger on top of this carnival ride any longer.

I jumped up, yelling at Ida Belle to cover me then get to the boat, and leaped off the top of the van as far from the bear as I could get without drawing her attention to Gertie, who was on the opposite side from the bear. Mama Bear took one look at me, stood on her hind legs, and roared. If I had not been trained to mock death, I probably would have had a heart attack right on the spot. She was absolutely terrifying.

Since I couldn't run for the dock without coming too close to the bear, I took off down the driveway to the road. There had been another house about a mile away. I didn't think I could outrun a bear for a mile but I was about to find out. In any event, I needed to draw her away long enough for Ida Belle and Gertie to get safely to the boat.

I heard a gunshot behind me and glanced back but all I saw was fur and teeth bearing down on me. I cranked up the speed and pulled my pistol from my waist, then I fired over my shoulder. I couldn't afford to slow down and aim and I really didn't want to have to kill the bear. But if things came down to me or her, we were going to be calling social services for those cubs. I fired again and glanced back but it hadn't slowed her one bit. In fact, she was gaining on me. And I didn't have any more turbo left to crank in.

I heard an engine racing behind me, clearly straining to keep up with its driver's demands, and a second later, Molly's van flew past me. The back door swung open and I saw Gertie staring down at me, a tie-down strapped around her waist. Ida Belle hit the brakes, and I dived into the back of the van, did a quick roll, then grabbed the back of the passenger seat as Ida Belle floored it.

The bear had just reached the van and had the door in her giant paws when it launched forward. The sound of twisting and scrunching metal filled the air and with a final roar, the bear ripped the door clean off and then stood there, holding it up like a game show display.

"Got it!" Gertie yelled and triumphantly waved her cell phone.

Then Ida Belle hit a huge hole in the road and the strap that had secured Gertie to the side of the van came loose. She stumbled toward the opening, flinging her phone backward and trying to find something to grab on to. I leaped forward, snagged the strap, and yanked her to the bottom of the van.

She sat up and shook her head. "Do you know how much makeup I'm going to need to cover the bruises on my thighs for the wedding?"

"Wear longer clothes," Ida Belle said. "No one wants to see your thighs."

I looked behind us and saw that the bear had managed to ditch the door and was coming after the van again.

"That is one determined bear," I said. "She's still coming."

"We've got another problem," Ida Belle said and started honking the horn.

I peered over the dash and saw Carter's truck approaching and since neither he nor Ida Belle showed any sign of slowing and the road didn't exactly hold two larger vehicles side by side, it wasn't going to be pretty.

"Hang on!" Ida Belle yelled.

I grabbed Gertie's strap and hugged the passenger's seat, hoping I had the strength to keep both of us from bouncing out of the van. The van swerved to the right and Gertie and I slammed against the side. Ida Belle yelled for Carter to move as we went by, and I looked back to see his truck throwing up grass and dirt from the side of the road. Then he must have reached the bear because the truck swerved hard to the side, hit the ditch, then flew into the woods. The bear stopped running, looked at the truck, and decided either she'd accomplished her goal or we were no longer worth her time. She turned around and sauntered off into the woods on the other side of the road.

Ida Belle slowed to a stop and looked back at me. "I guess we have to go check on him, right?"

"We can't exactly head back to Sinful in a stolen van," I said, just noticing the windshield was gone. "In a stolen, really broken van. What happened?"

"I shot out the windshield so I could hot-wire it," Ida Belle said. "We weren't going to leave you. You're fast but you wouldn't have outlasted that bear."

I sighed. "You got a good story for this one? Because that whole trailer hitch thing isn't going to work."

Ida Belle shrugged. "He can't prove anything."

"You mean besides trespassing and grand theft auto?" I asked.

Ida Belle waved a hand in dismissal. "It was an emergency situation. These things happen."

"Maybe in Sinful," I said.

Gertie nodded. "Remember the time Lester thought he was being chased by rabid raccoons and stole Sheriff Lee's horse? Everyone headed downtown to watch him circle around, trying to get the horse to go faster. Sheriff Lee was limping after them, yelling at the top of his lungs."

"So what was chasing him?" I asked.

"A couple of dachshunds," Gertie said. "He was drunker than Cooter Brown."

"Who is this Cooter Brown you keep mentioning?" I asked.

"It's a saying," Gertie said.

I shook my head, no longer trying to keep up. "We might as well head back and face the music before Carter adds assaulting law enforcement vehicles to our crimes."

"I'm still going with the trailer hitch story," Ida Belle said. "Trust me on this one. Carter is not going to throw me in jail when I'm about to marry his uncle."

"Oh, that's a great angle," Gertie said. "Shame we can only use it once, but there you go. Instant out."

I didn't think for a minute it was going to be instant or out, but I was happy to let Ida Belle take the lead. God knows, I couldn't come up with anything better and the truth was definitely not the way to go.

Ida Belle managed to get the van turned around and we headed back for the site of the bear-versus-truck showdown. Carter was out of the truck and frowning at it, probably trying to figure out how he was going to get it out of the ditch when he had two flat tires. This was not going to go well.

"What the heck were you thinking?" he asked as we pulled to a stop.

He strode up to the driver's door and glared at Ida Belle.

"We were thinking if we slowed down that bear was going to climb into the van and have us all for lunch," Ida Belle said. "She ripped the door clean off. I'm pretty sure it wasn't for fun."

He stuck his head in the window and looked back at the missing door and then Gertie and me. We waved and smiled. He didn't smile back.

"What are you doing here?" he asked. "And why are you in Molly's van? Why is that bear chasing you?"

"We went out in the boat to look for Molly," Ida Belle said.

"I've known the statistics on such things since before you were born so don't start preaching them to me. I wasn't ready to call it quits so we didn't. While we were out, I wanted to stop by Molly's place and take a look around her driveway to see if that's where my trailer hitch came loose. It's missing and I've already checked everywhere else that we drove yesterday."

"You expect me to believe that something wasn't secured properly on your SUV?" Carter asked. "*Your* SUV? That thing you value more than life itself?"

"I let Scooter borrow the hitch last week and didn't check it when he put it back," Ida Belle said. "I know that's not like me, but the next two weeks are going against a lifetime of digging my heels in, so cut me some slack here."

Clearly Carter had no idea how to respond to the 'I'm planning a wedding' excuse. Not when it was coming from Ida Belle. If I hadn't been worried about the destroyed van, the trespassing, the bear returning, Molly being missing, and probably a couple things I'd forgotten, I would have laughed at his expression and given her a high five for her ingenuity.

"Fine," he said, apparently not wanting to take on a bride, especially *this* bride. "So how did you end up stealing and destroying a van while being pursued by a bear?"

"Trash was scattered all over Molly's yard," Ida Belle said. "We looked around, figuring it was raccoons and maybe we could scare them off and try to pick some of it up before it blew all over, but the trash cans were nowhere to be seen. We walked toward the tree line, since the wind was out of the south and we thought they might have blown that way, when a pack of nutria came bolting out at us."

"A pack of nutria?" he asked.

I nodded. "I was not amused. You know how I hate rats, and there was a hundred of them—"

"Not a hundred of them," Ida Belle interrupted.

"Okay, two hundred," I said, even though there had probably been twenty at the most. "They were all running straight for us, so we got the heck out of there. We just made a bit of a miscalculation thinking the nutria were running at us when in fact—"

"They were running from the bear," Carter finished.

"She has cubs," Gertie said. "You know how territorial they can get. She probably pulled those trash cans into the woods and when the nutria tried to pick up an easy snack, she got after them."

"There was no way we could have made it back to the boat, gotten untied, and gotten away, because the bear was angled so she could have cut us off. So we ran for the driveway and climbed on top of Molly's van," I said.

"It was a good plan until she smelled us," Ida Belle said. "She rocked the van so hard Gertie fell off. That's when Fortune jumped off to distract her and yelled at Gertie and me to run for the boat. But no way were we leaving a man in the field."

"Of course not," Carter said, not looking even remotely surprised at anything we'd said.

"I shot out the windshield," Ida Belle said. "Then hot-wired the van and we hauled butt down the road where Fortune had taken off with the bear chasing her. We got her into the van, but the bear was so close, she ripped the door right off the back."

"You're lucky she didn't rip right into you three," Carter said. "Mother bears are nothing to play around with."

"We weren't playing," Gertie said. "That much, I can assure you. We were running like it was the Second Coming and spots on the elevator up were limited."

"Yeah, this was definitely not on my list of things to do in this lifetime," I said.

"Well, for someone who doesn't want to be chased by man-eaters," Carter said, "you've managed to do it somewhat regularly. And I might also point out that if you weren't sticking your nose into law enforcement business, you wouldn't have ever been chased."

"I told you—" Ida Belle said.

He held up his hand to stop her. "I know. Your missing trailer hitch. If you think the DNA in my family lends to gullible and stupid, why are you marrying into it?"

"One, I'm not planning on procreating, so unless God himself gets other ideas, I don't have to worry about your family's faulty DNA," Ida Belle said. "Two, Walter is gullible but not stupid. That must come from the other side of your family."

I watched Carter closely, wondering how he was going to handle this one. In less than two weeks the woman standing there lying to him was going to be his aunt. I was already his girlfriend and Gertie...was Gertie. Convoluted didn't begin to describe his life at the moment.

"Hey, at least we didn't have the rocket launcher," Gertie said.

He grimaced and shook his head. "I suppose I can let the grand theft auto go, and I'm not even going to try to convince a jury of trespass. They'll all see sweet little old ladies. They'll have no idea of the truth."

"Who are you calling old?" Gertie asked.

"I was thinking 'sweet' was the bigger stretch," I said.

"I'll pay to repair the van," Ida Belle said. "Or make up whatever difference insurance won't cover. Whatever the person who inherits wants to do. But I'm not sorry I took it and you shouldn't be either. Fortune is an impressive specimen but she's no match for a bear. Not with only a nine-millimeter on her."

I could tell he was unhappy—because he couldn't argue or because I'd almost been mauled, I wasn't sure—but finally, he pulled out his phone.

"I need to call for a tow," he said. "I have one spare. Not two."

"What do you want us to do with the van?" Ida Belle asked.

"I'll ask for two tow trucks," he said. "It can't sit in the driveway with no windshield and no door on the back. It's supposed to rain and her garage is full of junk. It will never fit in there."

"We need to get to the boat," Ida Belle said. "I don't want to leave it there."

"That bear has not gone far," Carter said. "Not with cubs. Do you really want to roll the dice on that one?"

"Have you seen the cost of Fortune's boat?" Ida Belle said. "You really want to leave it at an empty house?"

He sighed. "Fine. I'll drive you back to Molly's and get as close to the dock as possible. If there's no sign of the bear, then you three haul it to the boat, go home, and never return to her property before there's more loss than just a van. You can buy a new trailer hitch. Got it?"

We all nodded. It was safer than talking.

We piled into the back of the van and took a seat, none of us wanting to ride shotgun with a very irritated Carter, and after he made a couple phone calls, we headed back to Molly's, stopping only to pick up the discarded door. Carter just shook his head before shoving it into the back of the van with us.

There was no sign of the bear at Molly's house, or the nutria, which ranked only slightly below the bear in my book. I had Carter stop in the driveway so I could retrieve my cell phone, which incredibly didn't have a scratch on it, then he drove the van across the backyard as far as possible with the sketchy terrain and got us about thirty yards from the dock.

The boat was still there—thank God—so we climbed out of the van and all checked our weapons while Carter frowned.

"Be sure to tell that idiot boyfriend of Molly's about the bear," Ida Belle said. "Unless he's the one who killed her. Then maybe don't tell him anything at all."

"That would be a really good outcome," Gertie said.

"Just go home," Carter said. "This town has had more than its share of death. We don't need any more. Not even the stupid bear."

"Maybe the nutria," I said.

"They are a nuisance," Gertie agreed as we started walking off.

We were all on alert as we went but the walk to the dock was uneventful. We loaded up and I released the lines from the dock, and we were off. I glanced back to see Carter looking at us and frowning. I wasn't sure whether the frown was all on our account or a combination of a lot of things. Either way, I'd probably get an earful tonight over dinner. Or maybe after dinner. Carter said being angry interfered with his polite enjoyment of food, and he was grilling steaks tonight.

The wind from the boat ride felt good on my hot skin and I wondered if some of it was singed from being on top of the van. When Ida Belle slowed in a particularly narrow part of the bayou, Gertie leaned over the side and flung water back on us and herself. It helped take some of the heat off.

As we exited the bayou into the lake, I saw the two boats that had been dragging the night before. They looked like they were pulling the nets in.

"Looks like they're quitting," Gertie said.

Ida Belle nodded, her expression one of disappointment and resignation.

We'd lost operatives overseas. Men and women who'd simply vanished. I knew what it was like to come home with an empty seat on the transport and always felt a pain in my heart for the family that was going to get the awful news and the agent who had to deliver it. I'd been on the receiving end of that conversation once before. Twice now, I suppose.

I wondered who Carter had to deliver the news to and for just a moment, I was back on that transport plane with an empty seat.

CHAPTER NINE

WHEN WE PULLED up to my backyard, I was surprised to find we had a visitor. Nickel was sitting in a chair pushed far up under the tree and drinking a beer. Ida Belle drove the boat onto the bank and we got out, pulled it up a little more, and I tied it off to its post.

"Please tell me you did not break into the house of the deputy's girlfriend to acquire some beer," Ida Belle said. "Especially since you own a bar."

"Heck no," Nickel said. "I told you I was done with all the illegal stuff. My brother's been pulling the weight for long enough. Probably time I stopped being a screwup and gave him a hand. I snagged this from the bar before I left. Thought if I had to wait, I'd get thirsty."

I supposed taking the beer from your own bar was far better than stealing it from me, but I still wondered if Nickel was capable of getting it together. He seemed to have a lapse in logic when it came to right and wrong.

"And why are you hanging out in my backyard, drinking stolen beer from the Swamp Bar?" I asked.

He grinned. "Can't steal from yourself, can you?"

"The IRS thinks so," I said.

He gave me a confused look so I waved a hand in dismissal. "Doesn't matter. Look, we're more than exhausted. We've been out looking for Molly—with no success—and have been chased by a million nutria and an angry mama bear. Carter caught us stealing a van, and we sort of caused him to wreck his truck."

"The bear did that, actually," Gertie said.

"I don't think he sees it that way," I said.

Nickel's eyes widened. "You stole a van? That's hard-core. Carter must really like you if he let you go."

"We didn't steal it really," I said. "Just borrowed it to get away from the bear. Anyway, that's not the point. The point is it's been a long day. We're tired and chastised and in desperate need of a shower, and probably rethinking some of our decisions. So if you could just get on with your business or better yet, come back another time, that would be awesome."

"No can do on the reschedule," he said. "This is urgent. Why do you think I was ready to sit here until you got back?"

"Whiskey has my phone number," I said. "You could have called."

Nickel stared down at the ground. "I don't want him to know about this."

"Uh-oh," Gertie said.

"No," Nickel protested. "It's nothing like that. I would never ask you to do something wrong. I'm respectable now."

We all gave him the I-don't-buy-it-for-a-second look.

"Respectable for Sinful?" he suggested.

Still silence.

"Respectable for the Swamp Bar?" he tried.

It was an acceptable compromise so we all nodded.

"I want to hire you," he said. "You know, to do that investigating thing."

I blinked and stared. I hadn't even been able to imagine a reason that Nickel would need to speak to me and now that he'd delivered his kill shot, I was more than a little surprised. If I'd had the energy to speculate, that one wouldn't have even made the list.

"What do you want me to investigate?" I asked.

He glanced around, looking a little nervous. "Can we go inside? It's hot as heck out here and if anyone sees me talking to you, they'll start spreading the word."

"You've been sitting in my backyard drinking beer," I said. "It only takes one person to see you and talk. Ronald has probably already got a picture of you taped to his wall as a potential threat. But we can agree on the need for air-conditioning."

"And aloe vera," Gertie said. "Or we're going to be spotted up our arms for this wedding."

We shuffled into the kitchen and I grabbed some cold waters for all of us. Gertie headed for the medical supplies and came back with the aloe vera. I took a huge gulp of the water, giving myself a tiny bit of brain freeze, then looked at Nickel.

"So tell me about this case," I said.

"It's about Molly," he said. "I want to know who killed her."

Because I was former CIA, I could manage to avoid registering surprise in even the most questionable of circumstances, but so far, nothing about Nickel's visit had been remotely in the realm of normal. I was trying to imagine how he had managed a personal interest in Molly that had him sitting in my backyard all afternoon with stolen beer but couldn't even come up with a decent guess. I figured we'd get around to it eventually, so I moved forward with the business part of the discussion. My curiosity could wait.

"Molly? The caterer?" I asked, just to make sure we were both thinking of the same person.

"I don't know any other Molly around here," he said.

"I don't suppose you know her real name, do you?" I asked.

He gave me a confused look. "'Course I do. Mary Olivia Broussard."

"Molly for short," I said and looked over at Ida Belle and Gertie, who were shaking their heads. We'd just risked our lives, destroyed a perfectly good van, and angered a bear and more importantly, Carter, and all the while, Nickel had been sitting in my backyard with the very information we'd gone looking for.

"We don't know for sure that she was murdered," I said. "It could have been an accident."

"Bullsh—crap," he said. "Molly was no fool. No way she'd manage to get in a bind like that on her boat. You met her, right? Did she look like a woman who couldn't take care of herself?"

"She struck me as quite capable," I said. "But everyone can make a mistake, and sometimes those mistakes are fatal."

He shook his head. "Not Molly. Not on a boat. You have to understand, her brother Johnny drowned. Got caught out in a storm and just like that, he was gone. Being as Johnny was a commercial shrimper and pretty much wrote the book on boats, it was a big shock. And since Molly and Johnny was thick as thieves, him dying broke her up something awful, especially as it happened while she was in the joint. They wouldn't even let her out to attend his funeral. So when I say Molly was careful on boats, I mean careful like a surgeon or a pilot."

I glanced over at Ida Belle and Gertie, who looked as convinced by Nickel's words as I was. All three of us had problems imagining the obviously capable Molly getting caught unaware on the bayou, and given what Nickel had said, I was doubling down on that. The situation was growing stinkier by the second.

"How do you know all of this?" I asked.

"Yeah," Gertie said. "We didn't think Molly knew people in Sinful until she moved here, and she darn sure didn't go out of her way to hand out anything personal."

"I was good friends with Johnny," Nickel said. "Back during one of my stints in jail in NOLA, I bunked with him. Now, I see how you're looking and I don't want you thinking bad about the man. The truth was, Johnny was probably the only guy I ever met in the joint that didn't belong there."

"So why was he there?" I asked.

"He wrote a hot check," Nickel said. "Had an old buddy of his that he went into the shrimping business with. The loser wiped out the account, but Johnny didn't know when he paid the bills, and his buddy was long gone. The mayor was on a big push to crack down on hot checks at the time, so Johnny got a couple months in the joint in addition to a fine. They was making examples or something. Anyway, we got on real good and after I got out, I looked him up and we hung out mostly every week until I moved back to Sinful. He was the best guy I ever met. Well, him and Whiskey."

Most people around Sinful wouldn't put Whiskey onto a best-guy list but I knew a thing or two about the Swamp Bar owner that a lot of residents probably didn't. And I agreed with Nickel. Whiskey was a good guy. If Nickel put Johnny on the same level, then that was probably saying a lot because men like Nickel didn't just hand out compliments, especially about other men.

"Besides," Nickel continued, "even if something happened, Molly has a CB radio on her boat. Angel said her cell phone was cutting out."

"Who is Angel?" I asked, assuming she was the party on the other end of the call when Molly had made her cryptic statement about someone bringing about her death.

"Angel and Molly have been friends since they was kids," he said. "Angel had been dating Johnny pretty serious when he died. Her and Johnny was going to get married but was waiting on Molly to get out. Guess maybe you shouldn't wait on important things, right? Might not get another chance."

"That's really sad," Gertie said. "For everyone."

Nickel nodded. "And now Angel has to have another funeral with an empty casket. Seems like a lot for one person."

"What about Molly's parents?" Ida Belle asked.

"Her mom split when the kids was little," Nickel said. "They never mentioned her and if someone asked, they didn't really answer. I figured it was old wounds and I never got into it. Their dad is still alive, far as I know. I always got the impression he's a mean old cuss although ain't no one ever come right out and said so. It was more about what they didn't say, you know? He lives somewhere outside of NOLA. I only ever saw him once and that was at Johnny's funeral. Didn't shed so much as a tear and that ain't right. A real man shouldn't have no problem crying over the death of his only son."

"No. He shouldn't," Gertie said and patted Nickel's arm.

"Do you happen to know anything about Molly's will?" I asked.

Nickel shook his head. "Can't see Molly discussing that with someone like me. Whiskey maybe. He's got the head for business but they weren't on that kind of speaking terms. Why?"

"Because her crazy boyfriend showed up at Ally's house today threatening her," I said. "He's under the impression that Molly left Ally her catering business and apparently, he thought it should be coming to him."

Nickel's eyes widened. "Was Ally hurt?"

"No," I said. "He scared her more than anything. Carter locked him up but you know that won't stick for long."

Nickel scratched his head. "Molly's said before as how she thought Ally was the most talented baker she'd ever come across, which ain't no secret around here. And I know Molly's catering business was real important to her. I suppose if she was gonna do up everything legal and all, it would make sense she'd want it going to someone who could do it justice."

"You said Dexter was hitting on women at the Swamp Bar," I said, "but that you didn't think anyone had told Molly because they'd be afraid to. Did that include you?"

Nickel sighed. "I guess I kinda hedged on that one earlier. Yeah, I told her. I figured she'd go crazy on him but the next week, I stopped by her house with a bottle of specialty whiskey she'd asked us to get for her and that loser was still there. I didn't bother saying anything after that. Molly knew I wouldn't lie. Not to her, anyway. So if she decided it wasn't a problem, wasn't nothing I could do about it."

"Will Angel be willing to talk to us?" I asked. Maybe Molly's best friend could shed some light on things that Nickel couldn't.

"'Course!" Nickel said. "I talked to her about you before I came over here and she was all for it. Does that mean you'll do it? You'll figure out who killed Molly?"

"I'll certainly try," I said. "But you know I can't promise anything, just like you can't promise how many beers you'll sell on Saturday night down at the bar."

Nickel shook his head. "You'll do it. Whiskey says you're smart as hel—heck. And Whiskey don't go around bragging on people."

"You said you didn't want Whiskey to know about this," I said. "Why not?"

Nickel shrugged. "I figured he wouldn't want me messed up

in something like this, especially with police circling around. I'm trying to keep my nose clean and butting in on something like this isn't smart for a guy in my position. If the cops knew I was friends with Molly, they might make something of it."

"Where were you when Molly went missing?" I asked.

"Right where you guys found me when you was looking for her," he said. "I didn't know she was gone until you guys showed up and even then, I didn't think nothing about it. Figured Molly had got hot over something and went for a ride to cool off. I never thought..."

He stopped for a minute to cough, then took a swig of beer and I could tell he was trying to maintain his tough-guy persona. "Anyway, you see how I wouldn't want to draw attention to myself. My record...being in the same location...it don't look good. I promised Whiskey I was going to do everything straight when I got out last time. It's a promise I intend to keep."

"Okay," I said. "As a professional, I observe the rules of client confidentiality. No one will know you've hired me unless you tell them."

Nickel's relief was apparent. "Thanks. I really appreciate it. Do I sign a contract or something?"

He pulled a wad of hundreds from his pocket. "How much do I give you? I have two thousand here but I can get more."

We all stared.

"I promise I didn't take it from the Swamp Bar," he said, reading our minds. "I sold my Harley."

"You loved that bike," Gertie said.

He shrugged. "It's just a bike. I can get another one. But whoever did this to Molly has to pay."

"I'll take a thousand dollars on retainer," I said. "Let me go print up a contract. It will only take a minute."

As I headed for my office, warring emotions coursed

through me. Excitement over a new case. Sadness that the case involved the death of someone I think I would have really liked if I'd had the opportunity to get to know her. Anger at whoever had taken her away from the people who cared about her. And just a tiny bit of resignation over having to tell Carter that I had an official reason to be in the middle of his investigation.

But of all the things I felt, a desire for justice was at the top of the list.

———

NICKEL SIGNED THE CONTRACT, collected a receipt for the retainer, and then headed off. I wanted to question him more but Whiskey had called looking for him, so he needed to get back to the bar before his excuses ran out. We promised that if it ever came up, we'd tell Whiskey that Nickel had been out that day looking for Molly same as we were. It was sort of true. He'd been looking to find her killer, anyway, by hiring me.

The back door had barely closed behind him when Gertie threw her hands in the air.

"All that running and sweating and getting burned by metal and Nickel had her name all along," Gertie said.

"Don't forget the bear," Ida Belle said.

"Or the giant rats," I said. The nutria had still been the worst part of the day as far as I was concerned.

"I think those nutria are going to be the least of your worries," Ida Belle said.

I blew out a breath. "Yeah, Carter isn't going to be happy, but it is what it is. We both know that my work might overlap his. As long as I don't break the law, it's not his concern."

"Ha!" Gertie said. "If you didn't break the law, Carter

would hold a mirror in front of your mouth to see if you were still breathing."

"I attempt to follow the rules," I said. "Sinful just makes it hard."

Gertie nodded. "That reasoning has been the primary defense in a lot of court proceedings."

"How's it working out for people?" I asked.

"Better than you might think," Gertie said. "But I don't know that you're going to be able to pull off the uneducated fisherman routine as well as others."

"That might be a stretch," I agreed and grabbed my cell phone. "Let me try this Angel and see if we can arrange to talk. I figure this is best done in person. I want to get a look at her face and how she acts."

Ida Belle nodded. "Hard to get a read on people you don't know over the phone."

The call went to voice mail, so I left a message. Nickel had said Angel worked as a waitress so there was a good chance she was at work, it being well into dinner. Hopefully, she'd call me back by tomorrow morning and I could line up an interview.

"I just can't believe how all this turned out," Gertie said. "Never in a million years would I come up with Nickel and Molly as friends."

"Me either," I said. "It does make me wonder about something, though."

"What's that?" Ida Belle asked.

"Nickel telling Molly about Dexter hitting on other women," I said. "I'm sure she knew he wasn't making it up, so why keep that guy around?"

"No idea," Ida Belle said.

"Maybe so she could whup up on him in that cage," Gertie said. "He was mad as heck when we saw him at her house the other day. I bet given an opportunity, he'd return the favor."

"Possibly," I said. "But then we've only seen him twice and he was angry both times. For all we know, he might sing opera while petting kittens every night."

Gertie giggled. "Now there's an image. You definitely have a way with tall tales. Another forty years or so, and you won't be the newcomer anymore."

"Another forty years in Sinful and I'll probably be locked in a padded room," I said.

"Well, what's on the agenda for tonight?" Gertie asked.

My cell phone signaled an incoming text and I frowned.

"Looks like I'll be filling Carter in on my new case," I said. "The basics, at least. He's on his way over now."

Ida Belle popped up. "That's our cue. If he says anything about the van, tell him I meant what I said about making good on it. Seems even more important now if Ally really is inheriting the business."

"And see if you can find out if there was a will," Gertie said. "And whether the blood on the anchor was Molly's and how old it is. And if—"

Ida Belle yanked Gertie's arm. "Carter is two minutes away from this house and the last thing he wants to see right now is the three of us together."

"Fine, fine," Gertie said. "But only old people have dinner and turn in at this hour."

"Well, it's too late in life to make me into one of those bar whores," Ida Belle said.

"I have a good stereo system, plenty of wine and food, and we can talk about your honeymoon," Gertie said.

"Woman, no one is talking about my honeymoon. Not even me and Walter to each other."

I laughed as they headed out the back door, probably hoping to skirt the front of the house as Carter was walking in. Ida Belle was so done with wedding stuff I hoped she still showed up for the actual event. Carter called out from the front door and I told him I was in the kitchen. He had a key and could use it any time, but he persisted in the belief that warning an armed woman before entering her house was the right call. I was offended by his lack of trust at first until his mother told me he did the same thing at her house. Since I knew Carter had nothing but respect for Emmaline, I couldn't exactly hold a grudge.

He walked into the kitchen, his pace a bit slower than usual, and I could see the tired and sad in his expression. I pointed to the chair as I rose, and he slumped into it while I grabbed him a beer and a container of Ally's cookies. He took a drink of the beer but barely glanced at the cookies. I didn't even have to ask. I already knew.

"You talk to the DA yet?" I asked. The DA was young and enthusiastic, which was good, but sometimes all that enthusiasm was tough when you were a cop with few to no leads.

"I tried to get away with an email," he said, "but my phone rang about two seconds after I sent it."

"Murder cases are big feathers in DA hats," I said. "I don't suppose he's planning on hanging out in a small area any longer than he has to. The more he can beef up his résumé beyond assault and poaching, the better."

"I know, but it still seems wrong to be so excited about other people's loss, not to mention the victim. I mean, the funeral home benefits when people die but they don't seem eager about it."

"Probably because they have no intention of pulling up stakes for a bigger market and the added benefit of not having to seek out business. The clientele is kind of built in. But I get your point. I'm really sorry about Molly. I only just met her yesterday but I liked her."

He nodded. "I only knew her from a couple events she

catered. She wasn't much on law enforcement, as you can imagine, but she allowed as how she'd heard I was one of 'the good ones' so she would probably let me eat without arm wrestling her for the privilege."

I laughed. "That sounds like her. And you're lucky your reputation preceded you. You're no lightweight but I'd put my money on Molly in an arm-wrestling match."

"So would I."

"Listen, I know your day sucked probably more than mine even, although you didn't get chased by giant rats."

"I'd think the bear would have been a larger concern."

"I suppose in the bigger scheme of things, she was. But only if you're assuming death is the bigger scheme."

"I'm not quite sure how to respond to that."

"Anyway, I know your day sucked and tomorrow's probably not going to be any better, but I have to tell you something that's not going to help."

He stared at me for a moment, then sighed. "You have a new case and it's something I'm not going to like."

"We have the same case and it's definitely not something you'll like."

"What? Someone hired you to look into Molly's death? Who? And we haven't even announced that it was suspicious."

"You know I can't tell you who, but let's just say it's someone who knew her better than we do and was already suspicious."

"If you know someone who has information about Molly's disappearance, you can't withhold it."

"My client doesn't know anything about her disappearance except to believe it wasn't an accident."

"And obviously they don't think I can handle it. Is it that woman Molly called?"

I stared silently at him.

He sighed. "You're right. I don't like it."

"It's not the first time and it's not going to be the last time our jobs cross paths."

"Yeah, but this one is different."

"Why?"

"Because there's too many unknowns. Molly, Dexter, the whole Ally inheriting thing, and just the way it all went down. Unexpected death always stinks but this one has a particularly foul odor to it. There's so much undercurrent, I don't know that there's a bottom."

I nodded. On the surface, it didn't seem difficult. A cheating louse of a boyfriend and a woman who'd already sent the last man who crossed her to the cemetery. Molly's statement to her friend right before her demise. If this were a television episode, it would be a short one. The cops would round up the boyfriend, and because the criminal was always an idiot, he'd have left evidence that tied him to the crime, then they'd cut to the last scene where he confessed. On the surface, Dexter fit the bill. And maybe it was that simple. Heck, I hoped it was. Everyone who cared about Molly would still be sad and angry, but they'd be sad and angry with answers, and that was a world of difference.

"Look, nothing about Sinful has been face value since I arrived," I said. "Including me. And definitely nothing about my life prior to Sinful was face value, not even my personal life. If I was a regular everyday joe PI then I could see where you might be concerned about how I'd fare with a case like this, but that's not me. I'm trained for subterfuge. Heck, it might even be in my DNA."

He still didn't look happy but he couldn't argue. The reality was, I was probably better equipped to handle the twists and turns that Sinful crime threw out than a lot of law enforcement officers who had grown up in the area. And I knew

Carter had no issue with pride when it came to me solving a case before he did. Carter loved me but more importantly, he respected me and my skills. The only thing that had him frowning was worry. Would this be the time someone got the better of me? If things got sketchy, would he be able to intervene?

Carter might have been more advanced than the small-town bayou norm on what he thought women were capable of, but when it came to his own woman, the desire to be the protector was in constant conflict with his desire to let me be me. I could appreciate his dilemma but it was something he was going to have to figure out. Still, I found his worry to be endearing and not suffocating. He loved me and wanted to keep me from harm but no way was he going to suggest I drop the case. That ranked as high as taking a bullet for me from a guy like Carter, who was the natural-born hero type.

He reached over and squeezed my hand. "Be careful. I know I always say it and I always mean it, but something about this one bothers me."

"It's a potential homicide. It's supposed to bother you."

"I mean more than most. There's something wrong with it. More wrong than usual."

"What do you mean?"

He shook his head. "I don't know."

I nodded, completely understanding what he felt but couldn't explain. People like Carter and me had instincts about certain things. And if he thought something was amiss, more than what was visible, then I'm sure he was right.

"So we both watch our backs," I said. "And you keep Deputy Breaux in the loop. No playing James Bond, loner spy."

"You're one to talk."

"Oh, my back is always watched."

"I know. It's the two watching it who worry me the most."

CHAPTER TEN

CARTER ONLY STAYED LONG ENOUGH to finish off my left-overs, then he headed home for a shower and some sleep. We'd both decided to reschedule steak grilling for a better night. Neither of us was much in the mood for talking and given we'd been at odds most of the day, I figured we could use a break. We didn't spend every night together anyway and I was perfectly fine with that. I still needed my space and I assumed Carter felt the same way. Neither of us had been looking for a relationship when we'd met and although I don't think either of us could have picked a better match, the reality was our relationship was going to be an ongoing negotiation, probably for the rest of our lives. Or at least until one of us retired.

I actually slept decently for a change and even beat Merlin out of bed, which made him purr with excitement over the possibility of having breakfast a bit early. I indulged since he'd slept quietly rather than subjecting me to a night of pacing the halls or pouncing on threads on the comforter. As I put on coffee, I thought about Walter and Ida Belle. There was another relationship that was perfect and yet fraught with difficulty—mostly because of Ida Belle. Walter was the easiest-going man alive. And then I thought about Carter and me. Carter definitely was not the easiest-going man alive, or even second easiest. And I rivaled Ida Belle in stubbornness, so our future was likely to be even bumpier than Ida Belle and Walter's.

But it was still doable. And anything worth having was worth working for, right? Director Morrow always said that to me. He was talking about the job, of course, but I supposed it could apply to most anything in life. I was just sitting down to my first cup of coffee and a slice of toast when my cell phone rang. It was barely 8:00 a.m. so I figured it was Ida Belle, Gertie, or Carter, but was surprised when I saw Angel Denis's number come up on my display.

"Hello," I answered. "Ms. Denis?"

"Please call me Angel. I hope I didn't wake you. I'm taking some classes at the university and have to leave in a few minutes, but I didn't want to wait until after..."

"No worries. I was just having some coffee. Thank you for returning my call."

"So does this mean you took the case?"

"Yes. And I'd love to talk to you and get more information. No one around here knew Molly all that well and I'm hoping you can fill in the blanks about her personal life."

"And that's important?"

"Unless a crime is random, who the victim is almost always indicates why they were killed."

"That makes sense." Angel sniffed and I immediately felt guilty. I'd started right in on my desire for information and hadn't even thought that this woman had just lost her best friend.

"I'm really sorry for your loss," I said. "I just met Molly a couple days ago but I liked her. I wish I'd gotten a chance to know her better."

"Thank you. Molly was...something else." She let out a single laugh. "She was tough but kind and had worked hard to get her life together. I was proud of her and she was happy, for probably the first time since I've known her. This is all so unfair."

"It is. Do you have time today to talk to me? I can come to New Orleans if that makes it easier on you."

"That would be great. I only have an hour or so in between classes and my last one ends about two hours before my shift at the restaurant. I could talk to you in between classes or before I go to work."

"Let's do it before you go to work. I don't want to interrupt your studies."

And that would give me time to track down information on Molly's father and Dexter Nutters, both of whom were in the New Orleans area. We could make a day of investigating in the city.

"I really appreciate what you're doing," Angel said. "It's important to me and Nickel. More important than you'll ever know."

"Well, I can't do anything to bring her back, but I can certainly try to bring her justice."

"I'm not interested in justice, Ms. Redding. I'm interested in retribution."

———

Two hours later, Ida Belle, Gertie, and I were in her SUV and NOLA-bound. They hadn't so much as blinked when I'd told them that Carter was still looking into things. That didn't mean he was calling it homicide but it was sketchy enough to commit more time to.

After getting Molly's father's name from Nickel, we'd

managed to locate an address for him, and the old boy was still kicking. And I did mean old boy. Molly had been in her early thirties. According to the information I could drum up on the internet, her father was over seventy. And either he didn't like change or he didn't like to spend money because according to the property tax rolls, he'd inherited the property from his parents. I assumed it was the house Molly grew up in.

Dexter Nutters had been a bit harder to get a fix on. I'd found an apartment address, but the manager had told me, not so politely, that Nutters had run out on rent and if I saw him I was to tell him that Winky Bear never forgot a debt. The man I'd spoken to sounded like a heavy metal singer, practically growling into the phone, so I was sorely tempted to make a drive by the apartments and see what a man called Winky Bear but with a voice like thunder looked like. But our first stop was Silas Broussard, Molly's father. We'd already seen the document leaving the catering business to Ally, but we didn't know who the rest of Molly's belongings would go to. Without a will, next of kin stood in line, and as far as we knew, that meant Silas. Since I was certain Ally hadn't killed Molly to inherit, I was moving on to the next in line.

"Carter's probably notified Molly's father, right?" Gertie asked as Ida Belle hurtled us down the highway at one and a half times the speed limit.

"I'm sure he has," I said. "He had Angel's number and I'm sure she could provide his name and address, especially as he hasn't moved since birth."

Gertie nodded. "A lot of those old bayou people are like that. Sometimes multiple generations live out their lives in an old shack on a single plot of land. Heck, some never even leave their local town. There are people living out in the bayous around Sinful that have never even been to New Orleans."

I couldn't imagine hiding away from the world, but then I'd

traveled a lot of it and not the pleasant places, either. I could handle whatever was thrown at me. But for a hermit type, who'd never been out of the weeds, so to speak, a place like New Orleans was probably overwhelming. Quite frankly, based on some of the things I'd seen overseas in the sandbox, electricity could be overwhelming. A cell phone was straight-up the devil.

"I was going to try to get more information about Silas from Nickel," I said, "but he couldn't talk last night and I couldn't reach him this morning."

"Which means he's probably got Whiskey within listening distance," Ida Belle said.

"More likely, he hasn't gotten out of bed yet," Gertie said. "It's not afternoon."

"That's true," Ida Belle said. "I forget these bar owners keep late hours working and sleeping. And Nickel wasn't ever one to turn down a beer. I can't imagine him working in the bar is the best idea for keeping him straight, but I don't see that Whiskey has a choice in the matter, either."

"Has their father signed the bar over to them yet?" I asked.

"I don't know," Ida Belle said. "You'd think he would have done everything up legally when he first got sick but he's a stubborn old cuss."

"So based on the very limited information we have on Silas, what do you think we're walking into?" I asked.

"Someone who shoots trespassers on sight," Ida Belle said. "We're gonna need to park right in the middle of the driveway or dirt patch or whatever serves as parking and walk with our hands in clear sight as we approach the house."

"Yep," Gertie said. "And if there's a warning shot or even an indiscernible yell or grunt, we get the heck out of there. I'd sooner mess with gators than one of those rooted-in Creoles."

"I really hope he doesn't shoot," I said. "I'm not interested in killing anyone today. Well, most days, really. Unless they're bad guys and they start it. Then I'm good."

Ida Belle grinned. "As long as you have your standards."

"I've had to get a bit more stringent being a civilian and all," I said. "The CIA was surprisingly lenient when I had a few more hits than assigned. Of course, they sent me in dens of the worst criminals on earth, so it wasn't like I had to discern the nice florist from the mix and make sure he didn't take a stray bullet."

"Our legal system definitely gets in the way sometimes," Gertie said. "Makes everything harder and takes more time. The Old Testament was a lot more immediate."

"Well, it's been a while since God burned bushes and parted seas," Ida Belle said. "I think we're going to have to work this without hoping for a lightning strike to come down on the bad guy."

"Probably so," Gertie said. "But I've still got hope."

My cell phone rang and I pulled it out of my pocket. "Carter," I said, hoping he didn't lead off the conversation by asking what we were doing.

"Hey," Carter said when I answered. "Where are you?"

I smiled. This one I could answer. "We're on our way to New Orleans. Last-minute wedding stuff. What's up?"

"There's a video online of you three with the bear ripping the door off the van."

"Yeah, Gertie was videoing."

"You were in a stolen van!"

"No one knows that. Maybe we had permission from the owner to borrow it."

"The owner is missing."

"Which means no one can prove that we didn't ask beforehand."

"I give up. I just wanted to give you a heads-up that I had

to turn Dexter loose. Jails are full and the DA said he'll probably walk with a fine or minimal probation at best. Bail was so low, Tiny could have paid it."

Tiny was Carter's rottweiler.

"Well, crap," I said. "I was hoping he'd be visiting with you a bit longer than this. Did you call Ally?"

"First thing," he said. "And I gave Dexter a very stern warning before I let him go. She's at the café working today but this evening, we'll all be taking a pass by her house to make sure Dexter isn't as stupid as I think he is."

"Can he get back into Molly's house or is it considered a crime scene?" I asked.

"You know I can't tell you—"

"I just want to know if it's likely he'll still be in the area or if he's going to have to head back for the rock in New Orleans he crawled out from under," I said. "I think Ally would feel better if she knew he wasn't in the same parish any longer."

"Okay then," Carter said, apparently mollified. "Dexter has no rights to Molly's home. He's not on the deed or any of the utilities. He doesn't receive mail there that I could find, and his driver's license still shows a New Orleans address. I took his house key and told him I'd be changing the locks."

"And he didn't give you grief?" I asked.

"He groused about his personal belongings, and I told him I was happy to make him an appointment to collect them when an estate attorney and someone from the sheriff's department could escort him and would let him know when that could occur."

"You need to call Ally back and tell her all of that," I said. "Trust me, she'll rest a lot easier knowing Dexter is probably back in NOLA."

"You're right. Should have thought of it myself. Maybe I'll just have a late breakfast and tell her in person."

"Thanks," I said and disconnected.

"So Dexter is free and loose," Gertie said. "I wonder if he's going to try to head back to that apartment he used to rent."

"I don't know," I said. "Winky Bear is a silly nickname but the dude sounded like a demon. Dexter isn't the best of fighters, so if I were him, I'd just lie low until I could get some new friends and a new line of work. I don't think that cage fighting is going to pay the rent."

"Do you think he'll be stupid enough to razz Ally again?" Gertie asked.

"I hope not, but just in case, I'll have her stay at my place tonight," I said.

"Where's the fun in that?" Gertie asked. "If you stayed at her place, you could take out that idiot if he shows up."

"I don't need the hassle, especially over someone like Dexter," I said.

"Maybe we'll get lucky and he'll show up at your house and Godzilla will take care of him," Gertie said.

I shook my head. "Godzilla hasn't been back since he ate that guy. Maybe he's full."

"Or has indigestion," Gertie said. "Godzilla should be pickier about his diet. Eating terrorists can't be good for his stomach."

"Worked out great for the rest of us, though," Ida Belle said.

"There is that," Gertie agreed. "So you'll let Carter know Ally is staying at your house for the night?"

"Definitely," I said. "I still want them patrolling her house tonight but the sense of urgency is different if she's not actually there."

Gertie nodded. "Sure as you don't tell him, he'll show up at your place in the middle of the night and scare ten lives off of Ally."

"He always texts first if it's the middle of the night," I said. "If I don't answer, he doesn't stop by."

"I thought he had a key," Gertie said.

"He does," I said. "But he also dates a woman who is former CIA, sleeps with a gun, and has an itchy trigger finger when it comes to being ambushed."

"Smart man," Ida Belle said.

Gertie shook her head. "If you two are ever going to live together, you're going to have to figure that one out. The man can't sleep in his vehicle every time he has to work late and you've fallen asleep."

I felt my neck tense. "We are *not* moving in together." I looked over at Ida Belle. "You know I blame you for this. Before you agreed to marry Walter, no one was pushing me toward anything permanent."

"You'll get used to it," Ida Belle said. "After thirty or forty years, most people won't bother you anymore."

"Great," I said. "Something to look forward to."

"I think we're coming up on the exit," Ida Belle said. "Can you check?"

I pulled out my phone and checked GPS. "Yep, take the next exit, then head south. It's another ten miles to the town Silas lives in and his house looks to be a little south of that."

"Ha. Town," Gertie said. "You just wait."

Gertie was right. The town consisted of a convenience store that also served as a bar and a church. Two old men sat outside the store on rusted metal chairs, staring as we drove past. Fortunately, Ida Belle's tinted windows allowed me to do all the looking I wanted while no one else could see who was inside the vehicle.

"That's it?" I said. "Where do kids go to school?"

"They're bused to the nearest school," Gertie said. "Assuming they get to go to school. A lot of these embedded

Creoles don't come out much and they don't like their family to, either. Before I retired, I used to volunteer with a reading program over summers. We set up shop in places like that convenience store and taught people how to read—kids and adults. There's less distrust when it's a lone woman in your local hangout."

"Well, let's hope Silas thinks the same about three women," I said.

"I imagine he'll think we're a waste of time, but not a threat," Ida Belle said.

All of a sudden, Ida Belle slammed on the brakes. "Crap," she said. "I think that was our turnoff. Let me back up."

The sign for the road, such as it was, was lying over in the weeds, the name painted on the wooden plank weathered so much that you could only make out a couple letters. But they matched the letters we were looking for, so we went for it. The road was as weathered as the sign and typical of the remote bayou locations I'd experienced around Sinful. It was basically dirt, with a little bit of rock thrown in and holes big enough to lose a tractor in. Ida Belle drove slowly, winding around the holes when she could and dipping carefully in and out of them when she couldn't. I really hoped that Silas went for the waste-of-time option instead of the fire-first-ask-later option because no way could we speed out of there. A guy with a walker could get close enough to shoot a vehicle on this road.

The brush and trees finally parted and we found ourselves in a surprisingly large clearing. The house was barely more than the shacks people called camps, the roof sagging and much of the siding with paint peeling and some rotted wood along the eaves. The porch was the only thing that had seen a somewhat recent attempt at maintenance. At least one section of it sported planks that weren't rotted and sagging like the rest of the house. Since it was the section right in front of the door, I assumed Silas didn't bother with things unless it became absolutely necessary and then he did only the minimum required to keep it functional. An older-model black Dodge pickup was parked to the side of the house. It looked like it hadn't had a good washing since it was purchased. I could see a small shed off to the right of the shack and off to the left was a chicken coop and a garden.

"Self-sufficient," Gertie said. "Bet he doesn't have electricity."

"What about plumbing?" I asked, hoping that ramshackle shed wasn't serving as a bathroom.

"No city service out here," Ida Belle said. "He'd have a well. But there's a hose rigged over the clothesline. Likely that's his shower."

"Is that an outhouse?" I asked.

"Could be," Ida Belle said. "Wouldn't surprise me. If the plumbing went to crap, a guy like Silas wouldn't pay to have it fixed. He'd just go back to basics."

"A water hose and an outhouse are not basics," I said. "That's primitive."

Ida Belle shrugged. "He wouldn't be the only one living that way out in these marshes."

"How close is he to the bayou?" I asked.

"Maybe a hundred yards according to GPS," Ida Belle said. "Might be able to get decent groundwater or he could have a cistern behind the house. From the deed, looks like he owns all the way back to the water."

"Probably lives off those chickens, the garden, and fish," Gertie said. "And I think that might be a peach tree back there that I can just see the tips of."

"Great," I said. The less people needed to interact with other humans, the more they seemed to resent interacting with humans.

Ida Belle insisted Gertie leave her purse in the SUV, just in case Silas decided we were armed and dangerous, and we climbed out. Of course, we were still armed and dangerous, but with any luck, he wouldn't need to find that out. We walked slowly and with our arms and empty hands in clear sight of the house in case he was watching. We'd made it halfway to the porch when a man stepped out the front door, holding a shotgun.

CHAPTER ELEVEN

SILAS BROUSSARD WALKED to the end of the porch and glared at us.

Looked about eighty but I knew he was almost a decade less. Six foot five. Two hundred seventy pounds. He was definitely fitting a steak in his diet somewhere because that mass did not survive on lean meats and vegetables. Scar on his left elbow from an old break and his hip was higher on one side, indicating a likely back issue that had probably led to the obvious knee issues. It was clear to see where Molly had gotten her size.

"This is private property," he said. "You best skedaddle."

"Are you Silas Broussard?" I asked.

He narrowed his eyes at me. "Why you ask? You from the insurance?"

Immediately, my radar went up. This was the first we'd heard of insurance, so I needed to play it smart and see what I could get out of him.

"My name is Fortune Redding," I said. "I'm a private investigator looking into your daughter's disappearance. Insurance companies often hire people like me in order to get enough information to process claims."

"What about them?" He nodded toward Ida Belle and Gertie.

"They handle the paperwork," I said.

He lowered the shotgun a bit to study me. From his expression, he wasn't impressed.

"Molly ain't disappeared," he said. "She done gone got herself in trouble on them bayous like her brother. They ain't the place for everyone. You gotta know what you're doing or bad things happen."

"Of course," I said. "But I've been told that Molly *did* know what she was doing, and that she would have been extra careful given what happened to her brother."

He shrugged and spit chewing tobacco on the dirt. "Guess that depends on who you ask. I tried to teach both of 'em how to survive without needing other people. It's other people that brings trouble. But neither one listened. Took up with partners and Molly ran off with that crap she ended up killing. If they'd both listened to me and stayed put on the land that's held my family for generations, they'd still be alive."

"That's quite possible," I said. "When was the last time you saw Molly?"

He shook his head. "Can't say as I know. Saw her right before she went in the first time. She called after she got out—claimed she was checking on me—but I don't need no checking."

"So you haven't seen your daughter in years?" I asked. "Then why would she name you as a beneficiary on a life insurance policy?"

Gertie's eyes widened a bit but both she and Ida Belle kept their expressions blank.

"Don't got no idea," he said. "I got a call from that agent telling me I needed to come down and sign some papers. Had to be in front of one of those people with the stamps."

"A notary?"

"Yeah, that's it," he said. "So I went down and signed and that was it."

"And you didn't find it curious that she was going to leave you money even though you had no relationship?" I asked.

He took one hand off the gun and pointed his finger at me. "Listen here, I raised that girl best I could after her momma took off and left us. I don't know why she did half the things she did so I ain't trying to answer for her. All I know is she's gone and I'm due that money. Weren't no clause that said we had to have dinner every Sunday or fish together or anything else. She wanted me to have the money and I intend to have it. Now you get back in your vehicle and go tell the insurance company that. They best not think they can get away with keeping my money. I had people try that before. I know my rights."

He raised the gun again and aimed it right at me. "Go. I ain't got no use for private investigators or women round here. And don't come back unless you got a check."

"Thank you for your time," I said and we headed back to the SUV. Silas kept the shotgun trained on us until we were out of sight. He didn't turn to go back into the house until we were pulling away. I noticed his limp had gotten worse.

"You were a heck of a lot nicer than I would have been," Gertie said. "What a—"

"I think we all know what he is," Ida Belle interrupted. "But it was a smart move mentioning that insurance companies hire investigators."

I grinned. "I'm learning from the best. I didn't lie. I just stated a fact and he assumed the insurance company had hired me."

Gertie nodded. "One day, you might give me a run for my money."

"I'm pretty sure you will always be the reigning champion of misdirected conversation," Ida Belle said.

"So Silas appears as mean as Nickel described," I said. "And Lord is he a big dude."

"I bet I can guess why Molly's mother ran off," Gertie said. "With all his 'no use for women' and that attitude, it doesn't take a genius to figure the score."

"No," Ida Belle said. "It's not exactly an uncommon situation, but I always have trouble when a woman leaves her kids behind. If a man is so bad you have to run from him, why leave your children there to take up the slack you left behind?"

Gertie shook her head. "It's a sad state of affairs. Maybe Angel can fill in some holes. What time do we meet with her?"

"Not for another couple hours," I said.

"So what are we doing now?" Gertie said. "There's this party shop near Bourbon Street that has these blow-up man dolls. I was thinking—"

Ida Belle cringed so hard she hit one of the holes without slowing and we bounced a good foot out of our seats.

"I think we should hunt down that apartment manager and see if maybe Dexter left anything behind," I said.

"As mad as he is, he'd probably give us everything Dexter owned for twenty bucks," Ida Belle said.

I nodded. "And my guess is if Dexter did leave anything behind, he'll make a move to go collect it now that he's out of jail and can't get back in Molly's house."

"You think he was living with Molly?" Gertie asked.

"Hard to say," I said. "Molly didn't strike me as the type that would let a man move in on her space but then she might have loved the guy."

"I don't see how she could," Gertie said.

"I didn't say it was healthy," I said. "But these cycles of abuse tend to repeat, right? You said rumor was Molly's husband tuned her up and that's ultimately why she killed him. My guess is her father did the same thing and she fell into the same situation because it was familiar."

"Except it looked more like Molly was beating up Dexter, not the other way around," Gertie said.

"But I think Dexter would have gotten in any licks he could," I said.

Ida Belle nodded. "It's a frustrating thing to watch as it's repeated, but Fortune's right. I'm willing to bet Angel says as much when we talk to her. Tell me where the apartments are."

I gave her some general directions toward the area and would narrow it down when we got closer. Traffic was surprisingly light and we made it across downtown and into the Ninth Ward in about thirty minutes. I took one look at the apartment building and looked at Gertie.

"Bring your purse this time," I said before we climbed out.

A bar and a bail bonds business were directly across the street, which usually indicated trouble. Two empty spaces were next to the bar and then there was a small convenience store that cashed checks, and some sort of church. All of the businesses had bars on their windows and doors.

The office for the apartment building was toward the back of the property. It had a tree on top of the roof, which at first, I figured was from recent storms, then I realized it was mostly rotted through and might have been sitting there for years. I could only imagine why they hadn't been cited, and my imagination currently ran to payoffs that were considerably less than the cost of removing the tree. Likely, it was the only thing keeping a flood of rain from coming inside.

We headed for the office and I held my hands on my hips as I walked inside. To strangers, it looked like a mad woman walk. To people who knew better, it allowed me to access my pistol in seconds. Bells rang over the door as we walked in and a guy stepped out of an office behind the counter.

Six foot three. Two hundred sixty pounds and most of it solid. Shaved head. Piercings in his lip. So many tattoos he looked like a mural. No hindrances that I could see except his taste in artwork. Threat level high in an enclosed space. Much lower out in the open and if he didn't have a gun. If this was Winky Bear, I could see how he pulled off the nickname without getting any grief.

He never said a word. Just stood at the counter, staring at us, arms crossed in front of his chest. Obviously, Mr. Bear didn't feel the need to have his hands in a ready position.

"Hi," I said. "I'm Fortune Redding. If you're Winky Bear, I spoke with you earlier about Dexter Nutters."

"That's me," he said. "I guess you didn't give him the right message."

"I haven't seen Mr. Nutters," I said. "He was being hauled to jail the last time I laid eyes on him."

"Well, he's out now," Winky Bear said. "In fact, you just missed him. Showed up here about fifteen minutes ago, wanting to get some things he'd left behind. I told him when he came up with the rent, he could have his things. I got rights, you know."

"Of course," I said. "I can't imagine the difficulty of your job dealing with people like Dexter."

He tilted his head and gave me a long stare. "If you don't mind my saying so, you're not exactly the kind of woman that gets tangled up with Nutters."

He didn't ask a question, but I knew it was implied.

"I'm not tangled up with Dexter," I said and pulled out my ID. "I'm a private investigator and these two ladies are my assistants. Let's just say some of Dexter's behavior has caused my client to suspect he's up to no good, and they asked me to check him out."

Winky Bear snorted. "If Nutters is breathing, then he's absolutely up to no good."

"I don't suppose you'd fill me in on what kind of no-good behavior you're aware of, would you?" I asked.

He shrugged. "Hell, why not. We aren't friends and I never liked the guy, but you know, rent money's rent money. I can start with you're not the first people to come looking for him. Bill collectors come here on the regular. That was my first sign that rent was probably going to come up missing but I didn't have any legal grounds to evict him until he skipped. And then there was this one cat came by yesterday, looked like he'd been pumped up with air, you know the type? Like he was birthed by a gym and steroids?"

We all nodded.

"A friend of Dexter's?" Ida Belle asked.

"Dudes like Nutters don't have friends," he said. "My guess is the guy was his pusher."

"He was doing drugs?" Gertie asked.

"Steroids," I said. "Right?"

"Good call," Winky Bear said. "The guy comes in here thirty pounds lighter six months ago and then puts all that weight on in muscle? Come on. Not that it helped with all that flab around it."

"I suppose he needed the muscle for his job," I said.

Winky Bear laughed. "Job? Nutters didn't have a job to speak of."

"I thought he was a cage fighter," Ida Belle said.

"He wishes," Winky Bear said. "From what I heard, he did two bouts and got his butt kicked so hard in the first thirty seconds that no one will even give him another shot. I did my rounds in the cage back years ago. You can't just bulk up and win. It takes some actual ability and hard training."

"Did you know his girlfriend?" I asked. "Molly Broussard?"

143

He shook his head. "Not personally. By reputation, I did a little and I saw some of her fights on YouTube. Now that was a woman with some talent. It's a shame she quit fighting. I think she could have been a regional champion at the least."

"Have you heard that Molly has disappeared?" I asked.

"Yeah," he said. "Some deputy called me earlier asking questions about Nutters. Hey, do you think he did something to Molly? Because I can't imagine he could take her without a gun."

"We don't know exactly what happened to Molly," I said. "But Dexter has claimed that he was helping her with her catering business and that she was going to make him a partner."

Winky Bear stared. "That's some fine fiction right there. Look, Dexter couldn't manage to pay his bills even when he had money. And Lord knows, he didn't have the palate for good food or wine. I've seen what he drank—rotgut whiskey, and always cramming a hot dog in his mouth."

He must have caught our expressions at his choice of words like 'palate' and grinned. "I'm a bit of a foodie. I try to eat at one high-end place a month. There's some fine eating in NOLA but Nutters wouldn't know it from a microwave dinner. Does that sound like someone who could be a partner in a business furnishing quality food?"

"Not to me," I said. "But I'm just working with what I've been given. That's why we're here. No one really knows anything about Dexter, so I'm trying to get a feel for him. Understand what kind of man he is."

"He's no man," Winky Bear said. "He's a chronic loser who bounced from woman to woman, getting them to foot his bills. I don't have any idea why Molly would take that sort of thing on. I know she had her history and all with that murder rap but she just didn't strike me as that stupid. Still, I suppose there's no accounting for taste."

"Anything else you can tell me?" I asked. "You said he didn't have friends. What about relatives?"

"None that I'm aware of but if he had any, he's probably tapped them all out for cash and they avoid him now."

"What about hangouts?" I asked. "The bar across the street maybe?"

"Used to, but the owner banned him. Caused too many fights. He's a regular at the bar around the corner now. The owner there can handle a scuffle."

"What's it called?" I asked.

"The Bar," he said, then laughed at my expression. "It's a really classy joint."

"I'm sure," I said. "So Dexter came by earlier to collect his things. I don't suppose you'd consider selling them to me. I'm not paying his rent for them, but since you're unlikely to collect from him, anything is better than nothing."

He frowned. "Why in the world would you want to pay for that box of trash? The furniture, such as it is, comes with the rental. So do the dishes and pots and pans. This place was a motel before the owner turned it into apartments, so they just left the stuff in it that it had before. The only thing Dexter had was some cheap clothes, a couple books, bathroom stuff, and a bottle of Jim Beam, probably the only decent thing he owned. And since I already drank it, there's nothing left that amounts to anything."

"So twenty bucks and I take it off your hands?" I asked.

"Make it fifty and I never saw you, much less sold you his stuff," he said.

"It's a deal," I said and pulled the money out of my wallet. I also handed him a card. "I know the official story is that we never met, but if you can think of anything else about Dexter that I might find interesting, please give me a call."

He took the money and the card and stuffed both in his jeans pocket. "Give me a minute. It's in the storeroom."

He was back a couple minutes later with one medium-sized box of stuff. He hadn't lied. Homeless people had more belongings. I wondered if the bulk of his possessions were at Molly's house but figured there was no way I'd get that information out of Carter. Winky Bear insisted on carrying the box to Ida Belle's SUV and then we were on our way.

As Ida Belle drove, Gertie poked around in the box that was on the seat next to her. "This stuff isn't worth fifty cents," she said. "Fifty dollars was highway robbery."

"He could have held out for more," I said. "He knew we wanted it. The why doesn't matter to him. He just figured it was a way to make up some lost revenue, but in this case, in his pocket and not the apartment's."

"He definitely didn't like Dexter," Ida Belle said. "I'm sure he got a kick out of selling his things."

"So what's in there?" I asked.

"Some crappy clothes," Gertie said. "I mean really crappy and worn. A toothbrush and a bar of soap. No toothpaste, mind you. A pair of ratty tennis shoes and some books."

I frowned. "Did Dexter look like the kind of guy who reads books?"

"Not even remotely," Ida Belle said.

"What kind of books?" I asked.

"Old hardbacks," Gertie said. "I mean really old. The kind that didn't come with a paper jacket."

"Collectibles?" I asked, wondering if maybe the books were worth something and that's why Dexter wanted them back.

"No way," Gertie said. "I don't recognize the names of any

of the authors. Heck, one of them is a book on human anatomy from the early 1900s."

"Flip through the books."

Ida Belle and I both spoke at once.

"Okay, okay," Gertie said. "You don't both have to bark orders at the same time."

I looked back as she took one of the books and thumbed through the pages.

"There's paper in here," Gertie said. "Stuffed between the pages."

"Bingo," I said. "We just found Dexter's hiding place and the most likely reason he wanted his stuff."

"This looks like a financial statement," Gertie said as she unfolded one of the papers. "For Molly's catering company."

She handed me the sheet and I scanned it. "This is from two years ago, but wow! Molly was making a serious profit. Twenty grand in one month."

"What month?" Ida Belle asked.

"June," I said.

"Weddings."

Ida Belle and Gertie both replied.

"Still," Ida Belle said. "That's a good net. But then Molly didn't have employees. I think she was mostly a one-woman show."

"You forgot about her partner Dexter," Gertie said.

"Molly might have let him haul containers of food around," Ida Belle said, "but I guarantee you she wouldn't trust anyone else to prepare it. When I talked to her before she went to jail, she told me she was going to have to find an employee or two who was good enough or she'd never be able to scale up the business."

"Here's a couple more months," Gertie said. "If Dexter has

these, do you think that might mean he wasn't lying about Molly claiming she'd cut him in?"

"If he was legitimately in line to partner with her, why would he be hiding those financials in books?" I asked. "More likely he managed to access computer files or lifted copies from Molly's office and hid them here, figuring no one would ever check."

"But if he wasn't going to be a partner, why take financial statements?" Gertie asked.

"I don't know," I said. "Maybe just to try to figure out how much money Molly had. Maybe that was his end game—hit her up for funds."

"I wish we knew more about their relationship," Gertie said. "I can't help but think knowing the bigger picture where they were concerned would bring some things into us."

I nodded. "And that's what I'm hoping Angel can provide. Along with filling in some details about Silas."

"We've got about an hour until we meet with Angel," Ida Belle said. "You guys want to stop for a bite of lunch?"

"Heck yeah!" Gertie said. "I'm starving and there's no better place to fill an empty belly than New Orleans."

"I know a great place for po'boys close to Angel's apartment," Ida Belle said.

"The one with fried crawfish?" Gertie asked.

"That's the one," Ida Belle said and Gertie clapped.

"Do they have beignets?" I asked. Ever since my first introduction to the squares of powdery yumminess, I tried to have some every time I came to NOLA.

"Everyone has beignets," Gertie said. "The Catholic church probably uses them for communion."

"Awesome," I said. "Then we'll have some lunch and thumb through those books to see what else Dexter was hiding."

I smiled as Ida Belle drove. So far, it was a good day. We

had picked up some information on Silas and Dexter and even though it was only pieces right now, I had a feeling we were moving in the right direction. And we were about to partake of po'boys and beignets. The only pallor over the day was the reason for our investigation, but I'd made a deal with Nickel and I was going to see it through.

Molly's killer would pay.

CHAPTER TWELVE

THE PO'BOYS EXCEEDED EXPECTATION. I usually went for the fried shrimp but this time, Gertie talked me into the fried crawfish po'boy and it was excellent. A little bit spicier than the shrimp but after eating Gertie's cooking, I was used to worse. I only put down six glasses of iced tea to get through the sandwich, which was better than usual.

Gertie nodded toward my glass of tea that had just been refilled. "You're improving. I told you your taste buds would eventually adjust."

"To the food, maybe," I said. "But not that atomic, fireball, nuclear explosion version of your cough syrup. I don't know how people drink that and still breathe."

"You can't right away," Ida Belle said. "That's the fun of it."

"That one taste left my lips numb for a week," I said. "I'll stick to the mild version from here forward and I'll be giving you the side-eye every time you ask me to test something. I'm smelling everything first. If my eyes water, it's a no."

Ida Belle grinned. "Give it forty years or so. Everything on you gets a little numb and you'll welcome that additional kick."

"Well, that means I've got forty years to handle things," I

said. "Get my affairs in order, prepare a will, find someone to take the cat."

"Merlin isn't a real magician," Gertie said. "I don't think he'll be around in forty years."

"No, but I'll probably always have one," I said. "I kinda like them. They're ornery and independent and don't listen to a thing I say."

"So they remind you of yourself?" Gertie asked.

"A little bit," I said. "You have to respect a ten-pound animal that has convinced humans to wait on them for no apparent payoff."

"The payoff is no retribution," Ida Belle said.

The waitress came back with our large order of beignets, and silence ensued until we polished off the last bite of greatness. Then we spent the required five minutes popping our shirts to rid ourselves of powdered sugar remnants and once the table was cleared, Gertie pulled the books out of her handbag and we all took a copy to inspect.

As we flipped through the pages, we came upon page after page of financial and banking information for the catering company. I was starting to wonder what the point was of collecting all these months of activity when I found a letter in the back of the book I was checking.

"Jackpot," I said.

Ida Belle and Gertie looked up expectantly.

"It's a letter from a large catering outfit with multiple locations," I said. "They're thanking Dexter for the financial statements and will make an offer when their appraiser is finished reviewing the paperwork."

"Molly would never sell her business," Ida Belle said. "She quit cage fighting for that business. Besides, you met her and you see the numbers. Molly wasn't just good at cooking, she loved it. And her income was great. Why sell off when she's just getting started and she's winning out of the gate?"

"I know," I said. "It makes no sense unless Dexter thought that whole 'I'm a partner' claim was really going to fly."

"Well, if he did, then twenty bucks says he produces some trumped-up set of documents to stack his claim against Ally," Ida Belle said.

"Look at this," Gertie said and passed us a couple sheets of paper. "It's charts of all the waterways surrounding Sinful. And there's a big X on Molly's place."

"Dexter wasn't from there, so he'd need a way to learn the bayous if he planned on pulling off a boating accident," I said. "I'm making a copy of these and keeping them for myself."

"I wouldn't," Ida Belle said. "The main channels are right but at least a third are wrong. The weather changes a lot of things. But if you make a copy, I'll mark it up for you."

"Do you really think Dexter is stupid enough to think this half-baked plan would work?" Gertie asked.

"Yes."

Ida Belle and I both answered at once.

"Me too," Gertie said. "Which makes me even more angry. Still, you'd think he would have given it a little more time— convince Molly to let him help with setup and other things so that people saw him. At least then, when he claimed he was a partner, people would back him up in saying he was helping with their event."

"Stupid people aren't always the most patient," I said.

"Or..." Ida Belle held up a photo of Dexter and a woman. A woman who wasn't Molly.

"Who wants to place bets that Dexter promised this woman something that required money?" Ida Belle asked.

"That's a sucker bet if I ever saw it," Gertie said. "That woman is no looker but she's still too good-looking for Dexter and *way* too young. Lord knows, she isn't with him for his winning personality."

Ida Belle flipped the photo over and sighed. "No name on the back. Why can't people go back to old-school ways, like listing people, locations, and dates on the back of photos? It would make this so much easier."

"I wish there were a way to find her," Gertie said. "I'd love to know if she knew about Molly. I'm guessing that's a big fat no."

"Or Dexter passed her off as his business partner and made sure the two were never in the same place," Ida Belle said.

"We might be able to find her," I said.

"How?" Gertie asked.

"After we talk to Angel, we'll hunt up that bar that Dexter frequented," I said.

"You want to stroll into a bar in that part of town?" Ida Belle asked.

"We're armed," I said. "And probably far more dangerous than any of the patrons. They just don't realize."

"And because they don't realize, that's why we could have problems," Ida Belle said.

I narrowed my eyes at her. "Are you seriously suggesting that I back off of something just because there's risk involved?"

"Not at all," Ida Belle said. "I'm suggesting you weigh the risks of going to a NOLA jail against my upcoming wedding. There's not a big margin for error there."

"Hmmm." I considered this. She was right, of course. If I got into a scuffle, whoever started it wouldn't fare as well. Once the police found out I was former CIA, they would probably take me in just because it was a good time to razz a Fed. And an ambitious DA could sit on it for a bit, trying to make me sweat. I wouldn't shed even one drop of perspiration over sitting in jail. I'd sat in way worse places. But if I missed Ida Belle's wedding, that could lead to trouble I might never get out of.

"Okay," I said. "So we check it out and at the first sign of trouble, we scoot. And if the people there clearly aren't willing to talk to us, same thing. I have a feeling a couple of twenties might grease up lips and if we can get there before the regulars arrive, we can hit up the bartender before it gets crowded. If the bartender doesn't know anything about Dexter, that would mean Dexter just drank quietly and then went home. I have a hard time believing that."

"I think that's a good compromise," Ida Belle said. "I'm sorry this wedding of mine is causing such a shift in our norm."

"Hey, at least it's not the Swamp Bar," I said. "How bad can it be?"

————

ANGEL HAD ARRIVED at her apartment just minutes before we did and excused herself to change into her uniform as soon as we were done with introductions. We took a seat in her living room to wait and about five minutes later, she popped back in wearing a black skirt and white button-up shirt.

Five foot ten. One hundred eighty pounds. Based on the strain on her skirt and shirt, both of which looked fairly new, I'd say the weight gain was recent. Based on the five million pictures scattered around the living room, I'd put that weight gain down to her having a baby.

"Thanks so much for meeting me here," she said as she hurried into the kitchen. "Do you ladies want anything to drink? I only have unsweet tea and water, I'm afraid. Still trying to take off the baby weight."

"How old is your baby?" Gertie asked.

"Eight weeks," Angel said. "My husband works on the rigs

and is offshore right now. On days when I have school and work, the baby stays with my in-laws. They've been an enormous blessing in that regard."

Ida Belle grinned. "But not necessarily in others?"

"Well, you know how it is," Angel said. "One man, two women. Even if one of the women is his mother, it can get crowded."

"I waited to get married until his parents were dead," Ida Belle said. "Saves some trouble."

Angel laughed. "Well, we sort of put the cart before the horse with our son, so I didn't want to wait quite that long. When did you finally get married?"

"A week from Saturday," Ida Belle said.

"Oh, well, congratulations," Angel said.

"Molly was supposed to cater my reception," Ida Belle said. "I can't tell you how sorry we are. I know it must be taking a toll on you, especially with a newborn."

Angel nodded and I could see the tears in her eyes. "It's been horrible. Aside from when she went to prison...well, and jail, Molly has always been there for me. Ever since we were babies. We were practically raised together. My mom and her mom were friends and then after Molly's mom took off, mine took her under her wing best she could. Silas was worse than worthless."

"We talked to him earlier," I said. "And yeah, he isn't exactly the smile-and-handshake type."

Her eyes widened. "You talked to Silas? I mean, he actually said something besides ordering you off his property?"

"He thought I was from the insurance company," I said. "Naturally, I didn't correct the assumption, and what we got from him is that he thinks there's an insurance policy on Molly and she named him the beneficiary."

Angel shook her head. "No way. No way in hell. Not ever.

Molly hated him. He beat their mother until she fled and then he turned it on his kids. My mom called social services a couple times, but Molly and Johnny lied to get sent home."

"Why would they lie?" I asked.

"I asked her the same thing, and she said some places are worse and at least here, she had me," Angel said. "It broke my heart then, and I was only a kid myself, but now that I'm an adult and have my own child, I look back and I swear I'd like to kill him."

"I can understand that," Gertie said.

"Is Molly's mother still alive?" I asked.

Angel shook her head. "Me and Molly looked for her after Molly started her catering business. I think she wanted to find her and let her know that despite being left to deal with Silas, she still came through good. That he hadn't beat her down even though he'd tried. But she'd died a year or so after she left. Another man. Apparently one with a stronger punch."

"When Molly married, rumor has it she got herself back into the same situation she'd grown up with," I said.

"That marriage was a huge mistake," Angel said. "But Molly wanted out of that house so bad she was willing to believe Damon's lies, even though I think she always knew the truth. I think she believed if she managed to get away then she could break off without her dad trying to drag her back. But as long as she was there, he wasn't going to let her leave. Didn't want his benefits cut."

"I don't understand," I said.

"Molly was only sixteen when she married Damon," Angel said. "Twenty-five when she killed him. That's roughly two decades of taking a beating from lousy men."

"Holy crap!" I said. "Sixteen."

"That's horrible," Gertie said. "I didn't realize..."

"It's a lot more than horrible," Ida Belle said. "We knew

Molly had been to prison for killing her husband and rumor lent to the abuse, but we didn't know she'd put up with him for that long."

Angel sighed. "It was such an unhealthy relationship. They'd get into it and it would finally get so bad that Molly would leave, but then a couple months later, Damon would convince her that he'd get help or whatever. But every time she went back, it was eventually worse than before. I tried so many times to get her counseling, offered her a place to live or every cent I had so that she could leave town and find somewhere to start over, but nothing worked. She always ended up back there, in an even worse situation. Until..."

"Until she wasn't," Ida Belle said.

Angel nodded. "I was shocked when it happened. I think because Molly had never really fought back. Even after she took up cage fighting. She'd tear people apart in the ring but in her own home she stood there and took it, never lifting a finger."

"What made that change?" Gertie asked.

"She told me that on that day, everything shifted and came into focus," Angel said. "She said she looked him right in the eye and told him that he'd best make his next hit a good one because it would be the last one he got in. He laughed at her and backhanded her right across the cheek. Then he grabbed her and started to choke her and she reached out and snapped his neck."

"How long was she in prison?" I asked.

"Two years," Angel said.

"Why?" I asked. "He'd been beating her for almost a decade."

"But she never reported it," Angel said. "Never went to the hospital."

"But he'd hit her just that night," I said.

"And she'd had a fight three hours before," Angel said. "The prosecution claimed she got her injuries from the match. Unfortunately, that bruise on her cheek wasn't the only one, so they easily created doubt. Johnny and I told that sorry excuse for a public defender everything we knew, but the word of a brother and best friend don't hold up so well in court. And given her current profession, the jury wasn't lenient."

"They didn't believe that someone capable of fighting like Molly hadn't defended herself before then," Ida Belle said and shook her head. "And then when she finally did, they felt she went too far."

Angel nodded. "Exactly. So Molly went from the prison of her childhood to the prison of her marriage to an actual prison."

"I wouldn't wish that journey on anyone," Gertie said. "But it certainly produced an amazing woman. Anyone who could overcome all of that is someone who should be admired."

"You got that right," Angel said. "Everything she'd gone through and Molly was finally where she deserved to be. Successful, happy, not worrying about money or a loser guy. Well, for a little while, anyway."

"Dexter," I said.

Angel blew out a breath. "I think the worst fight we ever had was over him. I could tell after thirty seconds that he was no good. Rarely had a job, always bumming money, always an excuse for why he couldn't help with something around her house, even though he was practically living there. I always felt he was using her. Honestly, I don't even think Molly liked him all that well."

"Then why did she keep him around?" I asked.

"The devil you know," Ida Belle said.

Angel nodded. "I think that's partly it, although I don't think Dexter was foolish enough to try to hit her. I know they did their cage fighting but Molly could still kick his butt. Ultimately, I think it was a lack of self-esteem."

"What do you mean?" I asked.

"Molly wasn't what society considers a pretty woman. She was tall and big. She never wore makeup or girlie clothes. She had that crazy hair that she loves. I think she thought no good man would be interested. That men like Dexter were all she could get so she'd just have him around for what it was and not consider that she could have so much more."

"That's unfortunate," Gertie said. "Maybe with more time, she would have gotten that part of her life as straight as her career."

"That was my hope," Angel said. "I mean, look, I'm no wilting flower. I'm a tall girl and not a skinny one either, but I didn't settle. I found an even taller and bigger guy and probably just gave birth to a future NFL linebacker. He was such a big boy that the doctor brought me a trophy the next day. Natural birth."

Ida Belle, Gertie, and I all cringed a little and Angel smiled.

"He's worth it," she said. "So what else can I tell you to help?"

"Tell us about the phone call Molly made to you right before she disappeared," I said.

"Yeah, that was odd," Angel said. "Ever since our falling-out over Dexter, Molly hasn't so much as mentioned him to me. I figured she knew where I stood on the matter and also knew I was right, even though she wasn't ready to admit it. So saying nothing meant she didn't give me the opportunity to start in again on the subject."

"You don't need an opening to intervene when your best friend is making a huge mistake," Gertie said. "I butt in all the time and most of them are barely acquaintances."

"Lord, isn't that the truth," Ida Belle said.

"I know," Angel said. "And normally I would continue to push, but our big blowup was only a couple weeks ago, and I couldn't get her to answer her phone for days after that when I called. I know Molly. You have to let her sit with things a while, cool down and think about them rationally. She was a very logical person unless she was thrust back into her past. Then emotion took over and there was no arguing with her at that point until she came out of the weeds."

"What time did she call?" I asked.

"A little before three thirty," Angel said.

"And she called to complain about Dexter?" I asked.

"I assume so," Angel said. "I couldn't quite make out what she was saying. There was engine noise and the phone was cutting out a bit, which is why I figured she was on her boat. Cars sound different and even on the roads in Sinful you can get a decent cell phone signal."

"What could you make out?" I asked.

"She said something about not wanting to relive the past and then 'that man's going to kill me' and then 'hold on,'" Angel said. "The engine stopped, and I could hear rustling— like things being moved around. I kept calling her name, asking if she could hear me, but the signal was breaking up like crazy. I'd just get pieces of sound, then nothing for a few seconds. Then I heard her scream and the phone went dead. I called and called after that, but it went straight to voice mail."

"Like it had been turned off," Gertie said.

"Or thrown overboard," Ida Belle said.

"You think she was referring to Dexter?" I asked.

"That's what I thought at the time," Angel said.

"But not now?" Gertie asked.

"Well, now that I know about this insurance policy and Silas, I have to wonder," Angel said.

"Do you know if Molly had a will?" I asked.

"I'm not sure," Angel said. "About a month ago, she asked me a few questions about how that sort of thing was done. My husband and I thought we needed to get everything legally set because of the baby so she knew we'd been through the process. I encouraged her to look into it because of the business and the equity in the house. Plus, her van and one of her boats were paid for."

"Did it seem like she was going to pursue it?" I asked.

Angel shook her head. "I can't say for sure. I admit I pushed a little, which isn't always the smartest route with Molly, but it was because of what happened with Johnny. He didn't have a will and Silas ended up getting everything as next of kin. I knew she wouldn't want that."

"Nickel said you and Johnny were dating," I said.

She gave me a sad smile. "You could say that. We were engaged when he disappeared."

I felt my heart tug for her. First her fiancé and now her best friend. No one deserved that much pain in such a short amount of time.

"I'm so sorry," Gertie said and shook her head. "I can't imagine how difficult that was. I mean, it's hard enough when someone you love passes but when you never really have an answer—"

Gertie glanced over at me. "Sorry."

I waved a hand in dismissal. "My father was a federal employee and disappeared on a work trip," I explained. "But that was a long time ago. I was only a kid."

"But you know how it is," Angel said. "The not having answers can eat you up if you let it. You have to finally get to the point where you accept they're never going to stroll back through the front door, and then you can move on with your life. But it's always there somewhere in the back of your mind. The what-if."

I nodded. "That's true."

"Nickel tells me you made a good life for yourself in Sinful," Angel said. "If you don't mind my saying, you don't look like a CIA agent."

"Trust me," Gertie said, "she's the bayou version of Lara Croft."

Angel smiled. "That's what Whiskey said and Whiskey doesn't talk nice about anyone. That's why Nickel figured if anyone could help, you could. He also figures half the men in Sinful are afraid or in love with you, maybe both."

"Probably right," Gertie said. "Both things. But Fortune's heart belongs to Carter."

I felt a blush creep up my neck. "Yes, well. If I have to pick one, I'd prefer scared. Trust me when I say that one relationship with a man is quite enough to handle."

"I think most women feel that way," Angel said. "It's a shame Molly didn't trust herself to find a good man. I can't help but think everything would have been different if she hadn't hooked up with Dexter."

"If I told you that Dexter found a document in Molly's handwriting stating that she was leaving the catering business to a friend of mine, and he went nuts, claiming that Molly had promised the business to him...what would you say to that?"

"No way!" Angel's eyes widened. "Molly would never leave her business to Dexter. She loved that business more than anything. It was her salvation. Dexter couldn't even cook toast without burning it. What would he do with a catering business?"

"Sell it, maybe?" I suggested.

Angel frowned. "I hadn't thought...I was just thinking about the actual day-to-day work of the business, but I suppose it might be worth something to somebody interested in getting started or an existing company looking to expand. Surely Dexter wouldn't be stupid enough to think if he killed her that he'd get her business based on his word."

"Killing her might not have been planned," Ida Belle said. "Maybe he just got mad and it happened. We saw them both earlier that day. Molly had just worked him over in the cage and he didn't look none too happy about it. Maybe temper got the best of him and now he's trying to salvage something from it."

"That wouldn't surprise me," Angel said. "He's definitely a hothead. If you don't mind my asking, who did he claim Molly left the business to?"

"Ally Lemarque," I said.

"That name sounds familiar," Angel said. "Oh, she's a baker, right?"

"Unofficially, she provides baked goods all around the area," Gertie said. "But she's hoping to open her own bakery soon."

Angel nodded. "I remember Molly talking about her now. She said she'd brought her food to an event and they'd insisted she take a small dessert tray of Ally's goods home with her. She claimed it was the best sweets she'd ever had."

"The thing is, Ally had only spoken to Molly a couple times and it was only in a professional capacity," I said. "So she barely knew her and has no idea why Molly would leave her the catering business, assuming that's all legal and aboveboard."

Angel shrugged. "Well, I couldn't do it, and Molly knew that. I'm sure she wanted it to go to someone who loved and appreciated food as much as she did. Molly wasn't a complex person. Not really. If you understood where she came from and what she lived through, then she wasn't that hard to figure out."

"So the phone call is why you don't think this was an accident?" I asked.

"That's actually the least of the reasons," she said. "Molly was an excellent boater and after what happened to Johnny, she was extra careful about everything. She went over every square inch of her boats every single time she came back to the dock."

"How was she as a swimmer?" Ida Belle asked.

"Olympic good. Silas used to make Johnny and Molly swim back and forth across the channel, even when the tide was at its strongest. He said everyone living on the water needed to know how to handle it. Honestly, I think he was just being mean but it didn't turn her off from it. She had a gym membership somewhere close to the city. She drove in a couple times a week to use the pool and if she had time, she'd drop by for a visit. An hour of laps was her regular workout."

I watched her face as she delivered that information. She was so certain, so earnest in her words, that I had no doubt she believed something had happened to her friend besides a tragic accident. But was that correct or were she and Nickel just refusing to believe that the same fate could befall two people they cared about? Which made me wonder...

"Do you think Johnny's death was an accident?" I asked.

Her eyes widened a bit, then she stared at the floor, not speaking for some time before she finally looked back at me. "Honestly, I have my doubts there as well. I know what it looks like. I never got over Johnny's death—and I guess that's true enough on some level—so you think I refuse to believe that Molly could go the same way. But that's not it. You see, I *know* Johnny would have never taken his boat out that day. I told the cops that but no one believed me."

"Because of the storm?" Gertie asked.

Angel nodded. "And because there was no point. Johnny

was a businessman. Shrimp wouldn't have been running in that kind of weather. Every commercial shrimper knows it and said as much. No smart shrimper would waste his energy and gas on a trip out to make no money."

"Maybe he didn't think the weather was going to be as bad as it turned out," I said.

"Johnny was never wrong about the weather," Angel said. "It was kind of eerie, actually. The forecasters would all say one thing and Johnny would laugh and call them fools. He was never wrong. Not one single time. Got to be the standard around the dock for the others to go out based on his call. Besides, we lived together then and I'd talked to him that morning before I left for my shift. He told me he was going to work in the garage that day on an old lawn mower. Why would he lie about that?"

"So what do you think happened?" I asked.

"I don't know," she said. "All I know is a fisherman was leaving the docks when Johnny showed up, and he said Johnny was getting on his boat as the fisherman drove off. It was already starting to rain. The sky was already black. You see why it doesn't make sense?"

"Did the fisherman talk to him?" I asked.

"No. He only saw him from a distance, but he recognized Johnny's truck and his rain slicker. He had one with fluorescent purple stripes. Molly had given it to him. She loved the bright colors and he was so pleased with the gift that he wore it despite the ribbing he got from the other guys."

"And he was alone?" I asked.

Her shoulders slumped. "Yeah. I know. It sounds like exactly what the police said—he got caught out in the storm and something bad happened. They found his boat the next day and a piece of the slicker caught in a nearby buoy."

"Would he have been wearing a life jacket?" I asked.

"There were two missing from his boat," Angel said. "They found one some distance away from the buoy."

"I'm really sorry," I said, and I meant it. I could see how much Johnny's death still hurt her even though she'd moved on with her life. But I could also see how his death might have influenced her beliefs concerning Molly's disappearance.

But just because it could have influenced her didn't mean it had.

CHAPTER THIRTEEN

WE CLIMBED BACK into the SUV, all silent for a bit as Ida Belle exited the parking lot. We'd gotten a lot of information in one day and we needed time to process it all. Sometimes typing it up helped me piece things together. Sometimes I just got a wrist cramp out of it and zero inspiration.

"I'm confused," Gertie said.

"Me too," Ida Belle said. "And I hate to say it, but I'm not completely sure there's a crime here."

"You think Nickel and Angel are projecting?" I asked.

"It wouldn't surprise me if they were," Gertie said. "I mean, who could blame them after going through what they did with Johnny? Especially Angel. They were practically married. I can't imagine losing the man I love and not even having a body to bury."

Ida Belle nodded. "Me either. But it's no wonder she wouldn't want to do it again. She wants answers."

"And someone to blame," Gertie said.

"Yes," Ida Belle agreed. "After meeting Silas and hearing about the childhood those two had, I can't really blame her for wanting their lives to mean more. To know that they weren't

JANA DELEON

just two people who made bad choices that cost them everything."

"What do you think?" Gertie asked me.

"I agree with you and Ida Belle," I said. "But then there's strange things, like the insurance policy Silas thinks he's cashing in on. And Dexter trying to find a buyer for the catering business. I didn't think Molly would be interested in selling even before we talked to Angel, but I'm doubling down on that now. You heard her. She said the business was Molly's salvation. You don't just let something that important go. Not for any amount of money."

"So we keep digging?" Ida Belle said.

"We have to," I said. "If this was an accident, we're going to have to figure out how to prove it, for Nickel and Angel's sake."

"How in the world can you prove an accident that happens with no witnesses?" Gertie asked.

"By proving the only people who benefit from Molly's death couldn't have done it," Ida Belle said. "I think that's as close as we can hope to get."

I nodded.

"That's going to be harder than proving someone did it," Gertie said. "Especially if no one has alibis. And even if we started asking questions, I doubt Dexter and Silas are going to offer up where they were and what they were doing when Molly disappeared."

"Dexter was at the house when we left and when Carter went to check on Molly," I said. "So we know he had opportunity."

"Unless he went somewhere in between," Gertie said. "But then we'd need corroboration."

"Exactly," I said. "As for Silas, it's possible he wasn't playing hermit in his shack at the time Molly made that call."

"But unless someone saw him near Molly's house, we can't prove or disprove where he was, either," Ida Belle said.

I blew out a breath. "I hate to say it, but unless we can string all these incriminating pieces into a solid case, this might be the one that got away. Still, I'm not ready to throw in the towel. Not until we try to put those pieces together a bit better, and there are still plenty of angles to investigate, starting with finding out who benefits the most from Molly's death."

"Who *actually* benefits or who thought he would benefit?" Gertie asked.

"That's a good point," Ida Belle said. "If Dexter believed he'd get the business, that's as good as him actually being the legal heir. At least from his point of view."

"He looked pretty convinced when he was at Ally's house threatening her," Gertie said.

"He did," I agreed. "Which is strange in itself. Angel outright said Molly would never have given Dexter an interest in her business and based on what she described, it seems like Molly might have been reconsidering her relationship with him altogether."

"Then why would Dexter think he was due?" Gertie asked.

"I don't know," I said. "And it wouldn't do any good to ask. Even if he told us, we couldn't believe him, but I might know a place where his lips would have been loose."

"The Bar?" Gertie asked, getting excited.

"He does strike me as a big mouth," Ida Belle said. "If he thought he was coming into something big, he wouldn't be able to keep quiet about it. Especially if he'd been drinking."

"Exactly," I said.

Ida Belle nodded. "Then let's head that way."

———

THE BAR LOOKED as unimaginative as its name. The old brick building it occupied was on the corner of the street and didn't share walls with another business. Instead, it was located next to a cemetery. I wondered how many of its patrons were buried next door. There was a bit of concern about parking, and we ended up circling the block three times as we debated the merits of parking down the street so that Ida Belle's SUV was protected against the potential for having to flee for our lives.

Fleeing finally won out and Ida Belle pulled into a recently vacated space directly across the street. The number of cars parked nearby didn't at all equate to the amount of noise coming out of the building and we all hesitated, staring at the place.

"We manage the Swamp Bar all the time," Gertie said. "How bad can it be?"

"Don't ask that," Ida Belle said. "It's like inviting God's sense of humor while he's angry. The outcome is never favorable for us."

"Well, there's probably not an angry bear inside," I said. "So that's a plus."

The words had barely left my mouth when a man came hurtling through a window at the front of the bar and crashed onto the sidewalk. An even bigger man stepped up to the broken window and yelled something indiscernible at the one on the pavement.

Fortyish. Six foot six. Three hundred pounds solid. Shaved head. Too many tattoos to count. No visible shortcomings. Lethal as heck if he wanted to be.

"There's your bear," Gertie said.

"Do you think that guy's dead?" Ida Belle asked.

"I hope not," Gertie said. "It would mess up our questioning people if the cops show up."

"If the cops show up, there probably won't be anyone left to question," Ida Belle said. "It will look like a swarm of locusts leaving Egypt."

"Let's go check," I said. "I suppose we're duty bound to call an ambulance if needed."

"If he's dead can we hold off on the ambulance?" Gertie asked. "Just until the questioning part is over. And until I've had a chance to pee."

"You're not going to use the restroom in there and then get into my SUV," Ida Belle said. "We should probably be entering the place wearing hazmat suits."

"I'm wearing pants," Gertie said. "It's not like I'm going to roll naked on the bathroom floor, then strip down again and rub over every inch of your seats like a cat."

"There is so much wrong with that visual that I'm hoping he's dead so we can go ahead and leave and find a fast-food restaurant," Ida Belle said. "Why didn't you do this back at Angel's?"

"I didn't have to then," Gertie said.

"You should have gone anyway," Ida Belle said.

"Now you just sound like my dad on every vacation," Gertie said. "It didn't work for him either, by the way."

"You need to have a checkup," Ida Belle said. "This is getting to be a habit. Your parts are old. Get them checked out."

"My parts are fine," Gertie said.

"Sure they are," Ida Belle said. "Your kidneys are clearly as good as your eyesight."

Refusing to step into the middle of that one, I headed across the street. As I approached Sidewalk Dude, he moved and groaned. Alive, at least.

I peered down at him. "You want me to call for an ambulance?"

His eyes jerked open and he forced himself into a sitting position. "Hell, no! Like I need more trouble than I already got."

"You're bleeding from your side," I said, pointing at the dark stain on his shirt.

"I had my appendix removed a couple days ago," he said. "Probably tore a stitch or something."

"Or something," I said. "Maybe you should have that checked."

"My sister makes curtains for a living," he said as he struggled to get up. "She can sew me up good as any doctor."

"And probably offers a variety of thread color," I said. "It sounds like an excellent plan."

I shook my head at Ida Belle and Gertie, who'd come up after me and overheard the entire exchange. Sidewalk Dude headed down the street, leaning and clutching one side as he went. We turned back toward the bar and saw three guys staring at us from the broken window.

"Told you he wasn't dead!" one of the guys yelled back into the bar.

"He's going to be if he doesn't pay his tab," a voice answered.

"You should have told him to go outside," one of the guys said. "Now you're gonna have to pay for the window."

"He was insulting my wife," the guy who'd thrown the other man out the window said. "Things like that don't wait."

The other man waved a hand in dismissal and popped back inside.

"You still want to do this?" Ida Belle asked, glancing back at her SUV. She was probably mentally calculating what else could get thrown out the window and whether or not it would reach across the street.

"I think we need to," I said. "Seems like everyone is good and drunk. Maybe they'll be happy to talk."

"I don't think they're all that drunk," Gertie said. "But I'm still game."

"Let me remind everyone that this is the late-afternoon crowd," Ida Belle said. "They're supposed to be the calm ones."

"Then we'll make sure we're gone before the evening crowd starts drifting in," I said as I headed for the door.

A man and a woman shuffled up to the broken window and watched as we walked inside. The noise level dropped in half as soon as we crossed the threshold, and everyone in the place turned to stare. I supposed we looked a bit out of place. The average age in the bar was the forty-to-fifty crowd, so I was too young and Ida Belle and Gertie were too old, and we didn't exactly fit the look of the place, either. And nor, I supposed, did we fit with each other from a stranger's perspective.

"I need a beer and to see a man thrown out a window," Gertie said. "I'm halfway there."

Everyone laughed and turned back to what they were doing before. I looked over at Ida Belle, who shrugged.

"Good call," I said to Gertie as we made our way to the bar.

"Drunk people usually like to laugh. And old ladies being tough always amuses them. Look at Betty White. That woman is four thousand and eight years old and still killing it," Gertie said.

"I'm just a little surprised that you'd refer to yourself as old," I said.

"Oh, I'm not old," Gertie said. "But they think I am. Trust me, the more years that pass, the younger you realize you are."

"That makes absolutely no sense," Ida Belle said.

We grabbed seats at the end of the bar where no customers were around. There was a middle-aged woman working one end of the bar and a guy working the end we sat at. He glanced over at us and started our way.

Fortyish. Six foot two. Two hundred twenty pounds of solid muscle. Short, military-style haircut. No visible tattoos. Slight limp in right leg. Wouldn't be able to pursue for long in a chase. Could probably take him out by twisting the leg. Threat level currently unknown.

He studied us for a couple seconds after he walked up. "If you don't mind my saying so, you ladies don't exactly look the type for a bar like this."

"If you don't mind my saying so, neither do you," I said.

He smiled. "Well, my uncle opened this hole-in-the-wall thirty years ago. His liver finally called it quits and he left it all to me. It pays the bills."

"What branch?" I asked.

"Marines," he said. "I'm Glenn. You military?"

"Fortune Redding. Former Fed." I pulled out my ID. "Retired from government nonsense and happily on my own."

He raised one eyebrow. "What's a PI want in here? I mean, I'm sure there's all manner of lawbreakers but not a one of them worth paying a PI to shadow."

"I'm looking into the disappearance of Molly Broussard," I said.

He frowned. "That. Yeah, that sucks."

"Did you know Molly?" I asked.

"A little bit," he said. "When I first got out of the Marines, I thought I'd give cage fighting a try. Didn't have the skill set for much except fighting or shooting. Not a lot of jobs along those lines unless you're interested in law enforcement, and I'm not. The fighting looked fun and if you were any good, you could make some money at it."

"You've definitely got the build for it," Gertie said. "And good-looking guys always get the sponsors."

He grinned at her. "You saying I'm good-looking?"

"I'd say anyone in this bar was good-looking, just for safety reasons," Gertie said. "But yeah, you could pull off an advertising campaign."

He laughed. "What are you, like a relative or something?"

"Something," Gertie said. "Ida Belle and I are Fortune's assistants."

"That's an interesting gig you've got going," he said to me.

"You have no idea," I said. "So...Molly?"

"Right," he said. "When I first got started someone told me to look Molly up and pay her for a couple lessons. Said she was the best trainer in the business. I was apprehensive, of course. I mean, I'm not a small guy and I've had military training. I was wondering how in the world I was supposed to train with a woman. Then I met Molly. She like to have killed me that first session. Boy, she could fight."

"So you took lessons from her?" I asked.

"Only two," he said. "First time she twisted my leg, I knew it wasn't going to work. She knew it too. Had said as much during that first session. But in the second, she did a maneuver just hard enough for me to see that if anyone did it for real, I'd be leaving the ring on a stretcher."

"Bullet?" I asked.

He nodded. "They got it out and patched me up. I worked my butt off in rehab and then in the gym, but it was never quite right. Got the honorable discharge and came home, hoping I could figure out what to do with the rest of my life. The military was plan A. I didn't have a plan B."

"That sucks," I said. "So you didn't get a chance to know Molly very well with only two sessions."

"No, but I liked her," he said. "When Molly said something, you could take it as the gospel and know that it was meant for your own good. There nothing self-serving about the way she taught or handed out advice about fighting.

She liked to win and she liked to see people she knew win. I really admired her."

"Did you know about her past?" Ida Belle asked.

"More or less," he said. "It's common gossip among the fighters. I mean, probably nobody knows the real story except Molly and her dead husband. But I'm usually pretty good at reading people. I figure if Molly killed him then he had it coming."

"I like you," Gertie said. "If I were twenty years younger—"

"You could still be his mother," Ida Belle said.

He grinned. "I have a feeling you've left a wake of broken hearts. I don't think I could have handled you twenty years ago."

"You can't handle her now," I said.

He laughed. "So what is it you're looking for here? I heard about Molly but I can't tell you anything about her beyond what I just did."

"I don't want to know about Molly so much as I want to know what you can tell me about Dexter Nutters," I said.

His smile immediately turned to a frown. "*That* guy. You look up 'total loser' in the dictionary, and I guarantee you there's a picture of Dexter Nutters next to it. I never understood what Molly saw in him."

"That's a fairly common statement among the people who knew her," I said. "And having had the displeasure of meeting the man myself, I have to agree. I don't get it."

He narrowed his eyes at me. "You don't think he did anything to her, do you?"

"I don't know," I said. "But my client would like me to find out. It could be that this was just another tragic boat accident."

"But it might be something else," he said.

He stared at the wall for several seconds, then shook his

head. "Man, I just don't see it. Molly could whup that guy nine ways to Sunday. Nutters couldn't beat a grade-schooler in a fight. How's he going to beat someone like Molly?"

"Gun? Poison?" I suggested. "With no body, it's impossible to say. Did Dexter ever talk about the catering business when he was in the bar?"

"All the time," Glenn said. "Give him two shots of whiskey and you couldn't shut the guy up. Of course, no one believed half of what he was saying. Heck, I only believed he was dating Molly because she came in here once with him."

"Molly came to this bar?" Ida Belle asked.

"Only the one time and only for a minute," he said. "They were on their way somewhere and Nutters had forgotten his ball cap the night before. That's the only time I've seen her here, though. I imagine Nutters didn't want his two lives to cross paths."

"Two lives?" I asked.

"Other women," he said. "He was always hitting on women in the bar. Got clocked by angry boyfriends on a somewhat regular basis."

"Men in this bar are sensitive about their women," I said.

Glenn looked confused and I pointed to the window.

"Oh yeah, that," Glenn said. "That's just Tank being a fool. He keeps tearing up things over her, I'm going to eventually have a new bar on his dime."

"So if he gets that angry, why do people keep insulting his wife?" I asked.

"You mean, the woman who cleaned out his bank accounts, set his clothes on fire in his truck, and then ran off with his brother?" Glenn asked.

"Good Lord," Ida Belle said. "Doesn't sound like anything people made up could be worse than the truth."

He nodded. "But if old Tank admitted that, then he'd have

to face the rest of it. Easier to stay drunk, fish, and pay for repairs to my bar."

"It's a good life if you can manage it," Gertie said. "Unfortunately, those pesky bill things interfere—electricity, rent, food."

"Mineral rights," Glenn said. "He inherited some and a ramshackle set of townhomes a couple blocks from here. Between rent money and the rights, it's enough to keep him in utilities, food, and beer."

"So did Dexter have any luck with the ladies?" I asked.

"Not that I ever saw," he said. "Most women had his number right quick but then a couple months ago, he showed up with a younger one."

"How young?" Gertie asked.

"Twenty-one," he said. "I ID'd her. I don't want trouble in here."

I looked at the broken window again.

"I don't want *that* kind of trouble in here," he said. "The window is nothing compared to the trouble a young woman with a guy like Nutters could lead to."

"How often did he bring her in here?" I asked.

"Two or three times a week over the last month," he said. "A little less at first."

"And they were definitely in a relationship?" I asked, trying to fathom that there were two women in the world who would give Dexter the time of day.

"Oh yeah," he said. "It was disgusting. Her sitting there fawning over him like he was the Rock or something."

"Was she high?" Gertie asked.

"Could be," he said. "She had these beady eyes—like a rat —and they didn't look right. And she was super skinny—all arms and legs. She had some acne that you usually don't see by that age as well. If I had to guess, she hit the harder stuff somewhat regularly but hadn't gotten to that point where she was the walking dead, if you know what I mean."

"Probably meth," Gertie said.

"Well, that explains why she's with Dexter," Ida Belle said. "She wants money for a fix."

"That's the most likely explanation," he said. "But as long as they don't bring the stuff in here, I didn't care what kind of nonsense he got up to."

"Didn't he worry that someone would tell Molly about his new girlfriend?" I asked. "And doing it right in front of you when you'd trained with her? That's the height of stupid. Not that I'm saying he isn't that stupid, but you get it."

"I do," he said. "But I never told Nutters I knew Molly and that night when they came in, I was in the back getting more vodka when one of the servers asked where Nutters's hat was. They were on their way out by the time I got back to the counter."

"So you didn't see each other at all," Ida Belle said.

He shook his head. "And despite how it looks this second, I don't talk much about myself here. And I avoided all conversation with Nutters."

"So Dexter didn't know that you and Molly had met," I said.

"He didn't even know I'd tried cage fighting," Glenn said. "No one does. I get a lot of guys in here who've tried the ring or are still in it. Kind of a watering hole. You run a place like this, you don't want this lot to figure out all they have to do to get the best of you is whack you in the knee with a pool cue."

"Good point," I said. "So when Dexter talked about the catering business, what did he say?"

"He talked about how Molly had made him a partner and the business was going to be worth a fortune when they decided to cash out," he said. "Nobody much believed him.

Nutters couldn't tell the difference between carbonated water and champagne. There's no way he could produce quality food. What kind of catering was it, anyway?"

"Higher-end type stuff," Ida Belle said. "Crab cakes and dips, lobster rolls and salad, and the most amazing brisket. She did a lot of events."

"Did you know her?" he asked.

Ida Belle nodded. "She was supposed to cater my wedding next weekend. Gertie and I are some of the first people who met her when she came to Sinful."

"Ah man, I'm really sorry," he said. "I didn't realize you guys knew her personally."

"Thank you," Ida Belle said. "But I'm afraid none of us knew her as well as we would have liked. Molly was a very private person."

"I suppose someone with her past would be," he said. "So is Nutters trying to lay some claim to the business or something? Is that what started all this?"

"He seems to be under the impression that he was a partner and due the business if something happened to Molly," I said. "But a legal document he found when he broke into Molly's safe seems to indicate otherwise. Let's just say Dexter wasn't happy with Molly's choice and showed up at the woman's house threatening her. The woman named in the document only knew Molly professionally and just barely. She has zero idea why Molly would name her and since she's one of my best friends, I know she's telling the truth. Basically, the whole thing is both a mess and a mystery."

He shook his head. "Sounds like it. I don't envy you trying to sort it all out."

"Do you remember the last time he was in here?" I asked.

"Last week sometime," he said. "Can't remember the exact

day but it wasn't the weekend. Maybe Wednesday or Thursday."

"Was he alone?" I asked.

"No. He had his side piece with him."

"So Dexter must have still been using his apartment even though he stopped paying rent," I said.

"Hard to pay rent when you don't work."

"Is there anything else you can tell us about Dexter that might help us get a feel for him?" I asked.

"Honestly, it sounds like you already know everything there is to know," Glenn said. "Nutters wasn't that deep. What you knew and what I told you is probably all there is to it. He didn't have the smarts to be more."

"Do you think he could have planned to kill her and make it look like an accident?" Gertie asked.

"Honestly? No," he said. "Now, could he have gotten mad enough and done something stupid, then tried to cover it up? Sure. And would he have the balls to try to stake a claim on the business? Absolutely. Money was always Dexter's prime motivator. At least, that's how it looked to me."

"Except with the new girlfriend, who probably doesn't have any," Gertie said.

"Maybe he met the female version of himself," Glenn said.

I nodded. "But he'd need his own money to keep her. I don't suppose you remember her name, do you?"

He smiled. "Actually, I do."

CHAPTER FOURTEEN

I CLIMBED into Ida Belle's SUV, somewhat pleased that we'd made it out of The Bar without incident. It was both surprising and shocking. Usually places like The Bar combined with people like Gertie led only to trouble. The fact that Ida Belle didn't even wait for us to put on our seat belts before hauling it out of there told me she was looking to make sure it stayed that way.

"Home?" she asked as she headed toward the highway.

"No," I said. "I don't think so. Let's head back out toward Silas's place."

"You know I'm not one to back off from danger," Gertie said, "but do you think that's a good idea?"

"I have to agree," Ida Belle said. "I don't think you're going to get any more out of him."

"I wasn't thinking about revisiting Silas," I said. "I thought we'd make a stop at the gas station and see if those two guys sitting out front saw Silas leave Monday afternoon. I figure they sit out there a lot, waiting for something to talk about."

Ida Belle nodded. "That's a good idea. It won't tell us everything, but if those guys saw Silas leave and return, it might give us a window that he could have used to take Molly out."

"Exactly," I said. "Then our last stop is the exit to Molly's house. When we went to drop off Ida Belle's catering money, I noticed two boys in a tree house right at the exit. I assume they live in the house across the street."

"Oh!" Gertie's eyes widened. "They have a clear view of the road. They'd see every car that passed."

"If they were outside at the time our killer turned in," Ida Belle said. "And if they are the kind of boys who notice cars."

"I know," I said. "It's a long shot but it's easy to ask and won't take much time. I figure it can't hurt."

I pulled out my cell phone and did a quick internet search on Marissa Perkins, Dexter's side piece. I wasn't expecting to find anything unless it was a short mention about an arrest, but that wasn't even what popped up on my screen.

"Holy crap," I said. "Dexter's girlfriend was a competitive longbow shooter in high school."

"You sure it's her?" Gertie asked.

I turned my phone to show her the image. "Eyes like a rat, all arms and legs."

"Glenn sure nailed that description," Gertie said.

Ida Belle looked over at me, her eyes narrowed. "An arrow would explain why that hole in Molly's boat didn't go all the way through."

I nodded. "And it explains the variation in pattern. The arrow wasn't properly tuned. That's why it had that bit of a run on the right side."

"Longbow is smart," Gertie said. "No sound. Gunshots aren't uncommon around Sinful but they can attract the curious."

"So she shoots Molly from the bank somewhere and then

what?" Ida Belle said. "Molly falls overboard but then how did the hole in the boat get there?"

"Assuming Molly was taken out by an arrow, I can only guess there were two shots," I said. "If the first missed and Molly turned to look at it when it struck the boat, then the second could have hit her square in the upper back and propelled her overboard, which would explain why there was only blood on the side of the boat and not in the bottom."

"But there wasn't an arrow in the boat," Gertie said.

"She would have retrieved it," Ida Belle said. "That way, people assumed the hole was made by a bullet. Everyone has a gun. A bullet hole doesn't narrow things down just in case the cops started looking hard at Dexter and got around to her."

"Okay," Gertie said. "I'd buy it, but how do we prove it?"

"Great question," I said and did another search. "Of course, I can't find an address for her. But if we can pin down a location, I'd like to get a look at her."

"What will that tell you?" Gertie asked.

"Maybe nothing," I said.

"Maybe something," Ida Belle said.

Ida Belle made quick work of the drive back to Silas's hometown. The two men we'd seen before were still in front of the gas station in their chairs and perked up when we pulled in. As we climbed out of the SUV, they looked at each other, then began to rise.

It took a bit of time to accomplish and neither looked too steady on their feet, so I didn't even bother with a threat assessment.

"Evening, ladies," the first man said. "How can we help you?"

"We saw you earlier today," the second man said. "You need help finding someplace?"

Since the first man had locked eyes on Ida Belle and

seemed to have more than a passing interest, I figured I'd let her take the lead. I gave her a little nudge with my elbow and she smiled at them.

"No, thank you, gentlemen," she said. "We found the place we were looking for but then we had a question or two about the man who lives there. I saw you when we passed and thought, I bet there's two young men who have their fingers on the pulse of everything happening in this town. So we figured we'd come back and see if you could help us out."

I wasn't sure if calling them 'young' or telling them they had their fingers on the pulse of everything clinched it, but either way, it was clear from their expressions that Ida Belle had this one in the bag.

"Well, we're happy to help you ladies out if we can," the second man said. "I'm Jeb and this is my brother Wyatt. Who did you visit earlier?"

"Silas Broussard," Ida Belle said.

Wyatt whistled. "I hope it wasn't a long drive for you because Lord, trying to talk to that man is a waste of time."

"Not to mention it can be bad for your health if he's feeling that trigger finger," Jeb said.

"What can you tell us about him?" Ida Belle asked.

"Man's a—" Wyatt started.

"Now, now," Jeb interrupted. "There's ladies present. Let's just say Silas doesn't have many redeeming qualities."

"Doesn't have any far as I'm concerned," Wyatt. "Man's mean as a snake and sneaky as a feral cat. Treated his wife and kids so bad they all run away as soon as they could."

"Have you heard that his daughter recently disappeared?" Ida Belle asked.

Both their eyes widened and they shook their heads.

"Molly? What happened?" Wyatt asked.

Ida Belle explained that Molly had gone out on her boat

and never returned and it was found floating loose but without any sign of her.

"Well, that's just horrible," Jeb said. "That Molly was a good girl. My granddaughter was a tiny little thing—used to get picked on at school until Molly found out. She set them bad 'uns straight and my granddaughter never had any more problems."

Wyatt nodded. "Both those kids turned out good, especially considering the uphill battle they had."

"I don't suppose either of you saw Silas two days ago?" Ida Belle asked.

They both frowned and scrunched their brows.

"That was chili night at the VFW," Wyatt said.

"No, that was the night before," Jeb said. "Two nights ago was lasagna."

Wyatt made a face. "That's right. We always skip lasagna night. Gives us heartburn. So that means we were sitting right here, having day-old hot dogs and Frito Pie with spiced relish."

"Because that doesn't give you heartburn," I said.

"Of course not," Jeb said. "And as a matter of fact, we did see Silas. He was headed toward the highway that afternoon."

"You're sure it was him?" Ida Belle asked.

"Positive," Wyatt said. "Needs a new muffler on that truck of his. Thing's so loud you can hear him coming from a mile away. Probably hasn't done a lick of maintenance on it since he inherited it."

I made a mental note. They must be talking about Johnny's truck.

"Do you remember what time that was?" Ida Belle asked.

"Before two for sure," Wyatt said. "We watch our soap opera at two."

"Did you see him return?" Ida Belle asked.

They both shook their heads.

"Got our beer shipment in after the soap opera," Jeb said. "We were probably inside stocking."

"Thanks," Ida Belle said. "I really appreciate it."

"Can we ask what this is about?" Wyatt asked. "I mean, we don't have any allegiance to Silas—no one does—so we don't mind answering your questions. But I'm curious."

Ida Belle looked at me so I jumped in.

"We're investigators looking into the circumstances surrounding Molly's disappearance. You know how insurance companies hire out sometimes."

Neither of them looked like they completely understood but both nodded.

"Anyway, we're collecting data for a report," I said. "And one of the things we need to know is the whereabouts of any of Molly's relatives who lived in the area during the time when she disappeared."

Jeb stared. "The insurance thinks he killed her. Well, I'll be a son of a gun."

"I didn't say that," I said. "Insurance companies are like the government. There's all kinds of red tape to process before they handle claims. They pay people like us to make sure everything is thorough."

"If you say so," Jeb said, looking slightly disappointed. I assumed he was hoping we were going to find Silas guilty of something and haul him out of the bayou in handcuffs.

"I'm curious about something myself," I said. "Do you think Johnny's death was an accident?"

"I knew it," Jeb said. "You *do* think he killed her."

"When two children of the same man both die under similar and somewhat questionable circumstances, we're required to do a little extra footwork," I said.

Both men frowned.

"It does seem rather odd," Wyatt said. "I guess truth be

known everyone round here was shocked as heck that Johnny got caught out by a storm. He was smarter than that. One of the best shrimpers around and he knew his way around the bayous and his boat. A lot of us found it hard to believe that he got caught unawares."

Jeb nodded. "But we saw him drive by headed toward the marina and a fisherman saw him at the boat dock so it seemed like that's what happened."

"Did Johnny still live with Silas?" I asked, a little surprised.

"No," Wyatt said. "He and Angel lived in an old house she inherited from an aunt of hers. It's just down the road a bit. Angel sold it after Johnny passed and moved to New Orleans. I can't say that I blame her."

"You didn't happen to see Silas pass by that day, did you?" I asked.

They both shook their heads.

"What about a boat?" I asked. "Does Silas have one?"

"I suppose you could call it a boat," Jeb said. "But the thing hasn't run in probably ten years or better. Last time I saw it, there wasn't even a motor. Probably sold it or it stopped running and it finally fell off. He claims small boats are too hard on his knees so I guess he left it for dead."

Wyatt nodded. "Besides which, according to the police, Silas was on the phone yelling at the tax assessor around the time Johnny was headed for the marina. Called from his home phone so no doubt he was there at that time."

"And Johnny didn't have any enemies?" I asked.

"Good Lord no," Wyatt said. "Johnny Broussard was as nice a guy as they make. The only person that had a problem with Johnny was Silas, and that's because he has a problem with everybody."

"Was the problem specific?" I asked.

He shrugged. "Not sure of the particulars, but word had it

that Silas was always hitting Johnny up for money. I think in the beginning, Johnny obliged some—that whole he's-your-father argument. But as he got older and wiser, he wasn't so obliging. Mind you, he had no reason to be. If your parents are good people and you have the means, then of course you should help out when you can, but Silas wasn't due anything from Johnny."

"Except maybe a thousand butt whuppings to even the score," Jeb said.

"That's the God's honest truth," Wyatt said.

"So I understand that when Johnny went missing, Silas got all his things," I said. "You hear anything about that?"

"Oh yeah, we heard it," Wyatt said. "Silas had been behind on his property taxes for a coon's age. The town thought they were finally going to get rid of him and it all be legal and such. Then Johnny passed and he had cash from Johnny's accounts and the sale of the boat. He kept the truck, paid himself up regular on the taxes, and that was that."

"Why wasn't he paying his taxes?" Gertie asked. "They can't be much on a place like his. And since he's living mostly off-grid, Social Security should cover his expenses."

"There's two places Silas goes every week," Wyatt said. "He buys staples he can't grow, hunt, or fish at the Walmart up the highway. Won't buy anything local. Says he won't pay the markup."

"And the second place?" I asked.

"A bookie in New Orleans," Jeb said.

"Which explains why he got behind on his taxes," I said. "You sure about that?"

"There's been people come here looking for Silas a couple times," Wyatt said. "We knew what they were when they showed up, so we just directed them to his place and didn't try to start conversations. Safer that way, you know?"

Jeb nodded. "Had a cousin who got mixed up in that business. His wife ended up burying him before his fortieth birthday. That's not the sort of people you get crossways with."

"And two days ago—was that grocery or gambling day?" I asked.

"Neither," Wyatt said. "No idea what he was doing."

And suddenly, a thought occurred to me.

"Is Silas behind on his property taxes now?" I asked.

"Matter of fact, he's three years behind," Jeb said. "They were talking about starting legal proceedings again."

I looked over at Ida Belle and Gertie. "Let's grab some cold drinks and snacks for the ride home."

I knew the two men wouldn't take money from me in exchange for the information, but I also knew they were probably living on Social Security or some minimal retirement. Buying some snacks was at least one way I could pass some money their way.

Ten minutes later, we were headed for the highway, munching on stale potato chips and drinking flat root beer.

"Well, that was interesting," Gertie said.

"It most certainly was," Ida Belle said.

I nodded. "Ladies, I think we might have two cases to investigate."

———

WE'D JUST REACHED the highway when my phone rang. I didn't recognize the number. I pulled it out and answered.

"Ms. Redding? This is Glenn," he said, his voice somewhat muffled.

"Yes. Hello."

"You're not going to believe who just walked into the bar."

"Dexter and his girlfriend," I said.

"You got it. And neither of them looks overly happy."

"I'm about twenty minutes away. Do you think they'll stay that long?"

"I don't know. They were arguing about money when I went over to take their order so probably not."

"Give them a discount," I said. "I'll make up the difference."

"I'm not worried about the money," he said. "What is it you plan to do?"

"I'm still thinking about that one," I said.

I disconnected and told Ida Belle to head back to The Bar.

"Are you going to confront him with the girlfriend?" Gertie asked.

"No," I said. "I don't want to tip our hand."

Gertie sighed. "Yeah, I guess that wouldn't be smart. But man, I bet it would be interesting."

"Glenn's lost enough windows today," I said.

"It's going to be hard to do anything besides get a look at them," Ida Belle said. "We can't go in the bar. The place is tiny and Dexter knows all three of us. He'd know we were following him."

"But he might not know your vehicle," I said. "We were in my Jeep when we went to Ally's that day. So unless he looked outside when we dropped off the catering money, he doesn't know what you drive."

"That's true," Ida Belle said. "So we might be able to follow them when they leave."

"But what's that going to tell us?" Gertie asked.

"For starters, I can get some pictures of them together," I said. "Which will help the DA with the motive end of things. And if we know where they're staying, then it will make it easier on Carter when he needs to arrest him."

"So you think Dexter's our guy?" Gertie asked.

"He's certainly at the top of the list," I said. "I just can't make sense of his timing."

Ida Belle nodded. "Seems like if Molly was really going to make him a partner, he would wait to kill her after the ink was dry."

"And the heated-moment thing doesn't work if she was shot with an arrow," Gertie said. "Dexter's girlfriend would have to be on hand for that sort of thing and with her weapon. Based on her phone call to Angel, it sounded like Molly went off in her boat to take a breather, so Dexter couldn't have known she was going."

"Which is why I'd like to know where this girlfriend is holed up," I said. "I need to know if she was close enough to take advantage of a random opportunity or if this was somehow planned."

"If it was planned, it wasn't a very good plan," Gertie said.

"Have you met Dexter?" Ida Belle asked.

"I know, I know," Gertie said. "Most criminals are dumb and we should be thankful, but it's hard to be thankful when you knew the victim."

"We're going to find out what happened," I said. "And if someone killed Molly—which is what it looks like—then they're going to pay. We'll make sure of it. And I know that doesn't fix things but it sure makes them easier to live with."

Ida Belle circled the block around The Bar, then spotted a parking spot on the next block but with a clear view of the door. I pulled out my phone and called Glenn, who verified they were still there but looking as if they were about to wrap things up.

"Looks like we got here just in time," I said when I hung up.

We watched the entrance and about five minutes later,

Dexter and a young blonde came walking out. I snapped some shots of them crossing the road.

"Here we go," Ida Belle said as they climbed into an old white Hyundai with a rusted roof.

"That's not Dexter's vehicle," I said. "It must belong to her."

"Well, let's hope she's not a crazy driver," Ida Belle said.

Gertie snorted. "Like you'd have trouble keeping up."

"I could keep up with NASCAR drivers," Ida Belle said. "But not without them noticing."

"Hopefully she'll take it easy since they were drinking," I said.

Ida Belle and Gertie both stared at me. I couldn't blame them. Dating Dexter was proof alone that the woman wasn't all that bright, and if she'd been involved in a murder plot then that was additional points off her IQ. But then, by all accounts, Molly had been smart and she'd kept Dexter around even though she knew the score. For all we knew, Rat Eyes could have bigger self-esteem problems than Molly did, but I was betting the drug problem was her primary motivator.

We saw the brake lights flash on, then the car lurched forward, hit the curb, rolled off of it, and kept going. Ida Belle waited until they were at the end of the block, then started after them. Marissa took a straight route to the highway and headed toward Sinful. Ida Belle entered the highway some distance behind her but since it was flat and straight, it was easy to keep the car in our sights without getting close enough to call attention. Fortunately, Marissa was driving barely above the speed limit, and occasionally a random vehicle or delivery truck passed both of us. It looked like any evening on the highway.

"Surely they're not going to Molly's house," Gertie said as we got closer and closer to Sinful.

"I wouldn't think so," I said. "Look, she's got her blinker on."

"And we all know that exit," Ida Belle said.

It was a familiar one to us because it contained the closest motel to Sinful. And it was the height of seedy. It was also only maybe a ten-minute drive to Molly's house.

CHAPTER FIFTEEN

WE WATCHED as Marissa's car exited the highway.

"Try to follow them so we can see them go into the parking lot, but don't turn in after them," I said.

Ida Belle exited and remained some distance back until the car started turning into the parking lot of the motel, then she sped up a little to close the gap. As we slowly passed by, I saw the car park at the end of the building and the couple got out and headed up the stairs.

"They already had a room," I said.

"I wonder for how long," Gertie said.

"Let's go ask," I said.

Ida Belle made a U-turn and headed for the motel office. We'd dealt with this clerk before, if it was the same guy, and most things could be had for a little bit of flirting and/or a twenty-dollar bill. Gertie offered to do the flirting routine but before Ida Belle could shoot her, I jumped out and said I would give it a try first.

The clerk looked up when I walked inside and gave me a creepy up-and-down look. When he finally locked in on my face, his eyes widened.

"Oh no," he said. "I know about you now. You're that CIA chick."

"Former CIA. No chick."

"I don't want any trouble," he said.

"Then let's not have any. I just want some really easy information on a couple of your patrons."

"Ah, man, I'm not supposed to give out that kind of stuff."

"Because this place is steeped in propriety?"

"Whatever. Look, we both know this place is a dump, but it's a job. And there aren't too many jobs where you can game most of the day and still get paid."

"No one will ever know you've spoken to me. I'm very discreet. Remember, CIA?"

"Fine. Just promise me that you'll leave after."

"Sure," I said, not bothering to say exactly how long after I would actually wait until I left.

"Who is it?" he asked.

"Dexter Nutters or Marissa Perkins."

He shook his head. "I don't recognize either of those names."

"Of course not." People never used their real names at this motel. "Okay, dude is built like a tree stump, talks crap all the time, and can't fight worth a darn."

"No tree stump dudes staying here."

"The woman is skinny, blond hair, beady eyes."

"Oh, her. Yeah." He tapped on his keyboard and shook his head. "Registered under Jane Smith. These people really have no creativity."

"When did she check in?"

"Five days ago."

"That's a long stay for a place like this."

"True. Usually the oil field guys are the only ones who stay more than a day or two."

"Did you talk to her at all when she registered? You know, chat her up? Hit on her a little, maybe?"

He frowned. "No way. She's not my type."

I blinked. I had assumed that most women with a pulse would be his type. "Why not?"

"She's a user. I had a cousin who OD'd. I'm lazy and I'll drink beer like nobody's business, but I don't go near that stuff or anyone who does."

"We all have our line in the sand," I said. "That's a good one."

He nodded. "Anyway, I didn't ask anything and she didn't offer. Barely looked at me. Just asked for the weekly rate and shoved some cash at me."

"Have you seen her coming and going? Anything unusual? Any visitors—other than the stumpy guy I mentioned?"

"Haven't seen her since she checked in," he said and motioned to his laptop. "But if I'm not checking someone in, I'm usually on that. Got no window with a view out front and I'm not exactly the outdoor type."

Since his skin was as white as the paper on his desk, I figured he was telling the truth on that one.

I gave him my card and his eyes widened. "PI? Really?"

"My new line of work," I said. "If you see anything odd going on with that woman, give me a call. Or if you think anything is wrong."

"Like what? Hey, she's not dangerous, is she?"

"That's what I'm trying to find out," I said and headed for the door.

"Wait! How dangerous? What did she do? Do I need to get Mace or something?"

I just smiled as I walked out. It wasn't nice but he needed some way to burn energy. Lord knows, he wasn't working off ten calories a day sitting in that chair. A little worry might burn more.

I hopped back into the SUV and filled Ida Belle and Gertie in on the conversation.

"Five days?" Gertie said. "Then she was just minutes away from Molly's house. Dexter could have called her when Molly left in her boat, and Marissa could have gone after her in Molly's smaller boat."

I nodded. "That's what I was thinking. He probably knew where Molly kept the keys. I can't imagine she'd hide them."

"That's because you haven't lived here long enough," Ida Belle said.

Gertie rolled her eyes. "A lot of people have feelings about their boats like Ida Belle does about this car."

"Well, it's not like they'd be asking permission to borrow the woman's boat to kill her," Ida Belle said. "And unless she can pull one of those Jesus tricks like Fortune's dad, Molly isn't likely to come back and dish out some punishment for taking her boat."

Gertie stared at the motel and frowned. "I wonder what they're doing in there."

"Yuck," Ida Belle said. "No one needs those images in their mind."

"I don't think that's it," Gertie said. "They both looked mad when they left the bar, and when they got out of the car, they were walking single file, not next to each other. I wish we had a bug in their room."

"That's not a bad idea," I said. "Assuming the room next to them is empty."

Ida Belle shook her head. "The last time you tried that one, you fell through the ceiling and landed on a naked dude who thought you were the prostitute he ordered."

"So I'll knock first," I said. "If no one answers, I go in and see what I can hear. Those walls are paper thin, trust me."

Gertie clapped. "What do you want us to do?"

"Sit tight and be ready to haul butt," I said. "If either of them sees us, the jig is up. And I don't want them running."

I pulled on latex gloves and hurried up the stairs, then put an ear to the door of the room next door to Dexter and Marissa's. I didn't hear any movement inside so I knocked softly on the door. Silence. I pulled out a credit card and grabbed the doorknob, but it jiggled so much when I touched it that I tried turning it.

It was open!

I heard a noise at the end of the motel and saw the clerk walk outside and lean against a light pole at the edge of the parking lot. Crap! He wasn't supposed to be outside. I pushed the door open and slipped inside. The drapes were drawn on the front window so the room was dark as soon as I pulled the door shut behind me. I felt the wall for a switch but when I flipped it up, nothing happened. It figured. This place was falling apart. Why bother with things like light bulbs?

There had been lamps on the nightstands when I'd fallen through the ceiling, so I walked toward where the bed should be, using the front wall to guide me to the side. When I reached the far wall, I located the nightstand only a couple feet away. I found the lamp, then slid my hand up to turn it on.

And that's when I heard breathing.

I flipped the switch on the lamp and choked back a cry.

It was him!

The same skinny glowing-white dude I'd almost landed on the last time I'd been here. But this time, he wasn't naked. Exactly. He was standing in the middle of the bed wearing a mask and a cape. A Hello Kitty mask and matching G-string lay on the nightstand next to me.

"You!" His eyes widened. "No way! This is not going to happen again."

"It didn't happen last time," I said. "And pull that cape around the important parts before I shoot them off."

My tone must have scared him into action because he flipped the cape around to his front like something you'd see in a vampire movie. Except the back of this cape had lettering on it that spelled out *Super Lover*.

"I ought to shoot you for that cape," I said. "Get down off that bed and find some pants."

"You broke into my room, threatening me with death if I don't dress to your liking? This is *my* room. What are you doing here?"

"None of your business. Just get covered with something that's not so offensive. Or a lie."

He flushed deep red. "You don't know anything about me so you don't know what's a lie."

"I know if you're paying for it, there's nothing super about it."

"If you don't leave, I'm going to scream and call the police."

I shouldn't have done it but I couldn't take it anymore. I didn't know what was worse—his naked grossness, the creepy, inaccurate cape, or the fact that I could hear raised voices in the next room but I couldn't hear what they were saying because Naked Dude wouldn't shut up.

I yanked the comforter and his legs flew out from under him. As soon as his body connected with the top of the bed, I threw the end of the comforter over his entire body, rolled him up the bed like a burrito, and shoved the mask into his mouth, drawing the string tighter in the back. Then I hurried to the wall and stuck my ear to it. Naked Dude was writhing on the bed and trying to yell, but he wasn't making enough noise to mask the argument next door.

"You promised me we'd have the money," Marissa said. "But you've got nothing. Where's the legal documents she drew up? You said you signed something."

"I did sign something," Dexter said. "Jesus, you know I'm not lying about all this. You heard my conversation with Molly. I dialed you up and kept the call connected just so you would stop doubting me. And if you hadn't been so stupid and screwed up the recording, I'd have it as evidence that the business is supposed to go to me. Not some wannabe baker in this crap town."

"Maybe Molly was playing you," Marissa said.

"You think a woman can play me?"

"I think a lot of things. But here's what I know for certain —I held up my end of the bargain, and now you need to make good on yours. You promised me the money to get to Mexico and live high on the beach every day. And that's what I expect you to deliver or I'll just find someone who can."

"You don't want to threaten me," Dexter said.

"That's not a threat."

I heard footsteps, then the door opened and slammed shut. A couple seconds later, I could hear footsteps on the stairs, and I peeked out to see Marissa jumping into her car. Ida Belle's SUV was nowhere in sight. She tore out of the parking lot and then I saw Dexter step out, staring after her. He shook his head and pulled out a cigarette, then went to sit on the top step. Crap. No way was I sticking around in the room with Naked Dude until Dexter finished sulking. It was a brand-new pack of cigarettes. He might be there all night.

I was about to pull out my cell phone and see if Ida Belle and Gertie could figure out a way to get Dexter off the steps so I could get out of there before Naked Dude worked his teeth through that mask and started yelling for the police when I heard a whistling sound. A second later, a bottle rocket hit the steps right below Dexter's feet and exploded.

He jumped and whirled around as a second one hit him square in the back just as it exploded. He screamed as if he were being killed and bolted for his room door, but he'd managed to lock himself out. He shoved his shoulder against it but he wasn't even strong enough to take out a door at the worst-built motel in southern Louisiana. More fireworks exploded around him and down on the first floor and he looked my direction, clearly panicked.

Holy crap!

He was going to run for this room and I'd left the door unlocked. I grabbed the Hello Kitty mask and bolted for the door, but Dexter had already grabbed the handle so I tucked myself behind it, barely managing to get the mask over my head and my hands up to block the door as it flew open. Dexter stumbled in, and during his momentary distraction with the man on the bed rolled up like a burrito, I gave the door a hard shove, then jumped out and followed up with a kick directly in his back.

The kick sent him hurtling onto the bed, directly on top of Naked Burrito Dude, who started wailing like a cat in heat. I bolted out of the room and ran for the end of the balcony. I hit it with my midsection and flipped over, landing in the parking lot below, then took off running for the woods at the edge of the parking lot, which is where the fireworks were coming from.

I heard yelling behind me and figured Dexter had spotted me running away. More fireworks lobbed over my head, ensuring he didn't try to pursue. Not that he could have caught me. I was running like the wind. And gasping like a smoker in that mask, which had absolutely horrible air flow.

I yanked the mask off as I ran into the woods and spotted

Gertie with her handbag of goodies at the edge of the tree line. She grabbed the bag and took off through the trees, yelling at me to follow. We skirted the parking lot and then burst out of the trees behind the motel where Ida Belle's SUV was parked, the doors already open. We jumped inside but as Ida Belle took off, I heard a familiar hissing sound.

I looked back at Gertie as she opened her handbag in a panic.

"We have a live one!" she shouted.

CHAPTER SIXTEEN

THOUGHTS of all the hardware Gertie had pulled out of her purse at one time or another coursed through my mind in a flash. I grabbed it from her lap, opened the SUV door, and chunked the purse into the motel dumpster as we passed. We had barely gotten past it when the handbag blew.

The dumpster rose a couple feet off the ground before slamming back into the concrete. Debris flew into the air, then rained down, covering everything within a thirty-foot radius. Ida Belle took only enough time to shoot Gertie a look that would kill before flipping on her windshield wipers and flooring it. She launched the SUV over the curb and through a large gap in the hedge—courtesy of our last visit—then made a hard right into the alley.

"Thank God Mannie cleared that hedge the last time," Gertie said. "It would have taken you forever to wax the scratches out of the paint."

"As opposed to how long it's going to take to get the stench and stain of an entire dumpster off of it?" Ida Belle complained.

Gertie waved a hand in dismissal. "Drama."

"I've got your drama," Ida Belle said.

"Can we please just get out of here and hose down this vehicle before Carter gets here?" I asked. "He's going to take one look at this setup and I'm going to be the first phone call he makes."

"There are other reasons for dumpsters exploding that don't involve me," Gertie said.

"Like what?" I asked.

"An asteroid," Gertie suggested.

"Because asteroids are more common than your purse disasters?" Ida Belle said. "Might as well go with alien invasion or a Marvel comic book setup."

"Well, there *is* a guy in a cape back in the motel," I said.

They both stared.

"Well, right now, he's wrapped up like a burrito," I said. "Or at least he was when I left, and I seriously doubt Dexter is going to help him with that, so he's probably going to be like that for a while. At least as long as it takes him to chew through that mask I shoved in his mouth and call for help."

"Maybe you'd better fill us in," Gertie said. "I have a feeling we're going to need to know what we're denying."

I started with my explanation about Naked Dude, and before I could even get to the part where Dexter burst through the door, they were both laughing so hard they were crying.

"Oh my God," Gertie said. "You know Carter will take this call because there was an explosion. When he finds that guy trussed up and rolled, he's going to lose it."

"Not as much as when he unrolls the guy and sees what he's wearing," Ida Belle said.

"Or not wearing," Gertie said.

"I'm beginning to wonder if the sheriff's department

should have to offer hazard pay for seeing naked people," I said.

"The taxpayers couldn't afford it," Gertie said. "Do you know how many random naked people they run across in a year? And trust me, it's never the people you want to see naked."

"I don't want to see any of them naked," Ida Belle said.

"What about Walter?" Gertie asked.

"He's not random," Ida Belle said. "But I still wouldn't want a random sighting. I like to be aware that nakedness is coming."

"So if you popped over to the store one night after hours, and Walter was doing inventory in the nude, that wouldn't get you all excited?" Gertie asked.

"Why in the world would the man do inventory in the nude?" Ida Belle asked. "Where would he keep his highlighter?"

"If I could just continue," I said before any discussion could ensue about highlighter placement.

I finished telling them what I'd overheard.

"So it sounds like our theory was right," Gertie said. "Marissa was on hand to do the job just as soon as the right opportunity presented itself."

"But what is all that about Dexter signing things and the phone conversation that Marissa was apparently privy to?" Ida Belle asked.

I shook my head. I was as confused as they were by that part of the investigation. Everyone who knew Molly well said there was absolutely no way she'd leave her business to Dexter and I believed them. But Dexter seemed to be under a completely different impression and for whatever reason, I felt he was actually being honest about that. So either he misinterpreted something really,

really badly that Molly had said and made up the document part to placate his girlfriend, or Molly's best friends didn't know her as well as they thought they did. And if Marissa had actually overheard a conversation about that very thing, and the discussion was in Dexter's favor, then that muddied the waters even more. But then with Marissa being a user, she might have been easy to fool.

On the surface, it looked as if we'd found our answer to whether or not Molly's disappearance was an accident, and it appeared as if we'd found our culprits. But nothing rang completely true for me. There was too much muddying the waters, as people liked to say here in Sinful.

Ida Belle took a hard left, and I was so deep in thought I almost banged my head on the window. Gertie wasn't so lucky. I heard her slam into the door, then start cussing Ida Belle.

"What the heck was that for?" Gertie said.

"Car wash," Ida Belle said as she pulled up to an older man with a clipboard who was giving the SUV a disapproving stare.

"Darn kids," Ida Belle said when she rolled down the window. "Threw a bag of trash off the overpass and onto my vehicle."

The disapproving stare disappeared and he shook his head. "I don't understand what's wrong with kids these days."

"Their parents?" I suggested.

"You'd be right on that one," he said and stuck a ticket in her window. "No charge. Just pull up until that light turns red and we'll do the rest."

"So what do we do now?" Gertie asked. "Are you going to tell Carter about Dexter's girlfriend and the longbow thing? I don't guess you can talk about the conversation you overheard at the motel as you sorta broke in on that naked guy and tied him up."

"Not to mention you blew the motel dumpster sky-high

with your bag of things nightmares are made of," Ida Belle said to Gertie.

"You have a rocket launcher and he got over it," Gertie said.

"Because without it, Fortune would have died," Ida Belle said.

Gertie waved a hand in dismissal. "Details."

"At least it was trash this time and not the vending machines," I said. "Although I'm guessing that clerk is never going to give me information again. I kinda promised him I'd leave the premises. He didn't want trouble."

"Then he shouldn't be working there," Gertie said. "Everything about that place is trouble. We're just shining a light on it."

"You set off a bomb on it," Ida Belle said. "Twice."

"Details," Gertie said again.

"And this time it would have blown us to bits if Fortune hadn't thrown it out of the car," Ida Belle said. "And so help me God, if you say 'details' I'm going to shoot you right here in this car wash and pitch you out into those jets where all the forensic evidence will be washed away."

The giant turbines cranked up the wind on the SUV and I was happy to see that the trash seemed to have washed off. Hopefully, there wasn't anything that would mar the paint, or Gertie was never going to get to ride in Ida Belle's vehicle again.

"What happened?" I asked Gertie.

"I don't know," she said. "Something must have been hot enough to set off one of those bottle rockets, which sparked the dynamite."

"Something?" Ida Belle asked. "You mean something like you dropping a lit bottle rocket into your purse?"

Gertie shrugged. "Who knows? Does it really matter?

Everyone is good, even the dumpster, and I have a spare hand-bag. The only loss is the bottle rockets, which I was planning to use at your bachelorette party."

Ida Belle shot her a look of dismay and I laughed.

"You know if you keep talking about this party, Ida Belle's not going to attend," I said.

Ida Belle exited the highway and headed for the road to Molly's house. I scanned the tree line as we turned onto the road and spotted the two boys sitting in their tree-house fort. Ida Belle pulled over as much as possible without running into the ditch and I climbed out of the SUV.

"Hi, guys," I said as I approached, judging their ages at around nine and ten. "I was wondering if you could help me."

The first boy shook his head. "You're a stranger."

I pulled out my ID and held it up to the tree house. "I'm a private detective. Does that make a difference?"

"You don't look like a detective," the second boy said. "Where's your hat and magnifying glass?"

"It's too hot for the hat, and around here a good pair of binoculars comes in handier than a magnifying glass."

"That's true," the second boy agreed. "What do you want?"

"Were you guys out here Monday afternoon?"

"Unless it's raining or we're eating, we're usually out here," the first boy said. "Only got one TV, and Mom watches those daytime shows. Yuck."

"So you probably notice everyone who drives by, then."

They both nodded.

"We like cars," the second boy said. "Don't get to see too many good ones around here, although that SUV you got out of is way cool. You can hear the engine miles back. I bet it's fast."

"You have no idea," I said. "So, on Monday afternoon, did

you happen to see an old white Hyundai with a rusted roof drive by?"

"Yep," the first boy said. "It's a crap car but that don't mean you should treat it badly."

The second boy gave a solemn nod. "People who don't take care of their cars should have to walk everywhere."

"I'm going to buy a Lamborghini when I'm a grown-up," the first boy said. "And I'm going to wash and wax it every single day."

"That's a great plan," I said. "Did you see the car leave?"

They frowned and looked at each other, then shook their heads.

"No, but we got called in early because we had to take a bath," the first one said. "Our aunt was coming to visit. We always have to take a bath when she's coming to visit."

The second one rolled his eyes. "She complains about stinky boys but she lives with a hundred cats. You ought to smell her house."

"Yuck," I said, which made both of them giggle. "What about a black Dodge truck? Older model?"

They shook their heads, and I was about to thank them and leave when something occurred to me.

"Maybe you heard it—sounds like there's a hole in the muffler?" I asked.

"Oh, that one," the first boy said. "Yeah, we left the fort to go exploring, but we heard a big engine with bad exhaust. Could have woken the dead."

"Are those people the bad guys?" the second boy asked. "Because the person driving the truck isn't going to sneak up on anyone."

"No, I expect not," I said. "Tell you what, I'm going to leave my card down here wedged in the steps. If you see either of those vehicles pass by here again, can you call me?"

"What if our mom won't let us?" the first boy asked.

"Don't be such a baby," the second boy said. "Mom don't need to know. We're helping catch bad guys. That's more important."

"I don't want you to get in trouble," I said. "And under no circumstances are you to chase after those vehicles if you see them. Do you understand?"

They both nodded.

"I mean it," I said.

They glanced nervously at each other.

"Are they dangerous?" the first boy asked.

"That's what I'm trying to find out," I said. "So promise me you won't go anywhere near either of those vehicles or the people driving them."

The second boy shrugged. "Mom would kill us anyway if we got outside of shouting distance."

"Good," I said. "Thanks for helping."

"Will you come back and tell us when you catch the bad guys?" the first boy asked.

I smiled. "Sure."

I headed back to the SUV and as Ida Belle directed it toward Sinful, I filled them in. When I finished, Gertie threw her hands in the air.

"Of course they were both here that day," she said. "No way this could be easy and we could have narrowed it down to one."

Ida Belle sighed. "I figured after that conversation you overheard between Dexter and Marissa that we had our answer. But now we have to consider Silas all over again."

"I never stopped considering him," I said. "Maybe he's just a wife and child beater and an opportunist, but I have a hard time reconciling the fact that both of the man's children die in the same way and he benefits."

"Especially given that neither had a relationship with him," Gertie said. "I can see where Johnny wouldn't have had a will. Most men his age don't. It's just not something they think about, but I can't figure out why Molly didn't. Not with the way things turned out for her brother."

"And yet Silas claims he is the beneficiary of an insurance policy that Molly acquired," I said. "We need two things—the name of the insurance agent who wrote that policy, assuming there actually is one, and the name of the attorney who Molly saw about those documents Dexter claimed to have signed."

"Assuming there actually is one," Gertie said.

"Yeah, assuming," I said and shook my head. "I thought more information was a good thing. Now we have information overload."

"And everything makes all of them look guilty," Gertie said.

"Maybe they *are* all guilty," Ida Belle said.

"You think they are all in it together?" Gertie asked. "That doesn't seem likely."

"I can't see Silas colluding with anyone or anyone wanting to collude with Silas," I said. "But I do think all of them are hiding things. Shady things."

"So how do we sort it out?" Gertie asked. "We seem to have hit a wall getting information on Molly and Johnny. We've talked to everyone who knew them well enough to know anything."

"Are you going to tell Carter what we found?" Ida Belle said.

I blew out a breath. "I'm going to have to think on that. So far everything is circumstantial. Sketchy as heck but we don't have anything concrete. But since Carter *does* have access to Molly's house and records, he would know some of the things we're missing."

"Doesn't mean he'll tell you about them," Gertie said.

"Oh, I'm positive he won't tell me about them," I said. "But I'm wondering if the best thing I can do for our client is give Carter the information. It might fill the gaps he needs and he's the only one who can bring people in for questioning. All I really want is to get justice for Molly and answers for Angel and Nickel. I don't really care who ends up with credit for it."

"I really wish he'd just do that shady small-town thing and let you in on things," Gertie said. "You're not any more likely to be injured doing your job than he is doing his."

"Given that Carter doesn't spend much time around you and your handbags, that's not exactly accurate," Ida Belle said.

I laughed but I was already thinking about the conversation I needed to have with Carter. Then as if thinking about him summoned him, my phone rang.

"Someone blew up a dumpster at the motel," Carter said. "I don't suppose Gertie is short a stick of dynamite?"

"What motel?"

"The one with the exploded dumpster. I suppose you don't know anything about the guy rolled up in his comforter, either."

"That doesn't sound like something I'd be involved in."

"Given what he was wearing—or the lack thereof—it sounds exactly like something you'd do, and his description was rather specific, right down to your bra size."

"Gross."

"So you want to tell me why you broke into that guy's room and assaulted him with his own bed linens?"

I gave it a moment's thought. I was planning on telling Carter about Dexter and Marissa anyway. And given that Naked Dude and the clerk could easily identify me and I'd given the clerk my business card, it seemed like a waste of time to keep denying things.

"Dexter might be in the room next door to Naked Dude," I said. "Dexter and his girlfriend."

"What?"

"Look, we found out some things today that you need to know. And before you say it, I know you can't give me information and honor and police stuff and blah, blah, blah, but if those two were responsible for Molly's death, then I want them to go down. So does my client. The only manner I have to take care of that personally isn't exactly legal and probably not advisable."

"Probably?"

"Nobody likes Dexter."

"Okay. I'll take down some information and meet you at your house in about thirty minutes."

"Ally is at my house."

"Then meet me at the sheriff's department."

I hung up and sighed.

"Naked Dude ID'd me," I said.

"How could he?" Gertie asked. "There are plenty of hot blondes running around southern Louisiana."

"Probably not many that can single-handedly immobilize a guy in a comforter," Ida Belle said.

"He knew my bra size," I said.

"Gross."

They both spoke at once.

"My feelings exactly. Anyway, the description and the exploding dumpster pretty much had us dead to rights, so I couldn't see any reason to lie about it. When we get to Sinful, just drop me off at the sheriff's department and I'll go face the music."

"Do you think we have enough for Carter to arrest them?" Gertie asked.

"I think we have enough for suspicion of murder," I said. "But we don't have enough to make a case."

"Hopefully Carter has some evidence from the boat," Ida Belle said. "Put it together with what we have and he might be able to make a case to the DA."

I nodded. Everything we knew was damning but it still wasn't right. I was missing something, and I had a feeling that it was right in front of me but I couldn't see it.

CHAPTER SEVENTEEN

I FIGURED Carter would be a while getting to the sheriff's department, so I headed over to the General Store to grab a soda and chat with Walter. I hadn't stopped in since my last food pickup, and I was interested to see if he was as nonchalant about the upcoming nuptials as Ida Belle was. He looked up as I walked in and gave me a huge smile. Gertie was always saying if she were younger she'd go after some guy, but I had the opposite thought. If I were older, I'd be shoving Ida Belle in front of a bus and going for Walter.

Walter was thoughtful and kind and despite the fact that he didn't run his mouth, he didn't miss much. He was funny and smart and so handsome with his silver hair. No matter when I saw him, he always had a smile for me and he always had time. If I was being honest, Walter was the father I would have liked to have had. Life would have been so much simpler. But maybe simple wasn't part of my journey.

"You flying solo today?" he asked as I grabbed a soda and pulled up a stool in front of the counter to sit on.

"Nope. Been flying with company all day today but I have to meet Carter in twenty minutes, give or take. So I figured I'd pop in here and check your blood pressure. You ready for the big day?"

I didn't think Walter could get any cuter but the blush that crept up his neck was priceless. Ida Belle had really won the lottery with this guy. And even though I knew and respected her reasons for not marrying him sooner, I still found myself wondering why the heck not.

"I suppose I should be," he said. "Lord knows, I've had plenty of time to prepare."

"Couple decades at least."

"A bit more than a couple but I'm not telling."

"Ida Belle isn't telling either, so you're safe."

"What are you meeting Carter in town for? You having a bite over at the café?"

"I wish. Unfortunately, I'm in trouble."

He chuckled. "You don't say."

"I know. Shocking, right?"

"What are you in trouble over this time or can you say?"

"A naked guy tied up in a comforter and an exploding dumpster."

Walter's eyes widened. "That sounds like the start of the kind of joke you tell in a bar."

"It kinda ends that way too. Let's just say it's been an interesting day."

"So this naked guy—I thought the bachelorette party was this Friday."

"It is. And trust me, no one wants that guy rolled up in the comforter dancing there. Not even Gertie. We were actually on a case. There was this conversation I wanted to overhear at the motel and things didn't go smoothly."

He stared at me for a couple seconds, then started to laugh. "The three of you are going to be the death of Carter."

"What about you? Your lady is right in that mix."

He shrugged. "I know Ida Belle thinks she's going to give me a heart attack with her behavior, but the truth is I turned that one over to the good Lord years ago. Figured he was the only one who had a chance of getting through her hard head. I just try to keep my worry to a minimum and my knowledge of what she's doing to even less than that. Ida Belle does her part by refusing to tell me stuff."

"I wonder if Carter will ever get to that point with me," I said.

"Can't hurry these things. After all, it's hard for two old dogs to change their ways."

"Carter's not that old. His ways shouldn't be set in concrete yet."

"I was talking about me and you."

"Oh. Ha."

"The truth is, you've had a lot more adjusting to do than Carter. A lot more compromising. You had to realign the entire scope of your life. Relearn everything you knew about everyday living. About friends and family. That's a big load on a person in a short amount of time. Carrying that load can get a bit heavy."

"I guess. But you know, it hasn't been as bad as you would think. Honestly, the CIA weighed heavier on me than living here, even though I knew everything about the agency and nothing about this place and the people. And even though it seems like nothing fits quite right at times, it also feels like where I'm supposed to be. Does that make sense?"

He nodded. "Does to me. You're good people, Fortune. And you finally found your place among other good people. People who rely on you and people you can rely on. People who care about more than if you're good at your job. I don't doubt for a minute that you were a darned fine agent, but I'd hazard a guess that you're even better at what you're doing now. I know for certain you're more important to those around you. Important in the ways that count most."

I felt my chest tighten. Walter was right—I had been a darned fine agent, stellar if I was being honest. And I knew that my service was important to the agency and the country. Director Morrow and my partner Harrison cared about me beyond just the job, but it wasn't the same as what I had now. Not even close. This was home. It seemed as if my entire life had been structured to send me here.

"I see Carter pulling in," Walter said. "You need any ammo?"

"Not this time," I said. "I can probably talk my way out of it."

He laughed again. "I just bet you can."

I headed to the sheriff's department and walked inside. The newish daytime dispatcher was manning the front desk and gave me an apprehensive look when I walked in. He'd been on the receiving end of a ploy or two from Ida Belle, Gertie, and me and now automatically assumed something was suspect when one of us walked in the door. Since he wasn't exactly wrong, I figured I couldn't fault him for his feelings.

"Carter asked me to meet him here," I said. "Can you let him know I'm here?"

His shoulders slumped in relief at such a normal request and he called Carter. "He said to go on back to his office."

"Thanks."

Carter's office door was open and as I stepped in the doorway he looked up and motioned me inside.

"Close the door," he said.

"You going to arrest me?" I asked as I complied. "Because if so, I'm going to regret turning down Walter's offer of ammo."

"I just don't want anyone else to overhear and then wonder why I *didn't* arrest you. I'll deal with my traitorous uncle later."

"Fair enough. Did the naked guy want to press charges?"

"I'm sure he would if he knew who interrupted his...whatever the heck that was. But when I pointed out that everything—everything—had to go on record, he changed his mind."

"I'm sort of surprised given how outraged he was."

"Yeah, well, his *date* showed up shortly after I got him out of the comforter and back into clothes. Real clothes."

I laughed. "Nothing like a hooker to put a damper on filing a police report."

"I gathered from our naked friend that this isn't the first time you've interrupted his cape-wearing adventures."

"I don't know anything about his adventures or the cape," I said, putting on my best blank expression.

"Hmm. So what is it you want to tell me?"

"I have information on Dexter and his girlfriend and on Silas, Molly's father. My problem is it's all damning but I don't have a way to make it cohesive. I have theories but not proof. I was hoping since you were privy to things I'm not that you could take what I had and maybe have a case."

"Against who?"

I sighed. "All three of them?"

"I think maybe you'd better tell me what you have."

I worked through the basics of the information, not telling him the who or the how, ending with identification of both vehicles by the two boys in the fort. As I talked, Carter listened intently and sometimes jotted things down on a pad of paper. When I was done, he blew out a breath and leaned back in his chair.

"That is a lot to process," he said.

"I know. Can you put anything together?"

He rubbed his jaw and stared out the window. "I'm not

sure. I'm going to go ahead and tell you it was Molly's blood on the side of the boat."

Even though I'd already known the score, I felt my heart sink a bit.

"That sucks," I said.

"It does, and what makes matters worse, given the indicated parties, is that I've been unable to locate a will. As things currently stand, Ally will probably be able to make a case for the catering business since there's a legal document and I doubt she's going to get any opposition, as those opposed don't have the money to take things to court. But the way things stand right now, the rest of Molly's property will go to her father. And it sure doesn't sound like that's what Molly would have wanted."

"No. But if she never got around to making a will, what can you do about it?"

"Nothing." He frowned, then sat up straight. "Or maybe that's not entirely true. With the hole in the side of the boat just below where the blood was found, I have enough to call it a suspicious death, especially with Marissa being a longbow champion. I just can't prove homicide without a body or a confession. But as long as her disappearance is under investigation, her estate can't be settled, especially if the heir is also a suspect."

"So her father wouldn't be able to get his hands on her property?"

"Not right away."

"How long could you leave things that way?"

"I don't know. He could take it to court and make a case for an earlier declaration, just like he did with her brother. But I'm not sure if he'd get it. With all the questionable circumstances, I can't see a judge being willing to stick his neck out. Not this time. If he kept pushing, I suppose he might be able to move the needle if a year passes and I haven't made any progress, but that's just a guess."

"I was hoping for longer."

"How much longer?"

"Until he died?"

"Ha! Maybe he'll do you a favor and go early."

"You haven't met the man. He's mean as a snake. People like that always live forever."

Carter frowned. "I didn't meet him. I talked to him on the phone. But it looks like I need to make meeting him a priority."

"What do you think about this insurance policy he claims to be on?" I asked.

"Honestly? I have no idea what to make of that."

"Yeah. Me either. That one came clean out of left field. So what are you going to do about Dexter? Did he see you at the motel?"

"I'm sure he did but he never poked his head out of his room, so he has no idea that I know he's there."

"I wonder if he's figured out it was me."

"You said he saw you running away, right?"

"Yeah, but I was wearing a Hello Kitty mask that I, uh...found?"

Carter gave me a pained look. "He might figure he just got caught up in the middle of some mess in the room next to him. Wrong place at the wrong time. He definitely didn't go back to check on the naked guy, who managed to roll off the bed and was kicking the wall like a mule when I arrived."

"So maybe he doesn't suspect either of us of having discovered him," I said. "Can you get a search warrant for that hotel room? There's nothing left at his apartment except the box of things I bought."

"You're certain about that?"

"As certain as I can be without questioning the management talents of Winky Bear."

"Winky Bear?"

"Trust me, you don't want to make fun of the name. The dude is the size of the Rock and has a voice like a demon."

He nodded. "The facts surrounding the girlfriend and the hole in the boat are probably enough to get me a search warrant of the motel room. But if they were smart, they would have ditched the bow."

"They're not smart. And those bows aren't cheap. I'd bet money they have it. Make sure the warrant includes their vehicles." I rose from my chair. "If you don't have anything else, I'd like to get home and have a shower. Ally is already there and has been baking for an hour. I imagine I'm going to walk into heaven."

"I'm a little jealous that I can't join the party."

"You've got things to do."

He walked around the desk and kissed me. "Thank you for the information. I wish it could be a two-way street."

"You just worry about taking down whoever hurt Molly. I don't think my client cares how it's done. I know I don't."

———

ALLY WAS PULLING a sheet of cookies out of the oven when I walked in the kitchen. Another sheet full of yummy goodness was already cooling on the stove.

"Peanut butter?" I asked.

She smiled and nodded.

I groaned. "You know I'm going to eat all of them by tomorrow morning. I'll have to run half the day to work off the calories. I'm already fifteen pounds up from my fighting weight."

"Please, your fighting weight was necessary for what you did then. You look better with a few extra pounds."

"Are you saying I was too skinny?"

"Not at all. You were extremely fit and lean. I wish I had that body for a day just to see how it felt, but you don't have to maintain that level of leanness now. I'm not saying let yourself go—not that you would—but you don't have to be ready to take on the world."

"I ran from a bear yesterday and an alligator the day before."

Ally's eyes widened. "Okay, then maybe keep up the running regimen."

"It's either that or shoot more."

She laughed and shook her head. "What in the world do you ladies get up to that requires you to do all this running from predators?"

"We're on a case."

"Which means you can't talk about it. Well, please be careful."

"I always am."

She raised one eyebrow. "You're *your* version of careful. I think the rest of us mere mortals have other ideas."

"Not Gertie."

"Gertie is a force unto herself and a study in what not to do." She nodded toward the table. "I brought dinner. I wasn't sure how many of us would be here, so looks like you're in stock with chicken fried steak for a couple days."

My mouth started to water. Chicken fried steak was one of my favorite dishes from Francine's Café. "With the dumplings?"

"Of course. And jalapeño cornbread."

"Ally? Will you marry me?"

She laughed. "Things might get a little crowded around

here with three of us. Are you hungry now? I can pop these in the oven for just a couple minutes and they'll be good to go."

"Ready when you are. I'll use the time to throw in some laundry. I'll be going commando if I don't put a load on. I need to buy more clothes so I can do laundry less often."

"A completely valid reason."

I headed into the laundry room and started tossing lighter-colored items into the washing machine. I wasn't much for clothes that required a lot of care, so basically I had five types of loads—light, dark, towels, bed linens, and cleaning rags. Since the pile seemed heavier on lights, I started there. As I lifted a pair of gray yoga pants from the stack, I heard something crinkle. I reached in the pocket and pulled out an envelope.

Frowning, I turned it over and saw it was addressed to Molly. Then I remembered that I'd snagged an envelope from a bush and shoved it in my pocket just before the rat explosion, leading to the bear chase, leading to being chastised by Carter. I'd completely forgotten it was there. I looked at the return address and my pulse quickened.

Law Offices of Paul Jamison.

The envelope was empty but that didn't matter. We'd just struck gold. I pulled out my phone and did a quick check. His office was in the French Quarter and opened at 9:00 a.m. I'd be on the phone at 9:01 making an appointment.

CHAPTER EIGHTEEN

At 9:30 a.m. Ida Belle, Gertie, and I were on our way to New Orleans. I hadn't told Carter about the envelope. If he got there first, the attorney would never tell me anything. As it was, I wasn't sure he'd tell me anything now, but he'd agreed to see me so that was a good sign. All I'd told him was that I had some questions about wills that I thought he could answer. He said he'd be drafting documents all day and to drop in any time and he'd see if he could help.

His office was a stately brick building with a small balcony with an ornate iron railing on it. There was a plaque that indicated the business inside but that was it. We opened the door and stepped into a beautiful lobby. Parquet floors, leather furniture, marble columns, and what looked like expensive art. Paul Jamison was either deeply in debt or doing very well.

A silver-haired lady at a desk at the back of the lobby looked over her glasses as we approached.

"May I help you?" she asked.

"My name is Fortune Redding. I spoke to Mr. Jamison earlier and he said to drop by any time today."

"Of course. He said to expect you. Let me make sure he's not on a call."

She called his office and let him know we were there, then directed us down the hall behind her and to take the elevator to the second floor. His office was at the front of the building. The second floor appeared to be divided into only three rooms —two offices and a restroom. The walls were paneled with the same glossy wood as the downstairs and the art display continued down the hallway. I knocked quietly on the door and heard a voice inside calling for me to enter.

We walked inside just as the man behind an ornate wood desk hung up his phone.

Late fifties. Six foot even. One hundred ninety pounds. Excellent muscle tone but all gym quality. Threat level low, especially wearing a suit and dress shoes.

"Mr. Jamison," I said as I moved forward to shake his hand. "Fortune Redding. Thank you so much for seeing me. These are my two assistants, Ida Belle and Gertie."

"Please have a seat," he said and indicated a set of chairs opposite him. "What line of business are you in, Ms. Redding, that you require two assistants?"

I pulled out one of my cards and slid it across the desk. He picked it up and raised one eyebrow. "Private investigator? I don't think I've ever had a visit from a PI. What is this about?"

"Molly Broussard," I said and watched him closely.

His expression, which had been curious, shifted to worried. "Has something happened to Molly?"

I made a note that he had forgone formality when referring to Molly, which was a sign that he knew her personally and not necessarily professionally. Or not only professionally. I explained about Molly's disappearance and that I had a client who wanted me to pursue other angles aside from an accidental death.

"Your client thinks Molly was murdered?" he asked, looking a bit shocked.

"Let's just say my client finds it hard to believe that Molly let down her guard enough to die in a boat given that her brother went the same way."

Paul nodded. "I can see where that would be troubling for your client. To be honest, I find it troubling myself."

"I take it you knew Molly personally?"

"In a way. My wife was one of Molly's junior high teachers. She took a special interest in Molly and we discussed her situation at length."

"And what was her situation?" I asked.

"We had no firsthand knowledge of the things Molly dealt with as a child, you understand, but we'd both seen enough of that kind of domestic issue to fill in the pages of the story. My wife tried to coax information out of her but Molly wouldn't talk to anyone. I was able to find out that social services had been contacted multiple times but Molly and her brother had always denied any wrongdoing."

"And that was that," I said.

"Unfortunately," he said. "My wife did her best to encourage Molly in her studies and used to bring an extra lunch and snacks to share with her. Molly was always on the larger side but she was far too thin for her frame. My wife continued to look out for her throughout junior high and then prayed for the best when she moved to high school. When she walked into my office a month ago and introduced herself, I was more than a little surprised."

"But you'd never met before, right? Then why did she come here?"

"She said she had never forgotten my wife's kindness and that she remembered her saying her husband was an attorney. Since she had a lot of respect for my wife, she assumed she'd married a good man. I told her I was happy to help. Then she brought me up to speed on her life after high school."

"Were you shocked?" I asked.

"Yes and no," he said. "The continuance of abuse is unfortunately quite common when it's part of your childhood, but it's still rare for a woman to kill her abuser. Not that I take issue with it, mind you. I'm rather Old Testament in some ways even though I'm supposed to be a steward of the law. But despite all that had happened, it sounded like Molly had really put her life back together—that things were going in a positive direction."

"What was it that Molly wanted you to do?" I asked.

He frowned. "I suppose I shouldn't tell you that. The professional part of our conversation falls under privilege but with Molly missing..."

"I don't think anyone will fault you for trying to help her," I said. "My client just wants the truth and justice, if applicable. What you know might help with that."

He nodded. "Molly wanted to talk about her assets, particularly her business, and what would happen in the event that she passed. I asked some questions about the financial viability of the business and its assets, then about the people in her life —those who would have a legal basis for assumption if she were to pass without a will."

"My understanding is that everything would go to her father, correct?"

"Yes. By Louisiana law, the closest living relative would inherit unless there is a will stating otherwise. She told me outright that she was not interested in that outcome. That her father had gotten enough when her brother died. Then she explained that extremely sad situation to me."

"Did she mention her boyfriend?" I asked.

He sighed. "I found Mr. Nutters very concerning. Not

because of what Molly said, mind you, but more because of what she didn't say. I advised her to strongly consider the history and character of anyone she wished to entrust her business to. I was really proud of what she'd accomplished and I could tell she was as well, perhaps for the first time in her life. I didn't want her hard work to go to someone who wouldn't treat it the way she did, and I said so."

He looked down at the desk and tapped his fingers for a moment, then looked back up at me.

"I will confess that I did some checking on Mr. Nutters after she left my office," he said. "I suppose I felt somewhat parental even though she's grown, but Lord knows she'd never had an adult who took her interests into account. I have to say that I found him particularly unsuitable and that was only after a very cursory investigation."

"Did you tell Molly what you'd found?"

"I didn't have a chance to. She left after our discussion, promising to call, but she hedged on leaving me any contact information. I found her business address and sent her a letter, asking her to contact me at her first convenience. We were supposed to meet next week and I hoped she wouldn't be angry enough with my overstepping to ignore the information."

"What did you find?" I asked.

"The usual lot that comes with his sort—bad debt, bankruptcy, history of assault and domestic abuse. But the one that concerned me the most was money owed to a drug dealer. I didn't come by that information through usual channels, but I know someone who has a bent for pharmaceuticals that add muscle...anyway, Mr. Nutters is highly sought-after for collection reasons in New Orleans."

I looked over at Ida Belle and Gertie and could tell they didn't like that bit of information any more than I did.

"Do you think that man hurt Molly?" Paul asked.

"I think it's possible," I said. "He seems to be under the impression that Molly was going to make him a partner and if anything were to happen, she was leaving the business to him. But to the best of our knowledge, he hasn't been able to produce proof of those claims."

Paul flushed with anger and he shook his head. "I loathe men like him. My wife comes from a wealthy family, so I've spent years watching people try to take advantage. But it wasn't until I left criminal law and opened a family law practice that I realized it wasn't just the plight of the wealthy. You see, it's all relative. What one person might not lift a single finger to gain, another would go to great lengths to attain."

"So the less a con brings to the table, the lower the score they're willing to go for," I said.

He nodded. "My experience has led me to observe that it's usually one or a mix of three different things that dictate the extent to which a con will go—his current financial position, the risk and amount of effort associated with the con in relation to the payout, and the ability of the con to make a larger score in the future."

"Interesting," I said. "I hadn't thought about future earnings but I suppose it makes sense. Most people never hit the one that sets them for life, so if the risk of things going south isn't worth the payout they would leave for greener pastures."

"But where does that leave us with Molly?" Gertie asked. "Dexter seems to think he's due the business but has no proof and sounds like his money situation borders on desperate."

"And on the other hand, it seems that Silas *is* due her property and his situation borders on desperate as well, since he owes back property taxes," Ida Belle said.

I sighed. "I don't want to see any of them get anything. I really wish Molly had followed up on creating a will."

Paul gave me a sad nod. "So do I."

———

WE CLIMBED BACK into Ida Belle's SUV with more information but no closer to having an answer on what happened to Molly than we were before. Ida Belle started the SUV and fired up the AC, then guided it toward the highway.

"What now?" Gertie asked, voicing all of our thoughts.

"It does seem as if we're at a draw," Ida Belle said. "All three had motive and opportunity."

I nodded and stared down the street, rolling everything over in my mind. Unfortunately, one of the missing pieces could only be filled in by the man who'd drawn a shotgun on us before we'd even introduced ourselves.

"We have to talk to Silas again," I said. "Now."

Ida Belle took a left instead of a right onto the highway and headed toward Silas's place.

"I don't think Silas is interested in talking," Gertie said.

"He might be if I tell him my investigation is holding up his insurance benefits," I said.

"Or he might just shoot you, figuring they won't bother sending a replacement," Ida Belle said.

"I hope he's a good shot then," I said. "Because he's only going to get one."

"What is it you think you can get out of him?" Ida Belle asked.

"The name of the insurance company he claims Molly had a policy with," I said. "If there really is a policy, I want to talk to the issuing agent."

"You think he faked the policy?" Ida Belle asked. "But how?"

"I don't know," I said. "I just know that everyone who ever

knew Molly has said that without a doubt there is no way she'd leave her father anything. So this whole insurance business is shady."

"If Silas really has an issued policy, he has more motive than Dexter," Ida Belle said. "Dexter doesn't even have any legal documents to back up his claims."

"True. And there's that business with Molly's brother," Gertie said. "It all stinks to high heaven. I really wish there was a way to connect the three of them."

"I can't imagine Silas partnering with anyone, even for money," I said. "I don't think he has it in him. And even though he went to Molly's house that day, how would he follow her in the bayou? Dexter had access to Molly's boat keys and could have taken her smaller boat out or given them to Marissa, but I can't see Molly allowing Silas to dig around her drawers."

"If they were hanging on a hook, he could have slipped a set in his pocket when she wasn't looking," Gertie said.

"But that would assume he knew she was going out in the other boat," I said.

"What about Johnny?" Gertie asked. "No one seems to think that was an accident either, but we know for certain that the only person who benefited from his death was Silas."

"True," I agreed. "But that bad hip and knees of his have been around for a while. While he could have used a hoist to get Johnny from the boat into the bayou, how did he get him on the boat to begin with? That fisherman said he only saw one person getting on board and that was Johnny."

"He could have been hiding on the boat waiting for him," Gertie said.

"How did he get there?" Ida Belle asked. "The nearest marina is a good ten miles away. He couldn't have made a ten-mile walk with those medical conditions and if he'd been hiding there, his truck would have been in the parking lot. That fisherman said the parking lot was empty."

"And even if he could have walked the distance, he still made that call to the tax assessor's office shortly before Johnny was spotted at the marina," I said. "He couldn't have run there that fast, even with perfect knees, and if he'd driven there, the fisherman and Jeb and Wyatt would have seen him. So would Johnny, for that matter."

Ida Belle nodded. "Even if he had a working boat, the fisherman would have seen him and no matter what, we always come back to that phone call with the tax assessor that the police verified was made from his land line."

Gertie threw her hands in the air. "I need someone to be guilty. Actually, I need everyone to be guilty. I don't like any of them."

"Me either," I said. "Which is why I am looking for more dirt on Silas. If Carter can keep that suspicion on record, then maybe he can keep Silas from claiming Molly's property before that five-year mark."

"What about Dexter?" Gertie asked.

"Carter might not find enough to get a conviction, but Dexter isn't coming out of this with any of Molly's assets," I said.

"Not good enough," Gertie grumbled.

"We're doing everything we can," Ida Belle said. "People like Dexter get theirs in the end. They don't know any other way but the wrong one and eventually they step on the wrong back."

Ida Belle turned off onto the path leading to Silas's shack. "Hang on."

The SUV dipped and bumped along the makeshift road for what seemed like forever. Silas's truck was parked in the same place as before.

"Let me go by myself," I said. "But maybe angle the SUV so you're ready to haul it out of here. And cover me. If he doesn't feel like answering my questions, I'm going to push."

Ida Belle nodded and swung the SUV around in a circle, angling it where they could see the cabin and where it was easy for her to launch for the road. I climbed out of the SUV and headed for the porch. As expected, Silas stepped out with his shotgun before I was halfway there.

"Thought I made myself clear on visitors last time," he said.

"I'm not a visitor. If you have any thoughts of collecting that insurance money, you'll answer my questions. Or I can just tell the company that you won't comply, and they can sit on the claim for a while before they assign it to someone else and start this process all over again."

He glared at me but I could tell he was considering my words.

"What do you want to know?" he finally asked.

"You said you hadn't seen Molly in years, but people saw you driving to her house the day she disappeared."

"Still doesn't mean I seen her. Look, she called and said I needed to sign some stuff and she didn't have the time or inclination to make the drive out here. Said to meet her at her house that afternoon at three. So I did what I was told but she wasn't there."

"How do you know?"

"I banged on that door for a good ten minutes. Didn't no one answer."

"Did you go down to the dock to see if her boat was there?"

"Didn't even know she had a dock and I'm not interested in walking much, especially across uneven ground."

"But her van was there?"

He nodded. "There was a van parked in front. Why are you asking all these questions?"

"Because the police have ruled her death as suspicious."

He narrowed his eyes and I saw his hand twitch near the trigger. "You saying I did something to Molly?"

"I'm not saying anything, but the insurance company needs to make a decision on her death before they'll pay out. The policy was new. That always brings questions, and the way Molly disappeared and with no body, it's hard to wrap these things up."

"Look, I don't know what kind of game that insurance company is playing, but I went to that agent's office and signed those papers. He said Molly took out the policy herself. I didn't know nothing about it."

"Hmmmm. And you signed those documents in Stan Morgan's office?"

"No. That wasn't his name. Last name Kent. His office was just off the highway before you get into New Orleans. Has a big Coastal Insurance sign right there on the front. Now, I've told you everything I know about this. I suggest you put all that in your report and get to cutting me a check."

He turned around and limped inside.

I headed back to the SUV, unable to keep from smiling.

"I take it we're making a stop at this insurance agency?" Ida Belle asked as she pulled away.

"Definitely," I said. "But first, let's swing by that marina and see if there's anyone around who can talk about Johnny. I would like to make sure everyone has their stories straight."

CHAPTER NINETEEN

WE WAVED at our friends in front of the convenience store as we passed. I could tell by their expressions that they were disappointed we didn't stop, but I was like a dog on the trail of a scent. The turnoff for the marina was halfway between where Silas lived and the NOLA city limits and on the east side, like Silas's house. The road to it was maintained much better than the path to Silas's house, with a topping of rock to help fill in the holes that all the trucks and trailers created. When we exited the trees, we were in a decent-sized parking lot. Three docks stretched into the bayou in front of us, shrimp boats tied to pylons lining each side. A couple of older men were fishing at the end of one of the docks and looked back as we started down the pier.

"Nothing's biting but the heat," the first man said as we approached.

"Then why are you fishing?" Gertie asked.

"Because it beats sitting in the house with my wife," he said. "Been married to the woman for fifty-six years. There's nothing we need to say that hasn't already been said at least ten times."

The other man shook his head. "That's why I never remarried when my Jenny died. Shouldn't be a reason for fishing other than wanting to fish."

The first man reeled in his rod with a sigh. "And unfortunately, it's about time I head back. Got that thing at my daughter-in-law's this afternoon. Grandkid's birthday party. Bunch of screaming kids and sitting around in the heat. My daughter-in-law won't even let us have beer."

"That's just wrong," the second man said.

"Was there something you were needing?" the first man asked as he packed his tackle box.

"I was hoping to find someone who could tell me about the day Johnny Broussard disappeared," I said.

Both men frowned.

"That was bad news," the second man said. "Why do you want to go stirring it up again?"

I pulled out my card and handed it to him. "Because I have a client who asked me to stir things up again."

Both men's eyes widened.

"This is because of what happened to Molly, isn't it?" the first man said. "I said straightaway that it wasn't right—brother and sister going the exact same way. I don't believe in coincidence. Not that much of one, anyway."

"Neither does my client," I said.

The first man nodded. "Well, the guy you want to speak to about Johnny is sitting right here. Mel was the last one to see him. I best get going."

He took off with his tackle box and Mel motioned for me to take a seat. I figured it was more polite than standing over him and grilling him so I sat. Ida Belle and Gertie each sat on a piling.

"I told the police everything I could at the time," Mel said. "What is it you want to know?"

"You were here that day when Johnny took his boat out," I said. "Was anyone else here?"

He shook his head. "The commercial guys didn't even bother coming out, not with that kind of weather coming round. And the fishermen that thought they'd give it a try anyway had all packed up and left before I did."

"You weren't ready to give up?" I asked.

He gave me a sheepish look. "To be honest, as soon as everyone left, I reeled in and pulled out a book. I'd rather read than fish anyway, but you can't let this lot know things like that. When the storm clouds started rolling in, I packed up."

"And you saw Johnny when you were in your vehicle," I said. "Where were you parked?"

"I was parked at the back of the lot over there in the corner," he said. "My doctor gets onto me about walking, and since I'm not one to go walk around for no reason, I started parking away from things. Probably doesn't make a bit of difference but it gets the doctor off my back."

"And where did Johnny park?"

"Right close to the dock. I thought at first that maybe he'd come to grab something off his boat. I mean, the weather wasn't fit for shrimping and Johnny knew that better than anyone."

"Was it raining by then?" I asked.

"Not yet but it was dark like evening and it was sure coming. The wind had already picked up. But when he got on the boat, he untied it from the dock. I started my vehicle and he looked my direction and lifted a hand. Then he went to the wheel to start her up and left. I watched him go up the bayou a ways and then it started to come down, so I got out of there myself before the road got muddy."

"And you're sure it was him?"

"'Course. I know everyone's truck and their boat and Johnny's a big guy. Biggest guy on the docks. Besides, he was wearing that slicker his sister bought him. Bright purple stripes. Took a lot of razzing from the guys but couldn't no one talk him out of wearing it. Every time someone tried to make something of it, he just grinned and told them they were jealous. That boy and his sister were thick as thieves."

"Could you see his face?"

"Don't suppose I could exactly but who else would it be? It was his truck, his slicker, his boat, body size was right, and he waved."

"Was he carrying anything? Pulling a cooler maybe?"

"Nothing that I could see."

"Did you take part in the search?"

He frowned. "Yeah. That was a bad deal. I still don't understand. I guess I thought maybe he needed to move the boat. Take it for a repair or gas it up, even though I'm sure those things could have waited. But I never thought he'd head into the lake. Nobody did."

"But that's where the boat was found?"

He nodded. "Got hung up on a sunken boat along the bank. Tide pushed it in and then it got wedged on top of the wreckage."

"How far is the lake from here?"

"Not far. Just take this channel north about two miles, then you come around right another mile or so and you hit the lake."

"What do you think happened?" I asked.

"They said he must have hit his head on something. They found a bloody glove in the bathroom in the sink and it was Johnny's blood on it. They figure he cracked his head and went to check it then went back out on deck and fell over somehow. Could have been dizzy, balance off, if he'd cracked it good."

"And is that a reasonable assumption?"

"Sure. Plenty of things on a boat that a head wouldn't fare well against. And most people don't think a lake can get rough, but I've seen waters out there look like the Gulf when a storm is pushing against the tide. Anything is possible, even for an experienced man like Johnny."

I nodded. "Your friend didn't seem satisfied with that conclusion."

"None of us are, really. But truth be told, that's probably more about how much we dislike Silas than anything else. He was never a good daddy to those kids. We all knew it but wasn't nothing we could do about it. Johnny being so young, I figure he never thought about things like inheritance but I sure wish he would have. Angel should have gotten his things. Not Silas. That's what Johnny would have wanted."

"I'm sure you're right, but like you said, he didn't set it up legally and with them not being married..."

Mel nodded. "I tell you what, though. It prompted a lot of people to get their affairs in order, especially those working on the water. You never know what can happen. If a man like Johnny can get bested by water, then people start paying more attention."

"Then I guess one good thing came of it," I said. "I appreciate you talking to me."

"You know anything about what happened to Molly?" he asked.

"Probably not any more than you've heard," I said. "The sheriff's department has ruled her disappearance suspicious, though."

"But no body's been found."

"No, sir. I and my friends here worked on the search ourselves. Most everyone with a boat did. I can't tell you how much we all wanted a different outcome."

His eyes widened a bit. "Didn't realize you knew her

personally. I was real sorry to hear about it. We all were. If there's anything I can do, you'll let me know, right? Melvin Thibodeaux. I'm in the phone book."

I was somewhat charmed that he referred to himself as in the phone book. "I will. And thank you for talking to us. If you can think of anything else—no matter how insignificant it might seem—give me a call. Or if you ever need my help yourself."

He nodded and stuck my card in his shirt pocket. "I hope you find something. Anything that can explain why two good people had to go that way."

He stared out over the water and I could tell his thoughts were on Molly and Johnny as we left. As we headed out, we were all silent for a bit. Mel's recounting had been somewhat somber and had reminded us once again that people felt the loss of Molly now and still hadn't stopped feeling the loss of her brother.

"Well, that was a dead end," Gertie said, then sighed. "And that was a horrible way to put it."

"But accurate," Ida Belle said.

I stared out the window, recalling everything Mel said and trying to find something that led to an aha moment. Unfortunately, I was coming up short.

"You get anything from that?" Ida Belle asked me.

"No," I said. "I had this wild thought that maybe the tax assessor was wrong about the phone call and Silas had killed Johnny somewhere else, then carried him onto the boat to get rid of the body. But Mel nixed that theory by saying he didn't have anything with him."

"I don't think Silas could have gotten a body down that dock and into the boat," Ida Belle said. "Not with his health issues."

"Probably not," I said.

Ida Belle shook her head. "It's looking more and more like Johnny took that boat out and had some sort of freak accident. Especially with finding his blood on that glove."

"Do you really think he was going shrimping?" I asked. "In that weather?"

"No," Ida Belle said. "But we don't know what else might have been going on with him. Maybe he took the boat out to think. Plenty of people do. He probably figured he would be fine in the storm as long as he was in the cabin and secured somewhere or in the middle of the lake where he couldn't be lodged against something underwater."

"That isn't the worst idea," Gertie said. "It sounds like the boat was where he felt the most comfortable. If he had something to contemplate, then a storm might not be a deterrent."

"But Angel didn't say anything about contemplation," I said. "She said he was going to work in the garage."

"Maybe the contemplation was about Angel and he didn't want to do it at home," Ida Belle said.

"Maybe so," I said. "I guess it doesn't matter in the big scheme of things. He went out, he died, and the only person who benefited couldn't have done it unless he turned into Superman and the Invisible Man."

"I'd be okay with those as long as we could prove he did it," Gertie said.

I slumped down in my seat. "Me too."

CHAPTER TWENTY

THE INSURANCE AGENCY was easy to locate. In fact, we spotted the sign from the service road. Based on the hours printed on the door, the office was open so we all headed inside. No one was at the desk up front and based on the layer of dust on the top, I wondered if it was even used. There were two doors behind the desk. I figured one was probably to the agent's office and another to a restroom. That would be about the minimum amount of space to run the business. I was contemplating knocking on both doors when the door to the left opened and a gentleman poked his head out.

Age somewhere between Gertie and the grim reaper, five foot ten, a hundred fifty pounds including the suit and dress shoes, maybe the wallet. No muscle tone that I could see. Threat level less than zero unless I considered possibly having to perform CPR a threat.

I'm not sure if it took him a second to figure out there were really people standing there or that he should say something. Finally, he stepped out of the office, his hand extended toward me.

"Pardon my rudeness," he said. "I wasn't expecting anyone

so you surprised me. You know how it is when you get buried in actuarial tables."

"More riveting than golf," I said.

He nodded. "Isn't it though? My name is Norbert Kent. How can I help you?"

Deciding the PI hired by insurance companies was my best route of getting confidential information out of Kent, I pulled out my ID and a business card and handed the card to Kent. He leaned in to inspect my ID, his eyes growing even larger behind his thick glasses.

"As you know, the company hires PIs to check into policy claims from time to time, especially if anything appears irregular," I said. "These are my assistants, Ida Belle and Gertie. We're doing some fieldwork on a policy issued on Molly Broussard."

He shook his head. "I don't recall that name."

"Sorry," I said. "Mary Olivia Broussard."

"Yes, of course," he said. "That wasn't long ago. Come into my office and I'll try to clear up any questions the company has. Has something happened to Ms. Broussard?"

"Unfortunately," I said as we walked in and sat in chairs opposite his desk. "She's gone missing from her boat."

"Oh, how horrible. This can be a lovely place to live but also a dangerous one."

"Very true. Did you issue the policy for Ms. Broussard?"

"I'm the only one working in this office so there's no other option," he said. "Transferring to a small office was my idea of semiretirement."

I wondered briefly if his plan was to move from retirement straight to hospice but figured it was rude to ask.

"So you met with Ms. Broussard to write the policy?" I asked, making sure I was crystal clear on everything.

"Of course," he said. "That's the way it's done at Coastal. You always meet with an agent."

"Can you describe her to me?" I asked.

He shifted in his chair, looking more than a bit uncomfortable. "Well, I don't wish to sound indelicate but I suppose this is necessary. She wasn't a petite woman. Taller than me and large-boned. But the thing I remember most was her hair. It stood up straight on the top of her head. I'd never seen anything quite like it. And it was painted bright purple. I remember having to work harder to focus because it was so distracting."

I pulled out my phone and showed him a picture. "Like this?"

He nodded. "That's her. Very interesting woman. She said she used to fight in a cage. I don't understand the meaning of that but apparently she changed to cooking, which seemed a much nicer pursuit."

"So Ms. Broussard asked you to draw up the policy and she specifically asked for her father, Silas Broussard, to be the beneficiary?" I asked.

"Let me see," he said, and tapped on his keyboard. "Yes, that's correct. I remember now, Ms. Broussard said her father's health wasn't good and he was getting on in years. If something were to happen to her, he wouldn't be capable of running her business, so she wanted to ensure he was taken care of another way."

I glanced over at Ida Belle, who raised an eyebrow.

"So did Ms. Broussard indicate she was taking care of her father monetarily at that time?" I asked.

"I don't recall that she said that outright but that's what I took away from the conversation," he said.

"Did Ms. Broussard and her father ever come here together?" I asked.

"No," he said. "I had the original meeting with Ms. Broussard to go over the options and help her make her selections, then I contacted Mr. Broussard to come in and sign the documents."

"Is that normal?" I asked. "That a beneficiary has to sign?"

"I'm afraid in Mr. Broussard's case it was necessary. He can't write, so I needed to do some additional identification items so that no one could make a false claim in the event that something happened to Ms. Broussard."

"So what do you do for identification?" I asked.

"A driver's license or state identification and I take a few pictures for the file," he said.

I drummed my fingers on my chair. All of this sounded completely aboveboard unless you took into account the fact that Molly was supposed to hate her father. Then the train ran completely off the tracks.

"Did you get a copy of Ms. Broussard's driver's license as well?" I asked.

"Of course," he said.

"May I see it?"

"I really shouldn't," he said. "If you want documents, they should come from corporate."

"I only want to take a peek."

He opened a drawer in the credenza behind him and pulled out a file, flipped a few pages over, then handed it to me. Sure enough, there was Molly's face on her state-issued driver's license. I made a mental note of the number to verify later but the license looked like the real deal. I flipped the pages over and saw the last page contained her signature. I looked at the signature, then flipped back to her license. Then did it once again.

They didn't match.

Molly's license contained a scribble, then mostly a straight line. The insurance policy had a very definite signature in loopy, round lettering.

I gave Gertie an elbow to the side while Kent was fiddling with his file and she glared at me. I looked at Kent, then the door, and she got the hint.

"May I use your restroom?" Gertie asked.

"Of course," Kent said. "It's just next door."

Gertie stepped out and was back a couple seconds later. "The door seems to be locked," she said.

"Oh that thing," Kent said as he rose. "I keep meaning to change that doorknob."

As soon as he exited the room, I pulled out my phone and took pictures of the signature page and Molly's driver's license. Ida Belle motioned to me that Kent was returning, and I shoved my phone in my bra, flipped the pages over, and put the file back on his desk.

"Well, Mr. Kent," I said and rose. "I think that's all I need. Thank you for your time."

We all headed out of the office and waited in front of the reception desk for Gertie to exit the restroom.

"I really appreciate you seeing us without an appointment," I said loudly.

The doorknob on the restroom jiggled but the door didn't open. It jiggled some more and finally Gertie's voice sounded through the wood.

"Now I'm locked *in*."

———

IT TOOK another couple minutes of finagling with the crappy lock to get Gertie out of the restroom, then another minute of apologies from Kent before we were finally back on the road to Sinful.

"I hope whatever you wanted was worth it," Gertie said as Ida Belle guided the SUV down the highway. "He has this absolutely horrible room deodorizer in there. I'll probably have to take a Benadryl and smell coffee all night."

"Smelled like ragweed and dirty socks," Ida Belle said. "The odor rushed out of the bathroom the same time you did. I held my breath through all of Kent's apologizing. Thought I was going to have to make a bolt for it."

"It was rather off," I agreed. "Maybe his smell is starting to go."

"More like gone for a long, long time," Gertie said. "So?"

"Right," I said and told them about the signatures. "I know people don't always sign correctly, but this was such a big change that I thought it needed some looking into."

"Sure," Gertie said. "But we need Molly's signature to check against."

"I was hoping Ida Belle might have it," I said. "The catering contract, maybe?"

Ida Belle frowned. "She never sent it. I guess she went out on her boat before doing the scan."

I sighed. "Crap."

"There might be another way," Ida Belle said. "Sometimes Molly picked up the odd item at the General Store. If she paid by credit card, Walter would have a receipt with her signature."

"Perfect," Gertie said. "No way Walter is going to say no— not to the two of you."

An hour later we were standing in front of Walter at the cash register in the General Store and he was shaking his head.

"I'm not getting in the middle of this," he said.

"The middle of what?" Ida Belle asked. "You don't even know why we're asking."

"And I don't want to know," he said. "And as long as I don't get involved, then I never have to answer to my nephew about why I got my nose in with you three over a law enforcement issue."

"Look," I said. "This isn't what Carter is looking into. It's something else. Yes, it involves Molly but not her death."

He narrowed his eyes at me. "Then what does it involve?"

"Fraud," I said. "And unless you want to have to explain everything to Carter, then that's probably all you want me to say."

He stared at me for several seconds, then sighed. "I just got a load of toilet paper in that I need to get off pallets in the back. I don't suppose you three can watch the store while I do that? If anyone comes in wanting a copy of an order for the last week, they're in the box under the counter. I haven't had a chance to file them yet."

"Thank you," I called to his retreating back.

"Didn't do anything," he grumbled as he went.

I jumped behind the counter and pulled out the box, then shoved a stack of receipts at Ida Belle and Gertie. We all started flipping through them as quickly as we could, praying that no one needed to buy something and wondered what the heck we were doing.

"Got it!" Gertie yelled and handed me the receipt.

I pulled out my phone and took a quick shot of it just as the bell above the door jangled. Ida Belle shoved the receipts at me, and I used my arm to pull them all in the box, barely getting it back under the counter before Celia stepped up, frowning.

"Don't tell me Walter has left you in charge," she said.

"As a matter of fact, he has," I said. "Is there something I can help you with—prune juice maybe? You have that blocked look."

"How about the jaws of life?" Gertie said. "We can get that stick out of her butt."

Celia turned beet red and tried to reply but only managed a sputter. Finally she whirled around and headed out of the shop, slamming the door behind her. Walter appeared a couple seconds later and I gave him the side-eye.

"You knew Celia was coming in, didn't you?" I asked. "That's why you let us dig through the receipts."

Walter grabbed a rag and started polishing the cash register. "I don't know what you're talking about."

Gertie grinned. "Well played."

"Do you ladies need any groceries to go with your illegal activities?" he asked.

"No, I think we're good," I said. "We have illegal booze, Cuban cigars, and the usual store of dynamite."

"You have Cuban cigars?" he asked.

I waved a hand in dismissal. "You wouldn't be interested in breaking the law. Forget I said anything."

"The law isn't exactly up-to-date on certain things," Walter said.

Gertie shook her head. "So easily converted. Today, it's cigars. Tomorrow, it will be knockoff purses and hand grenade displays in the store windows."

Walter drew himself up straight. "I would *never* sell purses."

"Thanks, Walter," I said as I headed for the door. "We'll let you get back to business."

As soon as we climbed into Ida Belle's SUV, I pulled up the photos and showed them the signatures.

"They don't match," Gertie said. "Not even close."

"Nope," I said. "The signature on the insurance policy is fat and loopy. Molly's signature on the receipt is narrow and has points at the top and bottom of the letters."

"I know people's handwriting differs at times," Ida Belle said, "but this isn't even close."

"So what the heck is going on?" Gertie asked.

"I'm not sure," I said.

"But you have a guess," Gertie said.

I nodded. "My guess is that Silas got a fake license for Molly and had someone pose as her to take out the policy."

"If he's in with bookies, they'd know people who could get that done," Ida Belle said.

"But he'd have to pay the premiums," Gertie said. "And he was broke."

"Maybe he didn't plan on being broke for very long," Ida Belle said.

"But Kent ID'd Molly from that photo you showed him," Gertie said. "And his description was dead on."

"Was it?" I asked. "He seemed mostly taken in by the hair and that's the easiest part to fake. So a large, tall woman with a wig could pull it off. Kent didn't strike me as the most observant person."

"You think everyone over the age of forty is half blind," Gertie groused.

"No," I said. "I think you need to up your prescription. I think Kent was so distracted by the hair and her size that he probably didn't look closely at anything else."

"But who would Silas get to help him?" Gertie asked. "He hates everyone and the feeling appears to be mutual."

"I didn't say it had to be a friend," I said. "Like Ida Belle said, given his gambling habits, he probably had access to all types of people needing a quick payout."

"I can't see him going to all that trouble unless he knew something was going to happen to Molly soon," Gertie said.

I nodded. "He definitely had motive and since we know he was on-site that afternoon, he had opportunity."

"So what's the problem?" Gertie asked.

"I'm stumped on the how," I said. "And unfortunately, Dexter and Marissa are a much neater fit in the how slot."

Gertie sighed. "You know, on the television shows, no one could have done it. In our case, everyone could have done it. I'm not sure which is worse."

Ida Belle nodded. "I hate to sound like Gertie but what now?"

I stared down Main Street and blew out a breath. "I don't know. Maybe I need to sit on it a while."

"Then I'll drop you off," Ida Belle said as she pulled away. "I'm going home and washing my SUV. A real wash."

"I probably have some canning to do," Gertie said.

"No, you don't," Ida Belle said. "It's hot as Hades and everything is dead. You won't be canning for months. What you will be doing is helping me wash my SUV."

"But I hate washing cars," Gertie said.

"How would you know?" Ida Belle asked. "You've never washed yours."

"I've washed my car," Gertie protested.

"Who was president when it happened?" Ida Belle asked.

"Morgan Freeman," Gertie said.

"Good movie," I said and Ida Belle gave me a cutting look.

"What?" I asked. "It was a good movie."

She pulled into my drive and gestured at me. "Get out. Get on with your thinking. Somebody's got to figure this mess out and I don't think it's going to be me."

"I might figure it out," Gertie said.

"If we're waiting on you, we're all doomed," Ida Belle said. "Call later and let us know if you have anything."

I nodded and jumped out of the SUV. I was going to head

inside, take off my bra, pull on the thinnest pair of shorts and tank top I owned, then grab a beer and park my butt in my lawn chair under the oak tree and stare at the water until everything was clear. Except the water, of course. That would take a miracle.

I was beginning to think this case would as well.

CHAPTER TWENTY-ONE

I WAS on my fourth beer and still no closer to an answer on the case when Carter dropped into the chair next to me. He pointed at the empty bag of Cheetos and the equally not-full bag of Oreos and shook his head.

"You ate dinner without me," he said.

"That's what happens when you don't keep regular schedules."

He smiled. "That's what happens when you're stewing over something. It's ninety-five degrees out here and you're collecting quite a pile of debris there."

"This is just from the last hour," I said. "And I probably shouldn't admit that."

"Impressive. We have a hot dog eating contest at the fall fair. You could win a year's supply of wieners."

I made a face. "Why is it always hot dogs? If it was funnel cake, I'd be first to sign up."

"If it was funnel cake, diabetes would clog up the funeral home in a single day."

I studied him for a moment. Something was different. His tone was lighter. His body looser.

"You made an arrest," I said.

He smiled. "The DA will make an official announcement tomorrow morning. Dexter and Marissa have been arrested on suspicion of murder. They were transferred to New Orleans for holding."

So many emotions raced through me that I wasn't sure which one to dwell on. I was thrilled that an arrest had been made. That Molly's death wouldn't go down as just another unfortunate accident. But I was also disappointed that Silas would be collecting on a daughter he had abused. Life simply wasn't fair.

"Was what I had on them enough for the DA?" I asked. "Or did you find more?"

"I found the longbow," Carter said. "And Dexter's finger-prints were on the keys to Molly's small boat."

"That's damning but is it enough?"

"Ha. Get this. Those idiots were practicing her signature. I found some drafts of documents on a laptop. It looks like they were going to try to fake a will."

"Molly didn't have a will," I said. "I know that for certain now. I found the attorney she talked to about it, but she never followed up. I'll get you his information for the DA."

"That would be great. How did you find him?"

"Long story that goes back to the Great Bear Chase."

I looked out over the bayou and frowned.

"I thought you would be happier about this," he said.

"I am happy. I mean as happy as you can be when a good person is taken out before their time."

"But?"

"But I'm bent that Molly's father will inherit. He treated those kids horribly. Every person I talked to said so."

"I don't doubt that for a minute."

"And I know he was planning something. I just think

264

Dexter and Marissa beat him to it. Maybe by a matter of minutes."

"What do you mean?"

I told him about the insurance policy and showed him the signatures. He flipped the images back and forth, frowning the entire time.

"Is there anything you can do about that?" I asked. "At the very least, he shouldn't be collecting on a life insurance policy that was fraudulently made."

"Let me check something," he said and pulled out his cell phone. He made a call, giving the person on the other line the number on Molly's driver's license, then hung up.

"If he's committing fraud, he's doing a darn good job of it," Carter said. "The driver's license number is correct. I'll look up the license when I'm back in the office, but this looks authentic and the picture on the license is definitely Molly. You said the insurance agent was positive that this is the person he worked with, correct?"

"Yes, but that doesn't mean he's right. What if Molly's license was stolen so that someone could do this? Or it's a good fake? A copy of a good fake is hard to pick out. Silas is just as desperate for money as Dexter is. Maybe the whole thing was a setup."

Carter shook his head. "With the issuing agent ID'ing Molly as the client, and a valid ID on file, you'd have a hard time proving anything."

"You think I'm reaching."

"I don't think you're reaching. I think you don't want a despicable man to profit from the death of a child he never cared about."

I sighed. "Reaching."

He shrugged. "Maybe. Or maybe you just want things to be fair. I have the same issues and unfortunately, this line of work shoves just how unfair things are in my face every week."

"Don't get me wrong, I'm happy that Dexter and Marissa have been arrested. I'm happy to have answers for my client and hopefully justice for Molly. I guess I just wanted all the bad guys to go down."

"I can talk to the insurance company, give them my concerns. They might pay eventually, but they can drag things out a while. And if I know insurance companies, they'll be glad of any excuse to exercise their right to do just that."

"Thanks. That's something at least."

"And maybe they'll launch their own investigation."

"What are they going to find that I didn't?"

"Likely nothing."

"So in the end, Silas still wins."

"Maybe we can hope he dies before he can collect."

I shook my head. "The good guys are never that lucky."

———

WITH THE ARREST in his rearview mirror, Carter stayed the night. We had leftovers and polished off the rest of my beer, then we both showered and slept like dead people. He was up and off early to finish up paperwork and take care of things that had slid while he was working on Molly's case. I was up early but only off to the kitchen, where I poured coffee and sent a text to Ida Belle and Gertie to convene whenever they were ready. I hadn't filled them in last night. It was news that would hold and besides, I still wasn't clear how I felt about it.

I'd hoped a good night's sleep would put it all into perspective but no such luck.

They arrived about thirty minutes later, Gertie wearing Band-Aids on three fingers and sporting a large bruise on her right biceps. I pointed at the injuries as she poured coffee and she gave Ida Belle a dirty look.

"I broke three nails cleaning that car of hers," Gertie said. "And they're so far back, I don't even think a manicurist can fix them for the party tonight."

"And the bruise?" I asked.

"Ida Belle popped me with the hose when I rubbed the wax up and down instead of in circles."

"That was an accident," Ida Belle said.

"That's what she says," Gertie said, not looking remotely convinced. "So Carter stayed the night. Does that mean you have arrest news?"

I stared at her in dismay. "How did you know that?"

She shrugged. "People see things. They talk."

"It was just last night and the sun is barely up," I said.

"There's not a lot to talk about here," Ida Belle said.

"But we're changing all of that tonight!" Gertie said, finally perking up.

Ida Belle looked as though Gertie had just announced a funeral service.

"So who's in jail?" Ida Belle asked.

"Dexter and Marissa," I said.

"Well, we figured that was coming," Ida Belle said. "With what we found, and I'm guessing a search warrant produced more."

"Did they flip on each other?" Gertie asked.

"No," I said. "Carter said they're still denying any involvement in Molly's disappearance."

Ida Belle frowned. "That's surprising. I didn't take either for a pillar of strength. I was just vacillating on which would give it up first."

"Yeah, surprised me too," I said.

Ida Belle studied me for a bit. "For someone who provided

the information that set all of this in motion, you don't look very happy."

I shrugged. "I am. I guess. I don't know. I mean, I'm glad Molly will get justice and Dexter and Marissa will pay..."

"But?" Ida Belle asked.

"But there's still so many unanswered questions," I said. "Things that don't fit. And there's still the issue of Silas getting paid out of all of this."

"Did you tell Carter about the signatures?" Gertie asked.

"Yes, and he said he'd talk to the insurance agency. He's pretty sure they'd be happy for an excuse not to pay out or delay at least. But with the DA making a murder case, it will be easier for Silas to push Molly's assets through the legal system."

Gertie sighed. "Darn it. I didn't even think about that. If you can get a murder conviction with no body, then I guess you can't exactly hold up the asset distribution."

"Probably not," I said.

"Well, hell," Gertie said. "Now I'm unhappy too."

"We do seem at cross-purposes here," Ida Belle said. "I suppose we just have to go with the truth and let the chips fall."

"If only Molly would have followed up with that attorney," Gertie said.

I nodded. "At least there's that document about the catering business. With any luck, Molly had as many assets as possible under the business."

"I'll bet there's still enough left for Silas to pay his back taxes, though," Ida Belle said. "Our friends at the convenience store will be disappointed. I think they were hoping to get rid of him this time."

"Maybe the insurance company will launch an investigation," I said. "If they can prove fraud then it's possible Silas could go to jail for it."

Ida Belle shook her head. "The insurance company won't take things that far. It's simply not economical. It's much easier to refuse payment based on fraud and then see if Silas sues. And assuming it was all a setup, then he should go quietly away and collect nothing. At least not from them."

Gertie nodded. "And as for the rest of it—maybe we just have to chalk it up to stupidity."

"Maybe," I said. "But just how stupid can people be? If we assume that Dexter and Marissa have been planning to off Molly so that Dexter could take the business, then why did they do it before they had legal documents? I mean, I know Molly wasn't going to sign it over, but why were they just now trying to create fake documents? Why wasn't that already in place before they pulled the trigger...or the longbow, as it was?"

"Perhaps they saw the opportunity and went for it," Ida Belle said. "Maybe collectors were coming down on both of them and they didn't feel they could wait any longer. Maybe they figured they could manufacture the documents as easily after she was dead as before. It's hard to know, really. Dexter is clearly a user and con and Marissa is an addict. You can't attach logic to either of them."

I sighed. "I suppose you're right but man, it's really not satisfying at all, is it?"

"In many ways, no," Ida Belle agreed. "But in others—the most important ones—it is."

"I guess I need to keep reminding myself of those important ones," I said.

"Have you told Nickel yet?" Gertie asked.

"No," I said. "I didn't figure he'd be up and about until later today and I wasn't ready to go over it all last night."

"I would think not with Carter staying over," Gertie said.

"And who told you that?" I asked again.

"We all have our sources," Gertie said.

I narrowed my eyes at her. "You've made friends with Ronald, haven't you?"

She feigned an innocent look. "I'm sure I have no idea what you're talking about."

"Oh good God," Ida Belle said. "Like we needed more crazy in our lives."

"Has he been feeding that gator in my yard?" I asked.

"No," Gertie said.

I stared at her.

"I swear he hasn't," she said. "I mean, he's baked casseroles and stood out there for a while, but he said he hasn't seen Godzilla since that day he ate the terrorist."

"And what about you?" Ida Belle asked.

"I've seen him when I went out fishing," Gertie said. "But across the lake."

"If he gets hungry and lazy, he'll be back here begging," I said.

"Last time we fed him a terrorist," Gertie said. "Maybe he decided he didn't like the menu here."

"I didn't feed him a terrorist," I said. "He just happened to be in my yard."

Gertie shrugged. "He was trying to kill you. Godzilla was hungry. Worked out well for everyone. Except maybe the terrorist."

"Maybe?"

"You were going to shoot him anyway," Gertie said. "It was just a matter of time."

It was a valid point so I couldn't really argue.

"Well, now that this case is closed, I guess we're back to sitting indoors and griping about the heat," I said.

They both frowned.

"Boredom is the worst," Gertie said.

"People can't go and get themselves murdered just so you'll have something to do," Ida Belle said.

"Some of them could," Gertie said. "I could make a list."

———

I LEFT a message for Nickel later in the morning and finally heard back from him just before noon. He was doing cleanup at the bar to prepare for opening that night and asked if I could swing by there to give him an update. I wondered briefly what he planned on telling Whiskey about our meeting, but when I arrived, he told me Whiskey had gone to New Orleans to pick up a shipment of wine that was stuck at the dock because the transport had broken down.

He grinned at me as I walked in the bar.

"Not your usual hangout," he said.

"Oh, I've been here a time or two," I said. "It's...interesting."

"Can get a little crazy."

I shrugged. "I was in the sandbox for most of my missions. This place is like visiting a library compared to combat."

He nodded. "Kinda puts it all in perspective. I'm surprised you're not bored living here, given what you used to do."

"Have you met Gertie?"

He laughed. "You've got a point. Anyway, you said you had an update, and I'd like to get that over with before Whiskey gets back and starts asking questions."

"You're not afraid those guys are going to tattle on you?" I asked, indicating a table of men in the corner.

"They've been here since yesterday. Slept right there in those chairs last night. I'm pretty sure they don't even know where they are or what day it is."

"Okay, well, here's the deal."

I filled him in on everything that I'd discovered—about Dexter and Marissa, the attorney that Molly spoke to, Silas and his back taxes, the insurance agent, the overheard conversation in the motel room. And finally, I told him that Carter had arrested Dexter and Marissa and they were being held in NOLA.

"Wow!" he said when I finished. "The rumors about you weren't joking. I can't believe you found all that out in just a matter of days. And Dexter and Marissa are in jail. I guess that's something."

He sounded about as excited over the news as I was.

"I know," I said and slumped on my stool. "I hate that I couldn't get more on Silas. I really, really dislike the man."

"I think that's pretty much how everyone who's ever met him feels."

"I'm sure. And I know he was up to something with that insurance policy but maybe Dexter and Marissa beat him to the final play."

"Could be," Nickel said. "I guess they was up to plenty themselves. Seems like Molly was walking around with more targets on her back than she had shirt for."

"I know the feeling. The only difference is I was aware I was targeted, and it wasn't by anyone that was supposed to have my back."

"Can't pick your family. And she shouldn't have picked Dexter. But yeah, I wish Silas could have gotten what he has coming. You sure there's nothing else you could come up with there?"

I shook my head. "I wish there was, but I just don't see what it could be. And I covered the old ground too—about Johnny. I was hoping to be able to draw a correlation between the two disappearances."

"You didn't find anything there?"

"Nothing that mattered. I mean, his behavior that day is completely inconsistent with the man people who knew him well described, but based on the timeline alone, I can't see how Silas could have been involved. And that's not even taking into account his physical limitations."

Nickel sighed. "Yeah. That makes sense given how you laid it out. I guess I was just hoping you'd see something that someone else didn't. Or put things together differently and have that moment where you got it and no one else had. You know, like the movies."

"I wish I had done that too."

"Well, I appreciate the heck out of everything you did. I can't imagine anyone else could have done better. So I guess both matters are closed. Now everybody just has to figure out how to live with it."

I nodded. That was the hardest part.

CHAPTER TWENTY-TWO

I DIDN'T DO MUCH the rest of the day. Gertie was busy preparing for the upcoming party, and Ida Belle was probably over at the church praying or begging her doctor to commit her for the weekend. At the very least, infect her with a twenty-four-hour flu. Carter was busy wrapping up the paperwork on the case and I had absolutely nothing to do or avoid. Well, except laundry. I always had laundry to avoid.

I supposed I should have been happy but the truth was I was pouting. I couldn't do anything to bring Molly back but I was really hoping I could balance the scales just a little. Silas inheriting completely ruled out the possibility of remotely fair and I was pitching a toddler fit. Internally, of course. Merlin, who had sensed my aggravation and unrest, had promptly asked to go outside after breakfast and I hadn't seen him since. The fact that he wanted to be outside in a thousand-degree heat rather than inside with the AC and sleeping on something cushy spoke volumes about my mood.

I managed to pace, sleep, and sigh away the afternoon and finally headed up for a shower. I blow-dried my shoulder-length hair—finally my own and not extensions—and threw on

jeans, tennis shoes, and a T-shirt. I knew Gertie would probably come in a ball gown or something so slinky everyone else
spent the entire night blushing, but I was shooting for
comfortable. When Gertie was involved, you never knew if
you might need to run or fight, plus jeans allowed for easy
access to my gun and my cell phone.

I arrived thirty minutes early, in case Gertie needed some
help setting up, and thought for a minute that I was late. Vehicles lined the street on both sides and I could already hear
music pumping from inside. Gertie had apparently foreseen
the parking issue and had put cones in her driveway with a sign
indicating that it was reserved for Ida Belle and me. I jumped
out to move a cone on one side, then pulled in and parked. I
didn't bother knocking because no one would have heard it
over the music. Instead, I said a quick prayer and walked
inside.

Sinful Ladies Society members swarmed like ants, putting
up streamers and setting up snack stations. They all looked
over as I entered and called out greetings, wearing big smiles. I
located the stereo and turned the music down just a bit and
shook my head at them.

"I'm surprised you guys are so happy given that your fear-
less leader is crossing to the dark side," I said.

Myrtle waved a hand in dismissal. "This is Ida Belle and
Walter we're talking about. For all intents and purposes they've
been dedicated to each other forever. Besides, Ida Belle's too
old for Walter to change her."

"I'm pretty sure Jesus couldn't have changed her when she
was five," I said.

The ladies laughed and one of them shoved a container of
mixed nuts at me.

"Dump those in the pink bowls that you see around the
living room and kitchen area," she said. "We're spreading

things out so everyone doesn't have to lump in one place to get a snack."

I distributed the nuts, working my way through the living room and back to the kitchen. Gertie was busy taking mini pizzas off a cookie sheet and putting them on a serving tray. A bevy of other goodies were scattered across the countertops.

I drew up short in order to examine her outfit.

The good news was Ida Belle didn't have to worry about Gertie wearing the camo miniskirt to her wedding. The bad news was she was wearing it now. And that whole tuck-under thing wasn't working too well as Gertie had a typical white woman booty, which meant very little. The skirt ended a couple inches below the relevant parts but as she bent over to pick up a wayward pizza, I saw that all bets were off.

"Doesn't lime green clash with camo?" I asked.

Gertie straightened up and whirled around. "How did you know my panties were lime green?"

"How do you think?"

The rest of the outfit was just as scandalous. The tank top was black but cut so low that her panty-matching bra showed off a good inch of fabric and pushed-up cleavage, and it fit like a wetsuit would, leaving not even a mole to the imagination. She was wearing a wig of straight silver and pink strands that hung in a blunt cut at her chin. Her eyes were covered with silver glitter, and a row of lime-green sequins rested just beneath the eyebrow.

But her shoes were the real kicker. They were thigh-high black patent leather boots with a platform heel, giving her an extra six inches. I gave her thirty minutes max before she twisted an ankle and spent the rest of the night on crutches.

"How in the world did you get in those?" I asked, pointing to the boots.

"Myrtle helped. Myrtle and a little baby oil."

"Wouldn't that make your feet slide?"

"No. I got the boots a half size too small to help with the slipping. Trust me, I've done my research."

"Been talking online to strippers again?"

"They have a lot of beauty tips. I mean, they have to look perfect everywhere and without the benefit of filters and Photoshop."

"Where's Francis?" I asked, changing the subject. The last time Gertie had got going on the online stripper group she lurked in, I'd received entirely too much information about hair removal, and not from the locations you might discuss with other people.

"I moved him into one of the upstairs bedrooms," she said. "I'm afraid someone might accidentally let him out."

So Francis had the best seat in the house.

"Looks like no one will go hungry," I said.

"Oh, this is just the snacks," Gertie said. "I've got a truckload of barbecue coming."

"What can I do?" I asked.

Gertie shoved a wineglass at me and poured us both a drink. "You can have a quick drink with me and toast my best friend finally marrying the only good man left in Sinful besides Carter."

I clinked her glass and smiled. "I can drink to that."

Gertie tossed back a drink and sniffed.

"You're not going to get weepy on us, are you?" I asked.

"Maybe a little, but as soon as the games start, I'll be having too much fun to be emotional. And there's the big surprise."

I wasn't even going to ask.

By the time Ida Belle arrived, everyone else was already there and had thrown back a glass of something. A huge cheer went up when she walked through the door and even Ida Belle couldn't help smiling at the greeting. Before she could make it two steps inside, someone had put a sash over her shoulder that read *The Bride*. Another lady gave her a tiara and a glass of wine. I took a picture because I didn't give anything but the wine two seconds before they disappeared.

By the time Ida Belle made it to the chair reserved for her in the middle of the living room, Gertie was wearing the tiara, the sash was hanging on the lamp, and the wine was consumed. She took a seat and waved for a refill on her glass while I slipped onto the ottoman next to her.

"I haven't been this nervous since my last CIA mission," I said.

"Tell me about it," Ida Belle said. "Vietnam didn't have as many potential land mines as this party."

"Ladies!" Gertie yelled, and turned down the stereo. Everyone finally quieted and Gertie raised her glass. "To my best friend, Ida Belle. I never thought this day would come but here we are. And I couldn't be happier for you. To Ida Belle and Walter—may they live happily ever after!"

We all cheered and clinked glasses. Ida Belle looked a little concerned with the 'happily ever after' part of the speech, but then she had the Hallmark channel blocked on her cable service, so it wasn't surprising.

Gertie clapped her hands to get attention again. "And now, for the first game of the night—pin the macho on the male!"

A big cheer went up even though I doubted anyone knew what she was talking about. I wasn't sure I wanted to know but I was equally sure I didn't have a choice.

"Come on up, Ida Belle," Gertie called.

Ida Belle rose from her chair but the suspicious look was already in place. When she got to where Gertie was standing, Gertie pulled out a blindfold.

"No way," Ida Belle said.

"It's like pin the tail on the donkey," Gertie said.

"Oh no," I mumbled, having figured out exactly what was about to happen.

Ida Belle was running behind on her Gertie comprehension and finally allowed herself to be masked. Once she was blindfolded, Gertie put a poster of a naked man, missing a vital part, on her wall and then put the missing part, complete with double-sided tape, in Ida Belle's hand.

I saw Ida Belle stiffen and took a picture before the moment was over, and I had acted none too soon. Ida Belle tore off the blindfold and stared at the part, her eyes widening, then let out a yell and chunked the macho across the room. Francis, apparently deciding the party downstairs was more interesting than his quiet space upstairs, chose that moment to break out and fly into the living room. The macho hit him right in the chest and stuck. Francis, thinking he was under attack, flapped frantically around the room as half the women chased him and the other half collapsed on the floor in laughter.

I snagged some gelatin shots and passed two to Ida Belle before downing one myself.

"This is going to be a long night," she said.

After the macho fell off Francis, he retreated to his perch in the kitchen. Gertie gave him a grape and he seemed somewhat mollified, although he spent a good minute telling everyone about the hot place they were going to. Gertie ditched the boots in favor of tennis shoes and the party continued. The rest of the games mostly involved drinking and no body parts, so everything was reasonably calm.

Then at 10:00 p.m. Gertie called for everyone to head onto the back porch because it was time for the big surprise. Ida Belle and I were half drunk already, but we took one more shot for good measure before heading outside. Gertie's back porch looked as if it had collected every old folding chair from all of southern Louisiana. Ida Belle and I were directed to reserved seats in the middle of the porch, right in front of the steps. I was somewhat fearful because it appeared as if Gertie had constructed a stage in the middle of her backyard, but I couldn't quite make it out in the dark.

Once everyone had a chair or a place to squat on the lawn, Gertie went up to the stage and I heard a familiar hissing sound. A couple seconds later, fireworks lit up the sky over Gertie's backyard and exploded into a million colors. All the women yelled as though they'd never seen fireworks before. When the last of the embers had flickered out, Gertie turned on the lights. And I mean lights. Flood lights illuminated the stage in her yard as if she were hosting a concert. Then the music started—loud, thumping music, pumped into the air by enormous speakers on each side of the stage.

"How long until the cops get here?" I asked Ida Belle.

"They're not coming," Myrtle said, overhearing my question. "Carter already told dispatch to ignore all calls originating about this address."

"Smart," I said. "Carter doesn't want any part of the things happening here."

"I'm not sure *I* want any part of things happening here," Ida Belle said. "That stage scares me. I'm not doing karaoke."

"I don't think Gertie would qualify karaoke as a big surprise," I said.

"That scares me even more," Ida Belle said.

I nodded.

Gertie reached down and grabbed a microphone and tapped it, causing all of us to cover our ears with our hands.

"Sorry," she said. "Is that better?"

We all nodded.

"Tonight," she said, "we celebrate an occasion that none of

us ever thought would happen. And there's no way I was letting this moment pass without throwing the most exciting party I knew how to put together. So without further ado, I present to you—Tricky Ricky!"

As Gertie ran off stage, the music started up again and then smoke wafted from below the stage, the lights dancing in it. Then the lights changed colors and started flashing, and a man wearing a black suit and cape walked onto the stage.

Midtwenties. Six foot two. A hundred eighty pounds of nothing but muscle. The suit was kind of tight. And he was gorgeous. Should have called himself Pretty Ricky. Threat level high for all husbands whose wives got a look at Ricky. Fortunately for husbands, this group was devoutly single. Probably unfortunate for Ricky.

There was a split second of silence and then the women cheered. Ricky walked to the center of the stage and in a single move, yanked off his entire suit, revealing red bikini bottoms and a really great set of abs. The women went wild. Ida Belle gripped my arm and leaned in.

"We might have a stampede," she said.

"I might start it," I said.

She stared at me for a second, then laughed. "He *is* really good-looking."

I nodded. As far as big surprises went, Gertie might have finally hit a home run.

Ricky started dancing and then paused and we saw what the cape was for—apparently, Ricky was also a magician. First, he pulled flowers out of...well, somewhere. I didn't want to speculate. The women went absolutely crazy when he jumped off the stage and knelt on one knee to offer the flowers to Ida Belle.

I swear she looked as though she was blushing.

Then he jumped up and straddled her chair and all doubt was

removed. It was hot outside but Ricky was sending the temperature into the stratosphere. Ida Belle kept scooting lower and lower in her chair as Ricky gyrated above her and Gertie ran up and shoved some dollar bills in her hand. She looked momentarily confused, then her eyes widened and she shoved the bills at me.

No way was I going to be any part of stripper gossip, so I shoved the bills back at Gertie, who gladly took them and wooted before stuffing them into the back of Ricky's bikini. By this time, all of the women were either on their feet or standing on their chairs, creating an orthopedist's dream situation. No way this night was going to end without someone breaking a hip.

Ricky made a round across the porch, dancing with different women and giving everyone a thrill when he took off his cape and tossed it into the audience. I couldn't help but laugh when Marie, one of Ida Belle and Gertie's best friends and the current mayor of Sinful, snatched the cape up before the other women could grab it and then promptly threw it around her own shoulders.

A second later, the worn-out slats broke on Myrtle's chair and she fell right through it. Fortunately, she didn't break a hip, but much hilarity ensued as women crowded around, trying to get the chair off of her. Finally, Gertie broke out a drill and unscrewed the frame. Everyone cheered and Ricky went back on stage to finish his show. Gertie came back out during the cheering, caught sight of Marie in the cape, and mistaking her for Ricky, gave her a big slap on the rear.

I looked over at Ida Belle and grinned.

She struggled to keep a straight face but finally started laughing.

"Maybe this whole girls' night thing isn't such a bad idea," Ida Belle said.

"Are you prepared to see that again?" I asked and pointed to the lawn.

Gertie had climbed up on the stage and was dancing with Ricky. It probably would have been better on the eyes if the cape had been there to block some things. A rap song came on and Gertie bent over and started shaking.

"Is she having a seizure?" I asked.

"She's twerking!" one of the Sinful Ladies yelled.

Ida Belle and I looked at each other and spoke at the same time.

"No, she's not."

Then we collapsed in laughter again.

CHAPTER TWENTY-THREE

I WAS BACK *in the desert on a mission, except this desert had a river running through it. A river filled with alligators. I had to cross the river to get to my target so I started swimming, even though the water was moving fast. I made the other side and ran for an old shack. The smell of rotting fish hit me as soon as I ran inside, and I lifted my mask over my mouth and nose. I slipped to the back of the shack, careful to avoid the worst of the rotted wood floor, and peered out the window.*

There he was.

My target was standing on a rise behind the shack. I lifted my weapon and took aim but then he turned. It wasn't my target after all but the man who wanted to take over his command. He was wearing my target's gold band on his arm—the one given to him by his father, the terrorist cell's previous leader. Perhaps he'd already done my job for me.

I radioed in my position and the situation, then held until I got the order to abort. My legs ached as I ran through the sand and back to the river. I battled the current once more, then I sat behind a dune and waited for my retrieval unit.

. . .

I BOLTED OUT of sleep and promptly fell onto a shag rug that I was certain I didn't own. I yanked my pistol from my waistband and jumped up, tracking the room with my gun. It took a couple seconds to realize I was at Gertie's house and I'd fallen off her couch, which is where I'd crashed the night before.

Ida Belle was snoring in the recliner nearby and a couple of other women were scattered on the floor, but they all appeared to be breathing. My head was pounding so I went into the kitchen to grab some water and aspirin but drew up short as I stepped in the doorway. I'd found what might be Gertie's final resting place.

Her dining table.

She was in the center, arms stretched out like she was waiting to be sacrificed. Her shirt was pulled up, exposing her belly, and the skin around her navel was pink. Tricky Ricky was sitting in a chair, slumped onto the table, clutching an empty bottle of the red-hot brand of Sinful Ladies Cough Syrup. The reality of what had gone on after I'd crashed washed over me and made that aspirin run more important than ever.

Francis was on his perch in the corner, leaned against the wall and dead asleep. The tiara was draped around his neck. I was pretty sure he'd gotten into the gelatin shots. I hurried into the kitchen and grabbed the aspirin bottle from the pantry, dumping three of the lifesavers into my palm, then stuck my head under the sink and took a big gulp to wash them down.

"I hope you're making coffee next," Ida Belle said from the doorway.

"Actually, I was thinking of heading home for coffee," I said and pointed to the table.

Ida Belle looked at the table and blinked, then grimaced as if she'd just seen Celia's butt and threw one arm over her face.

"My eyes. Is that what I think it is?"

"It looks to me like Gertie and Tricky Ricky were doing body shots."

"I don't even know what that is and you're not going to tell me. Thank God we passed out before then, although I'm beginning to wish I'd made it home. Unfortunately, I think we might have gotten arrested for even attempting to walk."

I nodded my agreement, then groaned at the movement.

"I was having this bizarre dream where I was back in the sandbox on a mission but there was a river with alligators and my target was already dead..."

I stopped talking and stared at Ida Belle. Then I reached out and grabbed her shoulders.

"That's it!" I yelled. "Phone! Where's my phone?"

Francis squawked and flapped his wings to maintain his balance, blinking the entire time. I ran into the living room and spotted my phone on the fireplace mantel.

"Crap! It's dead."

"Stop yelling," one of the women on the floor said.

"Where's Gertie's laptop?" I asked.

"Probably her room. What is going on? You're starting to worry me."

I ran into Gertie's room and drew up short when I saw one of the Sinful Ladies in bed with the blow-up doll. Neither of them had on enough clothes. I grabbed Gertie's laptop off the nightstand and ran out, leaving Ida Belle standing in the doorway, staring at the sight on the bed with dismay. She was right on my heels when I got back to the kitchen and ran over to poke Gertie.

"Get off the table," she said. "We need to use it."

Gertie raised her head and smiled. "One more shot and I'm going to look twenty."

"If I were twenty years younger, Ricky," Francis said.

"Good God," Ida Belle said and rolled Gertie to one side.

I fired up the laptop and pulled up a satellite map of the area surrounding Silas's house. I zoomed in and located the marina, then tracked down to about where his shack must be. Then I looked at the channel in front of it and the strip of land separating it from the lake behind.

"What's happening, Fortune?" Ida Belle asked.

I looked at her and smiled. "I think I know how Silas killed Johnny."

———

IT TOOK us thirty minutes to rouse Gertie and another thirty to get Tricky Ricky and the other women out of her house, but finally the three of us were ready to roll. Except for one last thing.

I looked at Gertie. "Do you have more fireworks? And dynamite?"

"Is the pope Catholic?" Gertie asked.

"The pope wears a funny hat," Francis said. "Nobody prays for Celia. They don't want her in heaven."

I grabbed a grape off the table and tossed it to Francis before we headed upstairs.

It took a couple minutes for Ida Belle and me to get over the shock of what Gertie stored in one of her upstairs bedrooms and another fifteen minutes to find just the right combination of items—according to Gertie. I was more than a little concerned that one shelf in the room was dedicated solely to handbags, all with the retail tags still intact.

Finally, Gertie was loaded up with the latest in bottle rockets, smoke bombs, and enough dynamite to level a small office building, so we headed out. We had just turned onto the highway when Gertie leaned forward and looked at Ida Belle and me.

"So is anyone going to tell me where we're going and why you have me carting around things you normally don't want to know about?" she asked.

It was only then that I realized in my rush to get us out the door, I hadn't even told Gertie why.

"You rushed Tricky Ricky out of your house and don't even know why?" I asked.

"You said we had to hurry," Gertie said.

"And that's all it took?" I asked.

"Look, you wind up in the middle of a lot of drama," Gertie said. "But you don't instigate any of it. If you wake me up first thing and ask me to pack up dynamite and rush out the door, I figure there's a darned good reason."

I grinned. It was so great to have ride-or-die friends.

"So is anyone going to tell me why we're hurtling down the highway in the time machine at"—she checked her watch —"8:00 a.m.?"

"Fortune thinks she knows how Silas killed Johnny," Ida Belle said.

Gertie let out a huge yell, then grabbed her head. "Awesome! How?"

"She hasn't told me yet," Ida Belle said. "I just knew we needed to hurry."

"So where are we hurrying to?" Gertie asked.

"Silas's house," I said. "There's something I have to check before I go accusing the man of murder. I need evidence. It has to stick."

"And why do you need dynamite?" Gertie asked.

"I'm going to need a diversion," I said.

"So you can do what?" Gertie asked.

"Get Silas out of his house."

They both stared.

"You're going to go *into* Silas's house?" Ida Belle asked. "Do you think that's a good idea?"

"It is if he's not in it," I said. "Hence, the necessary diversion."

"Can we just blow up the house with him in it?" Gertie asked.

"That would blow us right past a trial and to the sentencing," I said. "I'd like to get evidence and let him rot in prison. I can't do that without the house intact."

"And what is it you think you'll find?" Ida Belle asked.

I told them.

———

IDA BELLE PULLED into the convenience store parking lot and as I'd expected, our friends were already in their chairs, having a cup of coffee. They perked right up when we pulled in, both grinning as if Publisher's Clearing House had just pulled up with checks. They both struggled a bit but insisted on rising as we approached. I couldn't help smiling. Old-school manners still charmed the heck out of me.

"Good morning, ladies," Jeb said. "You're out awfully early."

"We are, and we're here to see if you can help us with something," Ida Belle said.

"Of course," Wyatt said. "What do you need?"

"Do you have a boat?" I asked.

They both stared at me as if I'd lost my mind.

"Never mind," I said. "I need someone to take me down the channel in a boat."

"We can do that," Jeb said. "Can we ask why?"

"It's your boat," I said. "You can ask anything you'd like.

I'm going to have you drop me off on the land behind Silas's house. I want to sneak up on him."

They looked at each other, clearly worried.

"I don't think that's such a good idea," Wyatt said. "Old Silas is a mean one. He'd sooner shoot you as talk to you. I'm surprised you got away without some buckshot in your vehicle at least."

"It's very important," I said. "You see, I think Silas killed Johnny and if I can get onto his property without him knowing, then I think I'll be able to prove it."

Their eyes widened, and I would have bet money their pulses had just shot through the roof.

"You're kidding me!"

"Well, why didn't you say so!"

They both spoke at once.

"Of course we'll help," Jeb said. "Do we need weapons? Camouflage? I still have my sniper rifle."

"I don't have one of those," Wyatt said. "I flew copters."

Gertie smiled. "'Nam?"

"Any man our ages worth his salt did his duty," Jeb said.

"Ida Belle and Gertie did their duty as well," I said.

They both stared.

"Really?" Jeb asked. "Isn't that something. I knew there were ladies overseas but I didn't see any."

Wyatt nodded. "Now we know why we liked you guys straight off. What about you?" He looked at me.

"Former spook," I said.

They both stared for a couple seconds, then laughed.

"CIA? Good Lord Almighty, Silas doesn't stand a chance," Wyatt said. "Let me go put on my boots and hook up the boat."

"I'll get my rifle," Jeb said. "This might be the most

exciting thing that's happened since that buffalo fragging of 1964."

"When all this is over, you might have to tell me about that over a beer and one of those hot dogs," Gertie said as she followed him to the door.

He gave her a shy smile. "I'd love to."

"Lord help us all," Ida Belle said.

Wyatt shook his head as Jeb walked off. "He always gets the women with that sniper rifle thing. Nobody cares about helicopters."

"It's not the rifle," Ida Belle said. "It's the fragging. Gertie has a thing for explosives."

"Really? She looks so sweet," Wyatt said.

"Don't look in her purse," I said.

Wyatt looked a bit confused but nodded and headed for the store. "I don't have a sniper rifle but I've got a good shotgun."

"Load 'em up then," I said.

"They're not going to need weapons," Ida Belle said.

"I know, but they're too excited for me to say no."

Ida Belle grinned. "Maybe you should work in senior services instead of this PI thing."

"I'd have everyone in jail inside of a week."

"Bet they'd all be happy about it."

I watched as Jeb and Wyatt came back, both of them stepping lively and grinning as though they'd just won the lottery. There was something to be said for not growing old gracefully.

"How well do cell phones work on the bayou?" I asked.

"Usually pretty good," Jeb said. "But sometimes it can get sketchy."

"I have a CB in my SUV," Ida Belle said.

Wyatt perked up. "We have one in the boat."

"Put it on 1-9," Ida Belle said.

Jeb grinned. "I've always wanted to say 'Breaker 1-9.' My call name's Bullseye."

"Mine's Annie Oakley," Ida Belle said.

"I'm Vapor," Wyatt said.

"Vapor?" Ida Belle asked.

"What he was usually running on before landing," Jeb explained.

"I'm Hurricane," Gertie said.

I laughed. "That's appropriate."

They all looked at me.

"What?" I asked. "My real name's not Fortune. I got that in the CIA—soldiers of fortune..."

"You said that was your nickname and you made it legal," Ida Belle said. "But that doesn't mean it was your call name."

"Out with it," Gertie said.

"Keyser Söze," I said.

Everyone was silent for a moment.

"Don't suppose you need that rifle after all," Wyatt said to Jeb. "Looks like we got a younger pro on the job."

"Just when I thought you couldn't get cooler," Gertie said.

Ida Belle grinned. "I like it."

"Then let's get this show on the road," I said. "Ida Belle, you and Gertie head for Silas's place in the SUV but don't get close enough for visual. You'll have to stop and hike it for a bit to get line of sight for his place. Just try to position the SUV for a quick getaway if you need it."

"Silas isn't going anywhere quickly with his back and knees," Gertie said.

"He doesn't have to when he's pointing a gun at you," I reminded her. "Just shooting randomly into the brush he could get lucky. If you use the bottle rockets, position them some-where, then light and leave the area as fast as possible. Same for the dynamite. I'll signal when I'm in position and wait for the discharge before I move in."

"Then what?" Gertie asked. "We can't just leave you there."

"I'm hoping a large enough explosion will send him into the woods to investigate," I said. "I don't need much time— only a couple minutes."

"I don't suppose anyone figured on just calling the police?" Wyatt asked.

"And tell them what?" I asked. "They can't get a search warrant on speculation and if they ask questions, Silas will get rid of the evidence."

"To hell with that," Jeb said. "Let's do this."

"Don't worry," Gertie said. "We've done this sort of thing lots of times. I'm practically an expert with explosives."

CHAPTER TWENTY-FOUR

Jeb and Wyatt didn't look convinced of Gertie's claim to expert explosives knowledge and Ida Belle knew better, but no one was willing to let Silas out of their grasp now that I might have a fix on him. Heck, Jeb and Wyatt didn't even know what I knew but were still willing to stick their necks out, which just proved the point of how much people hated the man.

I climbed into an old Ford with Jeb and Wyatt and we headed for the marina. Ida Belle and Gertie took off for the road to Silas's house, figuring traipsing through the woods to find the perfect spot for the diversion might take a bit of time. Wyatt and Jeb were quiet as we drove, passing looks to each other that were both hopeful and fearful at the same time.

"You really think you can pin Johnny's death on Silas?" Wyatt finally asked.

"I hope so," I said. "That's what all this risk is about."

"What made you go on this search?" Jeb asked. "I thought you were checking into Molly's disappearance."

"I was," I said. "But I kept hearing the same things over and over again from people who knew Johnny well and I couldn't stand the inconsistencies. I never even knew the man but I have a hard time believing he had an accident."

"Me and Jeb always said as much," Wyatt said. "But we couldn't figure out how it could have been any other way. Did you figure out anything on Molly?"

"Oh yeah," I said. "Her boyfriend and his side piece were arrested for her murder Thursday."

They both hooted at once and then sobered. I understood exactly how they felt. Happy that someone was going to pay and yet somehow guilty for celebrating when a good person was gone.

"Did you have anything to do with that arrest?" Wyatt asked.

"I might have provided a deputy with some valuable information," I said.

"I bet he wasn't happy about a PI getting the best of him," Jeb said.

"He's rarely happy when it happens but it's not an ego thing," I said. "He's sort of my boyfriend."

They both stared for a couple seconds, then Jeb started chuckling. Then Wyatt. By the time we turned into the marina, they both had tears running down their faces.

"You are a pistol," Wyatt said.

"Probably going to be the death of that deputy," Jeb said.

"He was Force Recon," I said. "He can handle me."

"Oh Lord," Jeb said. "A spook and a Marine. It's like something out of a movie."

"Not until we get the bad guy," I said as we launched their bass boat.

A couple minutes later, we were speeding down the bayou and in no time, we pulled up to a dilapidated dock with a half sunken bass boat tied up to it.

"I see Silas keeps his dock and boat in as good a shape as his house," I said.

"He won't spend a nickel unless he has to," Wyatt said. "Unless, of course, it's gambling."

"You sure you're going to be all right?" Jeb asked.

"Positive," I said. "When I get close enough to make my move, I'll let Gertie know to start the diversion. As soon as Silas leaves his house, I'll make sure I'm right, then I'll head back here and we'll call the police."

"What do we do in the meantime?" Wyatt asked.

"Just sit tight," I said. "And turn the boat around and be ready to launch quickly, just in case."

They both nodded, not needing an explanation of what 'just in case' might entail.

I climbed onto the rickety dock, then looked back at them. "Promise me that no matter what you hear, you will stay put."

They glanced at each other and I could tell neither wanted to do it.

"I mean it," I said. "I'd be in a heap of trouble for getting you involved in this. You're not police or one of my employees."

"Well, we don't want you in any trouble," Jeb said.

"Good," I said. "This will all be over soon and then we'll celebrate."

"I like the sound of that," Wyatt said.

I pulled out my pistol and headed into the trees. I found Silas's path to his house and made quick work of traversing the wooded area to the back of the clearing where Silas's house stood. I worked my way around the tree line, checking both sides of the house to find the easiest point of access. On the left side of the house, near the front, I hit the jackpot. A section of the lattice that skirted the bottom of the house was missing entirely.

I pulled out my cell phone and sent a text to Gertie, then waited for the diversion to begin. A couple seconds later, I heard a bottle rocket go off and then a second later, it hit Silas's front door and exploded.

I heard cursing coming from inside and then Silas ran out onto the porch, his shotgun ready to fire.

"I know you're out there," he yelled. "Get off my property or I'll start shooting."

Another bottle rocket whizzed onto the roof and Silas fired off two shots into the woods. I hoped Ida Belle and Gertie were taking cover. A couple seconds later, more bottle rockets fired from a different location, but Silas didn't show any sign of leaving his porch. He just kept firing into the woods.

I sent Gertie another text.

He has to leave the porch. Draw him away somehow.

On it.

Silas paced the front porch twice, glaring into the trees, then leaned against the front wall of the house. I waited, wondering how long it was going to take Gertie to come up with something to budge Silas off the porch and what it was going to be.

Then the wait was over.

A giant explosion rocked the clearing, and the outhouse blew straight into the air and into a million pieces. Unfortunately, some of the pieces weren't wood from the outhouse. Silas threw his arm up in front of his face and ducked, but when the last of the wood hit the porch, he started yelling at the top of his lungs and lumbered down the steps and toward the woods near the site of the explosion.

"I'm going to kill you when I find you!" he yelled. "And I won't stop until I do!"

His limp grew more pronounced as he went, but he showed

no sign of stopping. As soon as he hit the trees, I ran for the side of the house and crawled through the missing lattice and under the house. I could hear the sound of the shotgun firing every ten seconds or so and wondered just how many shells Silas was carrying in those overall pockets. I scooted along until I reached the front porch, then looked up to find the newer of the porch floor planks. Then I pulled a spade out of my backpack and just to the side of the planks, I started digging. It didn't take me long because the grave was shallow.

I'd found Johnny Broussard.

I grabbed a bone, just in case anyone in law enforcement decided to drag their feet, and crawled out from under the porch, hoping that Ida Belle and Gertie had made their getaway. As soon as I made it to the trail to the dock, I pulled out my cell phone and sent a text.

Are you away?

No. Slight problem. Flat tire.

Crap! One of those random shotgun blasts must have gotten Ida Belle's SUV. I said a quick prayer that it was only a tire because if he'd marred her paint, she was going to be contacting the coroner rather than the police.

Pick up trail middle of backyard. Head for the dock.

10-4.

The makeshift path that led back to the main road was at least a quarter mile long. Making it to the boat was a better proposition. Even without knowing the terrain, Ida Belle and Gertie would be able to move faster than Silas. The problem was that no one could outrun a shotgun. Which led to a dilemma. Did I set off after them or wait for them here? I had no way of knowing how deep in the woods they were or how far away, and I didn't want to take up their time with more messages. When someone was after you with a shotgun, you didn't ask people to stop and text.

I spent another couple seconds mulling over the choices, then the universe made up my mind for me. A shotgun blast sounded and splintered the tree right above my head. I hit the ground, crawled behind a large cypress tree, and listened. I could hear someone moving through the brush, but it sounded like slow, deliberate thrashing. That must be Silas. I strained, praying that I'd hear another set of steps, but nothing came. Maybe they'd stopped and were hiding, trying to throw Silas off the scent.

A couple seconds later, I got my answer. I heard pounding steps and then Ida Belle and Gertie ran right past my hiding space and took off down the trail. I jumped up and headed after them, yelling at them to move it as another shot rang out. For a guy with a disability, Silas was moving pretty quickly. I could only assume anger was fueling him beyond normal capacity.

The only positive was that the last shot was farther away than the one before so we were making up ground on him. The question was would it be enough ground to get across the open space to the boat and get away. I could return fire but it wasn't going to look good for the home team—shooting a guy on his own property. And the last thing I wanted to do was give Silas a reason to request any form of leniency.

We hit the end of the tree line and burst out into the open. Wyatt and Jeb were waving and yelling for us to hurry. I turned on the afterburners and sprinted past Ida Belle and Gertie, in case I needed to provide them cover. When I got to the dock, I hit it with one step then leaped a good ten feet and landed in the bottom of the boat, crouching for stabilization as soon as my feet touched metal.

I whirled around, ready to do whatever necessary to protect Ida Belle and Gertie, and saw they were about twenty yards behind me. Unfortunately, Silas had just exited the tree line and spotted them. I was still holding the femur in my left hand so I pulled out my pistol with my right and took aim.

"Wait!" Jeb yelled and brought up an old Coca-Cola bottle full of fireworks.

He lit up all the fuses, pointed the bottle in Silas's direction, and a second later, they began to fire off. It was probably only ten or so that he'd managed to shove in the bottle, but it seemed like a hundred as they sizzled and flew. And his aim was great.

The fireworks began to explode all around Silas but one was a direct hit on his chest that dropped into his overalls. He threw the shotgun and grabbed at the straps on the overalls, but it was too late. The bottle rocket exploded and we heard Silas scream. Ida Belle and Gertie had reached the dock and Ida Belle made the jump into the boat as I yelled for Wyatt to prepare to launch.

Gertie took one last step on the dock to jump and tripped, sending her tumbling off the side of the dock and into the water. I looked up and saw Silas bent over, retrieving his shotgun. We had to leave now or get caught in the blast. The boat was floating away from Gertie and she swam toward us. I looked for a rope but couldn't see anything, then I extended the only thing I had available—the femur.

Gertie didn't even blink as she grabbed hold of the bone and I told Wyatt to start going. I tugged her close to the boat and Ida Belle grabbed her shoulders. As Wyatt took off, we pulled her over the side of the boat and she dropped into the bottom. She sat up, sputtering and clutching the bone.

"Is this what I think it is?" she asked.

I nodded. "Johnny Broussard."

Jeb and Wyatt looked at the femur, dumbstruck.

"Well, I'll be danged," Jeb said.

Gertie grinned. "Me first."

CHAPTER TWENTY-FIVE

IT ONLY TOOK a favor call-in to the state police from Carter—and a picture of the femur—to get them out to Silas's house with handcuffs, a warrant, and a forensics crew. Silas, predictably, threatened to shoot anyone who came on his land, but the state police just tagged him with a rubber bullet and that show was over. I made a mental note to add some rubber bullets to my office supplies. It was the perfect solution for disabling someone from a distance without killing them.

And fireworks, of course.

Gertie had hooked Jeb up with a supply at the convenience store and he raved about her, me, Ida Belle, and the entire mission to the state police, the forensics team, and Carter, and even called the local preacher. Wyatt, the older of the two brothers and apparently the one that usually kept things in check, didn't even bother to try to contain Jeb. He was probably too busy grinning. He hadn't stopped since Gertie had held up that bone.

The police and forensics team allowed us to stay on-site long enough to see Silas handcuffed and put into the back of a police cruiser. His overalls were completely blown apart at the crotch and he was covered with the remnants from the outhouse explosion. That cop was probably going to burn the car when he was out of it. Silas was leaning to one side in the back seat, so I figured at least he was suffering before the real suffering began. The arrest process took long enough for us to hear someone from the forensics team call out that they'd found the body. Like that was a shock. I'd been toting that femur for an hour before they'd shown up. Shortly after that, we were hurried off-site to await questioning.

We had to call for a tow for Ida Belle's SUV. The vehicle didn't hold a spare and the temporary wouldn't be safe to get us all the way back to Sinful. A flatbed picked it up and it was off to Hot Rod's shop to await a new tire. Ida Belle, Gertie, and I piled into Carter's truck and we headed out. Our friends Wyatt and Jeb were already in position in front of the convenience store, and Carter pulled in so we could wait on the state police to take our statements.

Jeb ran inside for more beer as we climbed out of Carter's truck and Wyatt practically jumped out of his chair, still smiling. They hauled out more lawn chairs and we all took a seat, everyone talking at once about the adventure.

"So can you please tell me now how you put this all together?" Ida Belle asked.

"It was the hangover, I think," I said.

Jeb nodded. "This sounds like the start of a really good story."

"I had far too many of those gelatin shots," I said. "When I woke up, I'd been having this strange dream. I was back in the sandbox on a mission. I had to swim across a river full of alligators, then traverse a shack with a rotted floor and the smell of decaying fish permeating the air. I locked on my target but it wasn't my target. He was wearing something that belonged to my target and I was about to eliminate the wrong guy. Then I woke up and things rushed into my head—Silas making his kids swim the channel with him every day, that woman who fell through the slats on the chair at the bachelorette party last night, Gertie slapping the wrong person on the butt last night because they were wearing the stripper's cape."

The guys all exchanged lifted eyebrows and Gertie smiled.

"That was a *really* good time," she said.

"And all of that made sense to you somehow?" Wyatt asked.

"I think I get part of it," Ida Belle said. "You realized Silas killed Johnny at his house, then drove to the marina and got onto his boat wearing his rain slicker. They were both large men and in the dim light of the oncoming storm, the witness couldn't see his face and just assumed it was Johnny."

"What about the phone call to the tax assessor?" Wyatt asked.

"He made that call right before he left," I said. "That way, he'd have proof he was at home and since no one saw his truck on the highway or at the dock, there's no way he could have followed Johnny or waited for him on the boat beforehand."

"So he set up his alibi then left for the dock," Jeb said.

"Exactly!" I said. "Then Silas took the boat into the lake and jumped onto shore, walked across that thin stretch that separated the bayou in front of his property from the lake, then swam across."

"But what about his back and knees?" Gertie asked. "How could he swim that channel in a storm after doing all that walking?"

"Because his injury gets worse with walking or standing but swimming doesn't put any pressure on his spine," I said. "I've seen it a million times, especially with compression injuries from parachuting. He parked close to the dock so he could manage the short walk to the boat without limping. It didn't matter if he limped after that."

"But it still would have been risky swimming the channel in the storm," Jeb said.

"Silas has swum that channel a million times," I said. "And remember, there were two life jackets missing from the boat. He threw one in and used the other for his swim. It wasn't like this was a timed event. He could take all the time he needed to get back home. No one was going to come looking for Johnny at his house. They were going to go to the marina first, then launch a search on the water."

"So how did you know the body was under the porch?" Gertie asked.

"Because there were slats on the porch that were newer than the rest," I said. "Silas didn't repair anything. He turned a shed into an outhouse rather than repair his plumbing. So why would he spend money on his porch? My guess is he called Johnny to his house, then hit him up for money, like he always did. Johnny refused and they argued. Silas probably shot him as he was leaving. Johnny died right there on that porch and since there was no way Silas could move the body, he cut the slats on the porch and let the body drop below. Then he dug a shallow grave and repaired the porch."

"And since everyone thought Johnny had died on the water, no one ever looked closely at Silas's house," Ida Belle said.

Carter sighed. "Diabolical. How could someone do that to their own kid?"

"Silas never cared about anyone but himself," Wyatt said. "Anyone around him for five minutes knew that much. But murder takes things to a whole other level."

"What do you think's going to happen to him?" Jeb asked.

"I think he's going to die in prison," Carter said.

"Does this change anything about Molly's murder?" Gertie asked.

Carter frowned. "I don't know. The fact that Molly died in

a similar fashion is going to be great fodder for the defense, especially with their father being Johnny's killer. And we already know he had motive and opportunity. It might be enough for reasonable doubt."

"Do you think Silas killed Molly and it wasn't Dexter and Marissa?" Ida Belle asked.

Carter shook his head. "I just don't know."

"Which means a jury won't, either," I said.

———

IT WAS A LONG, exhausting, but exciting day. The state police had finally shown up at the convenience store to take our preliminary statements, but I had a feeling they were going to need a much more in-depth and less excitable version of the events than what they got. Wyatt and Jeb made the entire thing sound like *The A-Team* and were still in the stratosphere with excitement when we finally got cut loose by the cops.

Once we got back to Sinful, I called Nickel and Angel and gave them the news. They were both overwhelmed with gratitude and both cried, although Nickel swore if I told anyone, he'd figure out a way to kill me. Neither of them seemed surprised that Silas had done the deed, but they were both shocked at how calculated he'd been with the cover-up and impressed that I'd worked out something that no one else had even considered a crime.

Unfortunately, none of it brought Molly back, and she would have been the person who wanted to hear that Johnny's death would be vindicated the most.

Carter dropped me off at home and had to head to the office to call the DA since I'd essentially just thrown a giant monkey wrench in his case against Dexter and Marissa. I didn't envy him that phone call. After my calls to Nickel and

Angel, I'd taken a shower until the hot water ran out, then eaten most of the leftovers in my fridge while watching a marathon of *Justified*. Sometime that evening, I fell asleep in my recliner. I awoke there the next morning with a crick in my neck and an angry cat glaring at me from the armrest.

I glanced at my watch. 8:00 a.m. I'd been in that recliner for twelve hours!

I rose and stretched, feeling every muscle in my body strain to loosen after being in the same position for so long, then trudged into the kitchen to feed Merlin and make coffee —in that order. I'd barely flopped down to my first cup when my phone rang.

"She's alive!" Gertie yelled as soon as I answered.

"Can we talk about whatever this is after I've had coffee?" I asked.

"Molly is alive!" Gertie shouted.

I dropped my cup and it broke on the tile floor, slinging coffee every direction.

"What?" I asked, certain that I'd heard wrong.

"Molly is alive," Gertie said. "She's in the hospital. Ida Belle and I are on our way to pick you up. Put some coffee in a thermos."

She disconnected and I stared at the coffee running over my kitchen floor for about two seconds before launching into action. I flew upstairs and threw on street clothes, then ran back downstairs and dumped the rest of the coffee into a thermos. The floor would have to wait as I could hear Ida Belle's SUV pulling into my drive. I dashed out and jumped in, taking note of the excited expressions and flushed cheeks my two friends wore.

"Fill me in," I said as we took off.

"According to our hospital contact," Ida Belle said, "early this morning, Molly walked into the emergency room. She said she'd fallen off her boat while trying to free it from some debris it got stuck on and was rescued by a Creole man who lived deep in the swamp. She said she vaguely remembered being pulled onto his boat and him pouring chicken stock down her throat."

"She didn't even know what day it was," Gertie said. "She said she woke up early this morning, before daylight, in a cabin in the middle of the swamp. The man realized she was awake and told her he'd take her to the hospital. He drove her to the hospital and let her out on the road in front of it, saying he didn't want to see 'no people.'"

"Is she all right?" I asked.

"She has a lump on her head and some bruises that are already healing but good Lord, those could have been from her fighting that day as much as having an accident," Ida Belle said.

"Did she say what happened?" I asked.

They both shook their heads.

"She claims she doesn't remember," Gertie said. "Said she remembers taking the boat out and calling Angel, but then the next thing she was really aware of was waking up in the man's cabin."

"I can't believe it!" I said.

Gertie grinned. "I know, right? Best ending ever. Molly is alive and okay. Silas is going to prison for killing Johnny. Ida Belle will have awesome catering at her wedding, and Jeb promised me he'd call me for a date. This has been one heck of a week."

"I assume Carter knows?" I asked.

"Of course," Ida Belle said. "The nurse at the hospital recognized Molly as soon as she walked in and called the sheriff's department. Molly's disappearance was all over the local news. Nothing like working the night shift and thinking you're seeing a ghost walk in the door."

"Yeah, I'll bet," I said.

And I'd bet Carter was elated but also dealing with a very unhappy DA. Once again, I was really happy to be a lone agent and not under the thumb of the red tape bureaucracy and career climbers that Carter dealt with every day. I imagined the DA wasn't going to be excited at all about Molly's return from the dead.

"Did someone call Nickel and Angel?" I asked.

"I'm sure Molly did as soon as they got her in a room," Gertie said. "We figure they headed that way as soon as they got the news, but Ida Belle thought you might want to be on hand because they're sure to tell her about Johnny."

Ida Belle nodded. "I think she'll have questions."

"Don't we all," I mumbled, staring out the window.

This was all exciting and I was thrilled that Molly was all right and even happier that she would finally have some answers about what really happened to her brother. But once again, I had that niggling feeling that I was missing something.

The hospital nurse greeted us as soon as we walked in and appeared as if she was expecting us. She directed us to Molly's room and asked that we try to keep our voices down. Apparently, all the excitement coming from Molly's room had been disturbing the other patients.

Angel and Nickel were sitting in chairs next to Molly's bed and they both jumped up when we walked in. Angel rushed over to give me a huge hug and whispered, "God bless you for everything," when she pulled me in. Nickel surprised me by following suit with the hug and saying, "I can't thank you enough."

Molly was sitting up in her bed. She was bruised but smiling.

"Get over here and give me a hug, skinny girl," she said.

A tiny tremor of fear ran through me, but Molly took it easy on my rib cage and I came out of the hug with everything intact. Molly sniffed as she released me and shook her head.

"I don't know how I'll ever be able to repay you," she said. "But I'll make you that dip every darn week, I know that."

"As much as I would love to live on that dip, I still have a couple items in my closet that don't stretch," I said.

She laughed. "I knew I was going to like you the first time we met. But when Nickel told me he'd hired you to look into my disappearance and that it led to you solving Johnny's murder, well, I've never been more overwhelmed. Nothing can bring my brother back but the three of us have suffered so hard and so long, knowing that the official story couldn't possibly be all there was."

"I'm glad I could help," I said. "And I'm really sorry that it turned out your father was responsible."

Molly sighed. "I know it's a horrible thing to have to say but that's probably the one thing in all of this that didn't surprise me. I wish my father had been a different person...a better person. But he is who he is. I've hated him most of my life. At least now he'll pay for one of the horrible things he's done."

Angel reached over and squeezed her hand and Nickel nodded.

"Got that right," he said.

"What about you?" Ida Belle asked. "How are you doing?"

"I'm going to be fine," Molly said. "They're keeping me overnight for observation but come tomorrow, I'll be shopping for your wedding food."

"You don't have to do that," Ida Belle said. "We can manage without stressing you as soon as you leave the hospital."

"I'd be more stressed sitting in my house with nothing to

do," Molly said. "It's only going to take me ten minutes to pack up the extent of Dexter's belongings and less time than that to toss them out the front door."

"I guess the cops had to let him and that woman out of jail," Gertie said.

Molly shook her head. "My not being dead kinda put a hitch in that whole murder charge, but it seems the DA thinks they have enough to get them on conspiracy to commit murder. Apparently, a night without a fix had Marissa rolling on Dexter and telling on herself. I don't know what the outcome will be, but the DA is determined to make something of it."

"You never intended to leave your business to Dexter, right?" I asked.

"Good Lord, no!" Molly said. "That man can't tie his shoes with both hands free. Why on earth would I leave someone like that my business? I had intended on getting everything drawn up legal and leaving it to Ally. I don't know her well but I know she's trustworthy and can cook. I heard Dexter showed up to give her some trouble."

"He did but Fortune disabused him of that notion," Ida Belle said.

Molly grinned. "Heard about that part too."

"So what happened to you?" I asked.

"I'm not sure," Molly said. "I remember leaving, thinking I'd take a boat ride and get some air. I was frustrated with Dexter but mostly with myself for not doing anything about it. And I was giving my best friends grief for even bringing it up. I remember being on the phone with Angel, complaining about Dexter. Then my boat got lodged on something submerged. I leaned over the side to free it and remember hitting the water, but then everything goes blank. I can see flashes of being pulled into a boat and remember chicken broth but nothing more than a second or two until I woke up in that cabin."

"Do you think Dexter and Marissa went after you?" I asked.

"If they did, I don't remember," Molly said.

"What about the hole in the boat, and the blood?" Gertie asked.

"The hole was my own fault," Molly said. "I chunked my new anchor in and put a little too much steam behind it. Cussed myself for two days over that hole and need to get it fixed. As for the blood, I don't know. I assume maybe I fell and hit my head. That's what the doctor thinks."

"You're lucky you didn't drown," Ida Belle said.

Molly nodded. "All they can figure is that I must have been aware enough to float."

"Well, whatever you did, we're really glad of it," Gertie said.

I nodded. "We're usually happy with catching the bad guy. Having your victim turn up alive is better than winning the lottery."

"Uh, Molly," Ida Belle said, looking a little sheepish. "There was an issue with your van during our investigation."

Molly grinned. "I saw the video. That was a narrow escape. You guys are resourceful. But don't worry about the van. I carry really good insurance and it's probably not the first time the insurance company has had a filing about a bear."

A nurse popped her head in and gestured at us. "That's enough visiting for now. The patient needs some rest if she expects to get out of here tomorrow."

"You heard the woman," Molly said. "Get the heck out because I'm not riding this bed another day."

CHAPTER TWENTY-SIX

WE ALL SAID our goodbyes and headed out. Nickel and Angel were going to grab some coffee and breakfast at the cafeteria and wait for the next set of visiting hours. Ida Belle, Gertie, and I headed for the parking lot but when we got to the lobby, I paused.

"I need to make a stop at the ladies'," I said. "Do you guys mind grabbing us some coffee for the drive back? And if there's doughnuts there, I'd be forever grateful."

"Now you're talking," Gertie said. "I'd only gotten one cup in before Ida Belle called. And no food at all. I'm starving."

"Find us something to tide us over until we can get back to Sinful and have a celebratory breakfast at the café," I said.

They nodded and headed off. I went back down the hall but instead of going into the restroom as I'd said I was going to, I headed back to Molly's room.

She was still sitting upright and smiled at me when I walked inside.

"I thought you might be back," she said.

"There's a couple things I thought you might be able to clear up," I said. "And I figured you might not like them to be general knowledge, although I have a feeling you didn't manage all of this alone."

She cocked her head to one side. "And just what is it you think I managed?"

"Oh, I don't know—setting up your boyfriend and his side piece to be arrested for murder, for starters, but I don't think that was the main purpose. I think the real reason you faked your own death was to get someone to look into Johnny's death again because you always believed that your father was responsible. You just couldn't figure out how he did it and you knew the police wouldn't look into it again. Not without a reason. And since they couldn't be depended on to make the connection between your disappearance and Johnny's, you hedged your bets and had Nickel hire me."

"Whiskey told Nickel that if you had a 10,000-piece puzzle missing a single piece, you'd turn the world upside down to find it."

"I'm not sure if that's a compliment or a character flaw, but it's probably accurate. Silas didn't have anything to do with taking out that insurance policy, did he?"

Molly put on a blank face and remained silent.

"You see, the interesting thing is that the agent identified the woman who took out the policy as you and he had a valid driver's license," I said. "We figured it was manufactured or stolen and that Silas had hired someone to play your role. It was a good assumption and exactly the one you were hoping we'd make, which is why the signature on that policy was so far off from your own. It needed to look like a legitimate attempt at fraud."

"I couldn't have taken out that policy. When that document was being signed, I was catering a party in Mudbug."

"I'm sure you were. But Angel wasn't. She's almost as tall as you with similar features, and when the policy was taken out, she was pregnant. She told us she gained weight all over and was still working on losing it. With baggy clothes and a fake hairpiece, that ancient and half-blind insurance agent would have sworn he was looking at you."

Molly remained silent.

"It's a big risk, you know. The cops will pursue that angle as part of their murder conviction—to try to prove that Silas was successful once so he was going to try again. They'll run those documents. If Angel's fingerprints are on file for any reason..."

Molly finally broke her impassive expression and smiled.

"She was careful not to touch anything except the pen, and she took it with her when she left," she said.

"Then you called him from a burner phone and told him to meet you at your house about the policy. That way he was on-site when you disappeared, giving him motive and opportunity to cash in again. And with the back taxes owed and the bookies sniffing around, motive was increasing in urgency every day."

"So what do you plan to do with all this knowledge?" she asked.

"Nothing."

Her eyes widened. "Why not?"

"Because the only law broken was the fraud with the insurance policy and with no fingerprints, no one will ever prove who set that up."

"And if there had been fingerprints?"

"I still wouldn't have said anything."

"I figured you to be one for justice."

"I am, and Johnny finally got some. I don't blame you for what you did. In fact, I admire your cleverness. It was well planned. The biggest gamble you took was in counting on me to dig in and figure it all out."

"I did my asking around," Molly said. "Whiskey isn't the

only person who speaks highly of you. Back when I first started cage fighting, Big Hebert helped me out with some funds to get started."

"Big Hebert?"

"He's some sort of fifth cousin three times removed or whatever. You know how Louisiana families are."

"So much about this is making more sense. I suppose it was Nickel who gave you a ride out of the bayou that day and stashed you somewhere—their camp, maybe?"

Molly frowned. "My one regret about all of this is that we lied to you. But I didn't see any other way. I didn't think the cops would dig deep enough, but everyone who knew you said you would."

"Then why didn't you just ask me to look into Johnny's death?"

"Because you would have gotten the same information the cops did and said there wasn't anything else. And I wouldn't have blamed you. But with me missing in the same way and Silas looking to cash in again, I figured you'd keep digging longer than the evidence called for. And I needed someone really smart because none of us could figure out how he did it even though we were all certain he did."

I thought about it for a bit. Was she right? Would I have done my due diligence and dismissed the claims like everyone else? If Molly hadn't disappeared and set up that fake life insurance cash-in for Silas, would I have focused my laser attention on him as a murderer? Would I have questioned Johnny's death, or would I have assumed that three grieving people couldn't cope with the truth?

I wasn't sure.

And if I wasn't sure then there's no way Molly could have been. For all her manipulating and lying, she'd come up with the one way to get me to literally dig out the truth. And I didn't blame her for that.

"How did you know?" Molly asked.

"Small things. Things that gave me that feeling that something wasn't on the up and up."

"Like what?"

"When we talked to Angel, she would refer to you in present tense, then past tense. It's not uncommon with a recent death, but it makes more sense when you put it in the context of you still being alive. Then there was a statement Ida Belle made about unless you can pull one of those Jesus tricks like my dad. He has a thing for rising from the dead. And there was a statement that Angel made—that she wasn't interested in justice. She was interested in retribution. And the thing that never fit at all was your father's insistence that you had taken out the policy and called for him to meet you. It was no more outlandish than Dexter's insistence that you were going to leave him your business. And yet both of them said those things with a ring of truth in their statements."

Molly smiled. "You know, I feel sorry for any criminal that thinks he's going to set up shop under your radar. This town is a much safer place with you on the job."

"You *did* lead Dexter on, didn't you?"

"Of course. Even had him sign a fake document that I burned afterward. That idiot had always cheated on me, but when he hooked up with Marissa, he crossed a huge line. She kept bugging him to get money from me and then started asking if he got everything if I died. She fed him the idea of cashing in if I bought it, so I started stringing him along by making him think there was something in it for him if I died."

"And how did you know all of that?"

She shrugged. "A friend overheard them talking and let me know."

"Uh-huh. This friend wouldn't be a regular at The Bar, would he?" I asked, remembering that Glenn had said a lot of current and former cage fighters frequented the joint.

"I suppose it's possible."

"If you knew what Dexter was up to, why not just dump him?"

She thought about this for a bit. "I think because Dexter was going to be the last time a man used me. After everything I'd gone through, and he was actually trying to figure out how to kill me to get money for a junkie. I guess you could say it was the final straw."

I shook my head. "So much went into this. So many people searched for you, grieved for you."

Molly nodded. "And that's the one thing I feel bad about. Well, and lying to you. But if I had it to do over again, I'd still do the same thing. You managed to do what no one else would have, and without those circumstances, I don't think that would have been possible."

"I don't have any hard feelings about what you did. I probably would have done the same thing in your situation. But I want you to make me a promise."

"Anything."

"If you ever need my services again, tell me the truth. I won't stop until I have answers. I can't promise they'll be the answers you want, but I can't let things go until I know the truth about them. Character flaw."

Molly sniffed. "It's a good one to have."

"Also cumbersome."

She extended her hand to me and I placed mine in it. She squeezed and a single tear ran down her cheek.

"Thank you for finding Johnny. It means everything to me."

CHAPTER TWENTY-SEVEN

SATURDAY WAS bright and clear and hot as heck, but that didn't put a dent in the celebration at all. All of Sinful had cheered Molly's return to the living and now half of Sinful was in my backyard, anxiously awaiting the wedding that was never supposed to happen. The backyard had been transformed by me, Gertie, Ally, Marie, Emmaline, and Carter with some assistance from the local florist. There were a ton of white chairs in neat rows and a pretty arch with flowers draped around it at the end of the rows where Ida Belle and Walter would stand and make everything legal. A white satin runner split the chairs into two sides and residents had some fun arguing over whether they were guests of the bride or the groom, as they'd known them both forever.

Gertie and I were everywhere—outside ensuring people found places to sit and that the water stations remained filled with ice and bottled water, and inside, making sure when the time came, everyone was treated to some of the finest food Sinful had to offer. My kitchen didn't have one square inch of counter space left, and it smelled as though heaven had opened up and officially catered Ida Belle's wedding.

Molly was there and helping get the food staged for distribution. We'd figured she'd drop off everything and run but she surprised us all by showing up in a bright purple pantsuit that matched her hair and claiming that no way was she missing Ida Belle's nuptials as it was the equivalent to spotting a unicorn.

Although Gertie had spent a month teasing Ida Belle with her wardrobe choices for the event, she was turned out in a beautiful satin-and-lace dress in a soft green. She said due to the double layers, she was already sweating before she put it on, but she looked lovely. I had chosen to go with a simple blue dress with tiny white embroidered flowers. It might have been the girliest thing I'd worn since I'd come to Sinful but based on the look Carter gave me when he arrived, I'd made a good choice. Or maybe I should say Ally talked me into a good choice.

Ally was as pretty as ever in pastel pink and looked so young she would have been carded if she'd tried to buy alcohol. Emmaline was as elegant as always in a soft butter-yellow dress with pearl buttons up the back. Carter was looking very casual James Bond in his tan slacks and light blue button-up that matched my dress. We were going to make a nice matched pair when we walked down that aisle ahead of Ida Belle. Walter was so incredibly handsome in his suit, and nothing could have erased the smile on his face. Ida Belle was inside, waiting for the big reveal. None of us had seen her yet, and I couldn't wait to see what a bride in camo looked like.

But the real kicker was Ronald. He'd come completely decked out for a princess wedding, wearing an actual princess dress in shiny silver. It had more ruffles than I'd ever seen on a single garment. His shoes were a tribute to every foot problem known to man with silver sequins and six-inch stilettos. He even had a matching cone hat with a long train of lace trailing behind him as he flitted from person to person, probably more nervous than the bride.

The surprise guests were Big and Little Hebert, who arrived in their typical black suits. I moved my park bench from the front porch to a seat in the front row, and everyone took their turn passing by to greet the man who silently ran Sinful's underworld.

Finally, Pastor Don rang a bell and called out to the crowd. "If everyone could take their seats, please. It's time to begin."

Everyone hurried to their seats and Walter took his place up front next to Pastor Don. Gertie, Carter, and I went to the back porch to release the curtains over the arch that Ida Belle would walk through. That way, no one saw her until she walked down the aisle. Carter and I were the bridesmaid and groomsman. Ida Belle had asked Gertie to give her away.

I gave Gertie a hug before I placed my arm in Carter's. "The Dance" by Garth Brooks started to play, and Carter and I walked slowly down the aisle, smiling at all the attendees as we went. When we reached the front and moved to our respective sides, the music switched to the bridal march and I prayed the video was going to capture the expressions of everyone when they saw the bride in camo.

I heard the back door open and a small cry, then a couple seconds later, the curtain parted and Ida Belle and Gertie stepped through.

Everyone gasped, including me.

Ida Belle wore a gown of ivory with rows of pearls around the neck. Her feet were clad in matching ballet slippers, and she wore a spray of baby's breath and pearls on her head. Gertie was beaming at her as if she were an angel, and she definitely looked the part. Walter's eyes had already misted up, and I felt a little choked myself. Ida Belle smiled to the crowd as she walked with Gertie but her most special smile and that light in her eyes were all for Walter.

When they made it down front, Gertie gave Ida Belle and Walter both a kiss before taking a step back to stand next to me. Pastor Don began his wedding introductions and then looked at Gertie.

"Who gives this woman in holy matrimony?" he asked.

Gertie squeezed my hand. "Fortune and I do."

That was it for me. The tears that had been threatening to fall spilled out of the corner of my eyes. Gertie reached into the top of her dress and pulled out some tissue to hand to me, and everyone laughed.

"Get on with it, Preacher," Walter said. "We're not getting any younger."

Everyone laughed again and Pastor Don began the ceremony. When he got to the vows, he said, "The bride and groom have elected to skip the traditional vows because let's face it, Ida Belle was never going to stick to that plan. They've written their own promises to each other that more befit this later-in-life joining."

Walter and Ida Belle turned to face each other and he took her hands in his. "Ida Belle, I promise to refrain from offering an opinion on the choices you make, knowing good and well it won't make a difference."

Ida Belle grinned. "Walter, I promise to share my freezer space, except in deer hunting season."

Everyone chuckled and they turned to face Pastor Don again, waiting for that final declaration that changed everything and yet probably nothing. But as he opened his mouth to speak, one last guest arrived.

Godzilla.

The gator rushed out of the bayou and onto land, creating a small wake. The smell of awesome food had him lifting his snout and then he proceeded directly toward us. Guns came out of holsters, pockets, purses, and bras. I had a moment of probable impropriety when I removed mine from my thigh holster, but the move got an appreciative wink from Carter and a whistle from someone in the crowd.

"Don't shoot!" Gertie yelled. "It's Godzilla. He just wants something to eat."

Ronald jumped up and dug something wrapped in a dishrag out of his enormous handbag. "I brought a small casserole, just in case."

Of course he did.

"Well, get down there and fling the thing so we can finish," Ida Belle said. "Pastor Don, get on with it."

Ronald looked over at Gertie. "May I?"

"Knock yourself out," she said.

"By the power vested in me," Pastor Don started up again as Ronald set out with his wares.

He eased toward the beast, holding the casserole out in front of him like an offering to the gods. When he got within pitching distance, he cocked the casserole back to throw and that's when Godzilla launched. Ronald threw the casserole straight up in the air and ran. The charging gator didn't even see it land behind him as he rushed after Ronald, trying to lock in his snack. Everyone watched as Ronald ran across the lawn, the cone hat lace streaming behind him. I figured he'd kick off the shoes and make a better go of it, but he surprised me by moving reasonably quickly in the insane heels.

As he ran, he yelled, "Pronounce them, for Christ's sake! This dress is Dior!"

For more adventures with Fortune and the girls, try Fortune Funhouse.

To sign up for my new release newsletter, visit my website janadeleon.com.

Made in United States
North Haven, CT
23 June 2022

20552359R00183